DROGONS 5
GERMAN FORTESS OF ICE
THE FINAL SAGA

HELLS LEFSE

DEDICATION

To my canine partners Sven, Lena and Tesse whose love and devotion is shown to me every hour of the day. Never to be forgotten and always remembered is my other inspiration Einer and his human.

A special thanks are in order to my new agent Joe. Always there and always helpful in getting things to look appealing so that people will want to pick up my books and check them out.

With utmost respect for a talented song writer, musician and singer we have made reference to Roy Orbison and some of his songs. He is and will always be one of our all-time favorites.

To all the fans and historians of the Clyde Puffer ships. Right or wrong we have taken some liberties with our Puffer the Carolsea in the writing of this story. Some may think the Carolsea is as real as the Loch Ness monster. Maybe so. The Carolsea has a galley which we added by removing a bit of the cargo hold. The porthole in the crew's quarters was added for light. As for a sea going ocean travelling vessel, unlike Nessie we didn't want to keep the Carolsea bound to one body of water. It was with all respect to help our readers and the world to enjoy one of Scotland's floating treasures.

Fourteen books in fourteen years were written with

My best friend and partner 'Sven"

With heavy heart and love forever

I hope all of you will join me

In prayer for Sven who passed away this year

2006-2020

Rest in Peace in Doggie Heaven

DISCLAIMER

To all or any of you who happen to read this book please take note that Hells Lefse does the proof reading. Any errors are either intentional or unintentional depending on the mood he is in. If you think any fictional character in this book resembles you then that would mean that you are also fictional. If you find any spelling, grammar or fictional mishaps, please address your comments, complaints or praise directly to Hells.

Other books by Hells Lefse

Dogpire

Dogoyles

SvenSagas

Zomdoggies

Drogons

Booger Fairy

Buffole

Drogons 2

Sven Kabone

Drogons 3

Buffole Robyn Deadwood

Drogons 4

Buffole the Legend of Coyote Carol

Buffole Legend of the Golden Buffalo

Thanks a Slot

CHAPTER 0

Puppylude.

Hello, it's me Sven the handsomest, smartest saga telling Shih-Tzu the world has ever seen. I'm here to introduce you to our saga of The German Fortress of Ice by means of this Puppylude or for those who are not of the canine persuasion, it may be referred to by humans as a prelude.

I and my human partner Ole have been helping to save the world from the onslaught of Nazi Germany for some time. We have teamed up with some very unique characters from the past and the present. In case you have not read our previous four adventures I'll introduce our friends before the start of this saga.

Of course there's Ole and me. Ole's my human partner. He was a history teacher from a small town in Minnesota who was craving some time away from the mundane life of a small town and the snickers and jeers of his peers as he was shall we say an oddball in a town of so called normal people.

Asil, well, she was once a human as humans would describe a human. Only she had been recruited many hundreds of years ago to oversee a rare animal called the Drogons. She is under the guidance and guardianship of the Norse God Odin. We had partnered up with her on a quest to stop Hitler and his war machine from completely taking over Europe and maybe even the whole world.

Einer. Einer is a canine Drogons. He has a fair amount of Border collie in his blood plus traces of a few other breeds. His full name is Einstein, because no one is sure of his exact relativity. Somewhere along the line he became a Drogons. Drogons are ice breathing Canines that can fly. Einer and Asil are devoted companions to each other. Thankfully he is on our side and has saved us from many a life-threatening situation.

Krympe. What can one say about Krympe? She is a four foot high troll, pretty as far as long nosed, big eared, long armed, short legged trolls go. She is the devoted assistant to Asil and would do anything to protect and serve her mistress.

Captain Kavan Hammerbeck. Kavan was training the Japanese in submarine wolf pack tactics when the submarine he was on attacked and sunk the ship we were on as we headed for Pearl Harbor. The Japanese wanted to kill us but the Captain saved our lives and later joined up with us to fight the evil that was besieging his German homeland.

Parkurkarkus. We first me Parkurkakus when he was hired to guide us in Norway to Asil's secret hideaway. He was jovial, well versed in many occupations and a bit of a scoundrel. We soon learned that we could trust him because he also believed in our cause of saving the world from the Nazi regime.

So it was that the seven of us have banded together under the guidance of Odin to do our best to make this world a better place. This next adventures will be the last we would share as a team. So, sit back, put your feet up, grab a cup of hot chocolate and enjoy our final Saga. The German Fortress of Ice.

CHAPTER 1

We had left the future and saved the United States of America from a President who wanted nothing more than to destroy the country he was elected to protect. He had promoted the increase of foreigners who did not want to assimilate into our country but wanted to take it over and make it into the same as the country they had left. It was a bad time for the people whose Christian values and morals had shaped America into what at one time was the greatest nation in the world. Coming as we did from the 1940's we knew only too well that we and our fellow Americans had to fight to protect the freedom of the world. Nazi Germany was a good example, as was communism. The new threat that we hoped had been quelled was the takeover of the world by Islam. But for now we were back where we belonged in the 1940's.

We were sailing our Viking Longboat along at a nice clip. The sails billowed like clouds moving on a windswept day. Asil and Ole were at the helm, Ole's arm was around Asil's waist as her long dark hair blew in the wind like ravens on the wing. It was a beautiful day and for the time being none of us had a care in the world.

I for one was looking forward to the party that Odin had promised us. If Odin was throwing a party you can bet it would be one heck of a humdinger.

Suddenly the sky began to darken. The clouds turned grey. The waves increased in size and started to splash water onto the deck. Lightening flashed and illuminated a shadowy figure on the deck.

The figure waved his hand and the sky and the sea went calm. He was a giant of a man, at least seven foot tall, his long hair and beard were snow white and he carried a spear with two sharp barbs along its edge. He walked over to a barrel that was lashed to the deck and sat down. He looked at Ole and Asil as he spoke.

"You there at the rudder. Ole, I believe they call you. Lash the rudder in place and come here. Asil, you I know. You come and sit on the barrel next to me."

Ole did as he was told and I joined him at his side as we stood in front of this unknown being who had invaded our ship. Asil did not hesitate to follow orders and of course Einer was soon sitting next to her as she took a seat on an empty wooden barrel.

"I am Aegir Norse God of the deep. King of all the oceans and seas that cover the earth. Do you have no manners man? Fetch some grog for Asil, the Drogon Einer and me. Be quick about it. I don't have time to waste with mere mortal business."

Ole quickly located two drinking horns and a wooden bowl and filled them with grog. He handed the first to our visitor, the next to Asil and put the bowl on the deck in front of Einer.

"Do you recognize me human?"

Ole: "I'm sorry sir. I do not."

"You do not! Foolish mortal I am a Norse God." Then there was a long silent pause. "Well, I was a Norse God, until the one true God retired us and turned the world to Christianity. But, no matter I am still the King of the deep. You do know who the King of the deep is? Don't you?"

Ole: "I believe it would be Neptune or Poseidon. But, you your Kingship are new to me."

Asil decided to speak up to save what was turning into a very sticky situation for Ole.

Asil: "Aegir my Kingship. You must forgive this foolish mortal for he knows not of your greatness. His knowledge of the Norse Gods is not what it should be."

Aegir: "Not as it should be? He is Norwegian is he not?"

Asil: "He is. However he is the new breed of Norwegian, he comes from a future well beyond the time when the people worshipped the Gods of legends and Sagas. He was brought up with the belief in the one true God long after you and your brethren were retired. If you would be so kind, he is my friend and I would hope for my sake that you will forgive him."

Aegir: "For you my dear Asil I will overlook the mortal's lack of knowledge in those of us who shaped a world for his future kind."

Ole and I gave a slight bow in reverence to Aegir's power. Ole quietly asked for forgiveness.

Aegir: "You are forgiven, but remember this. Those other creatures of oceans and seas you mentioned. Poseidon and Neptune. They are nothing more than jellyfish that I allow to swim in my waters. Poseidon is nothing more than a mean-tempered, moody Greek demi-god. As for Neptune he prefers the fresh water of the seas, sprinkle him with a bit of salt-water from my oceans' and he will whimper for my mercy. I was a God of the Norse, powerful and mighty. Revered by the Vikings for my aid in helping them to navigate the waters of the world.

Asil took a swig of her grog in the best of Norse maiden tradition. She wiped the foam from her lips with the back of her hand. Leaning forward with her elbows on her knees she looked at Aegir. It was her way of showing Aegir that she was one of the no-nonsense warrior breed of Viking. Aegir looked at her with approval in his eyes.

Asil: "Aegir, may I ask just what brought you to my humble long boat. I'm sure this is not just a social call.

Aegir took a big swig of grog, the excess golden liquid ran out of the sides of his mouth and down his beard, where it then dripped onto his belly. He threw back his head and bellowed out a hearty laugh as he slapped his knee with his free hand. He finally gained his composure and gave Asil a serious look. "Asil, I've always liked you. You are a no nonsense woman of the warrior breed. They should have made you a Valkyrie instead of a Drogon keeper. Never the less, let's get down to business."

"Odin has a new assignment for you and your friends. I cannot go into the details. I was sent here to convey a message and to deliver you to your cavern as quickly as possible.

Ole: "I thought there was supposed to be a celebration party for us for defeating that evil President of America's future."

Aegir: "Humans. All they think about is themselves. Parties and recognition. Such silly creatures they are. Never any consideration for all we gods have done for them in the past. However, if it will appease you the party is taking place and has probably already started. Odin can be rather impatient when it comes to celebrating. Most likely we are already late. So hang on. Here we go!"

The wind increased, our sails billowed out to their breaking point. Our ship began picking up speed. The barrel Aegir was sitting on tilted at a forty-five degree angle. His powers of being a demi-god must have kept him from tipping over, although his grog was sloshing out of his drinking horn and splashing over his smiling face. His long hair flew into the wind and his beard parted in the middle and blew around his cheeks as he bellowed out a hearty laugh as he hollered loud enough for us to hear. "Steady yourselves matey's, we're picking up speed. We don't want to miss any more of the party then necessary. Although I must admit I'm already having fun."

Asil had fallen off her barrel as it tipped over and rolled to the stern of the ship. Her barrel was followed closely by Ole and myself. We crashed into the loose barrels that had rolled to the stern of ship with a sickening thud.

Asil had grabbed onto the ships mast and wrapping her arms around it she managed to regain her footing. Her raven hair undulating with the wind like dark waves on a stormy sea. She had a true Vikings smile on her face as she hollered out. "This is what I call sailing!"

Einer had unfolded his wings and was soaring just above the deck. His tail was at full wag and I could tell he was enjoying himself.

Although the wind made it seem as if we should be in a major typhoon the skies were filled with sunshine and the sea was calm as glass. The wind seemed to be confined to just our ships sails and deck. Our longboat was gliding over the water with such speed that just the center beam below the ship occasionally touched the water.

We were going too fast for Ole and I to regain our footing on the deck so we settled into a narrow open space between two barrels, curled up together, closed our eyes and prayed to the one true God that he would bring us to safety from this mad ride that Aegir was taking us on.

Although it seemed like forever it was probably less than half an hour before we entered the cove outside of Asil's' cavern. The longboat didn't even slow down as it entered the entrance to the cave that lead into the entrance of the mountain that held Asil's hidden home. Our speed remained the same as we took a high speed roller coaster style ride through the cave, each twist and turn pushed the wooden barrels against us until we were sure we would be squashed like bugs under a troll's foot. Suddenly we came to an abrupt stop. The ship dropped from the air with a mighty splash. Ole and I were tossed into the air and came down on our derrieres with a thump.

The crowd of party goers were watching us and a laughter at our plight reverberated off the walls of the cavern. Odin was sitting on a throne in the midst of the revelry and he was laughing the loudest of all.

A few moments passed as the laughter began to subside. Odin pounded the butt of his sword on the ground to quiet things down. All laughter and noise quickly deceased. Everyone's attention was diverted away from us and towards Odin.

Odin sat back on his throne. He took a long swig of grog from his drinking horn. "Our guests of honor have finally arrived due to the expedient assistance of our friend Aegir." Aegir stood up on the deck of our ship and made a sweeping gesture of a bow to the audience which gave him a thunderous applause.

Odin: "Please welcome our guests of honor. Asil, Einer, Sven and Ole." Another round of applause. "Saviors of the United States of America from a President who was hell bent on destroying its republic and turning its people against each other. A President who we can only hope will go down as one of the most evil despots in the history of the world."

"As all of us here know that now that we have been retired by the one true God that the Christian way of life is the best way. The Ten Commandments are an excellent way to lead our lives. The President that was disposed of by our band of heroes' was bent on turning the United States and then all of the world into a stronghold of Islamic beliefs where Christians would need to fear for their lives and women would be treated as a class lower than the lowest of animals."

A unicorn from the audience could be heard as he hollered out. "What's wrong with animals, Odin?"

Odin was taken back for a moment as he stumbled for his words. "I am sorry, that was a slip of the tongue on my part. Many Islam's treat animals as possessions which all of us here know is wrong. They want their animals only for working them to death or eating them. Their women are considered to be worth less than their animals. Please forgive me for my fauxpas.

Odin's apology, something that would have been unheard of before the one true God had humbled and retired the gods of old seemed to have been graciously accepted by the crowd of party goers. After all this was a time for celebration.

Odin's wife Freya walked up next to husband, a drinking horn in her hand, which from the looks of things she had frequently indulged in. She sat on Odin's lap as she addressed the crowd.

Freya: "If there is one thing all of us here know, men and women are equal in our world, be they human, or one of the many creatures gathered here tonight. We revere and respect each other as it should be. Working together there is nothing we cannot accomplish. Now to our honored guests." She lifted her drinking horn high into the air as did everyone in the room. "Skol to Asil, Einer, Sven, Ole and all those who helped them in their last quest."

Everyone present raised their drinking horns and hollered 'Skol" as they downed the golden liquid.

Asil was whisked from the ship amid cheers from the crowd by a glittering skinned handsome Merman and a Muscle bound Minotaur as Einer followed them down the gangplank to shore, Ole and I were quietly escorted to shore by Asil's companion and lifelong friend the diminutive troll Krypme.

The cavern was filled with hundreds of retired gods, deities and beings of myth and legends. Most of those present we had seen before at other parties thrown by Odin, however there was one individual we did not recognize from any of the previous parties. She, at least I assumed from the shape of her center torso and the presence of breasts that it was a she was by far the scariest most grotesque creature I have ever seen. Although I regretted my thoughts as soon as they entered my mind. I had been around Asil and her friends long enough to realize beauty was in the eye of the beholder. Also, anyone that was here was here because no matter what kind of lives they had led before retiring the one true God had given his son Christ Jesus over to death to allow those of this world a chance to change and redeem their sins.

Krympe had left us to get us some refreshments. I nudged Ole to look at the creature I have just told you about. It had the body of a women with a serpent's tail instead of legs which allowed her to balance and move much like a snake except with her body standing upright. Her head was covered with a shiny black snake skin looking scarf that hid her hair. However the scarf was moving about as if it was restraining something alive underneath it. Her eyes were covered with mirrored lensed sunglasses.   Krympe returned and handed us our drinking horns filled with grog. She noticed us staring at the creature.

Krympe: "You two seem mesmerized by the lady over there. You know it's not nice to stare."

Ole: "You must admit she seems a bit different than everyone else that we have seen."

I added in with. "Ole's right, and we've seen a lot since we were drafted into the service of Odin, Asil and Einer."

Krympe: "She has been confined for centuries to a life alone in a cave without any contact with anyone. Some of her mythical friend's felt sorry for her so they devised a way for her to leave the cave and come to this party. It is like a coming out party that humans throw for their children as they come of age. It was really a very nice gesture on the part of her friends and everyone here is doing their best to help her assimilate back into our world."

Ole: "That sounds like everyone here really cares about each other."

Krympe: "Of course we care. All of us here are unique in our own way. Since the one true God retired us we have to stick together. We are the living past, there will be no new individuals allowed to become the myths and legends that we fulfilled for so many centuries. We are the last of our breed. We have been privileged to retire in peace as long as we no longer let humans worship us and we do not interfere in human affairs unless we are asked to do so. Of course you know how that works with you being chosen along with Asil and Einer to occasionally help save this world from being ruled by an evil that always seems to be lurking around and bent on ruling the world or destroying it."

I spoke up, a little miffed at being put off from our original discussion. "All right already. Enough of the niceties of good fellowship, togetherness and saving the world. Let's get back to the original subject. Who's the lady with the wicked tail and the undulating head scarf?"

Krympe: "I'm amazed neither of you recognized her. She is famous in Greek legend."

"Just in case you forgot, we're not Greek."

Krympe: "Sven, don't you want to guess, I gave you a great hint in the fact she's Greek. I bet Ole knows who she is."

Ole: "Yes, I believe I do know, but I'm not saying until Sven figures it out."

"All right you two, that's just about enough. Remember I'm a dog, I don't have a whole lot of background in Greek mythology, and my partner Ole didn't do a lot of reading of Greek history to me when I was a puppy. I give up. Who is she?"

Krympe: "It's Medusa."

I gave a doggie gasp. "You mean the Medusa of Greek legend. The Medusa with snakes for hair who turns you into stone Medusa?"

Krympe: "One in the same. Come along and I'll introduce you to her. She's very shy, so many centuries of being alone have had an effect on her social skills."

I wasn't so sure about Ole but I for one was a bit nervous to meet her. What if her sunglasses fell off? If I was to get stoned I would rather it be from drinking too much grog instead of being turned to stone by looking into the eyes of a Greek legend.

Krympe led us over to Medusa and introduced us. Medusa shyly lowered her head a bit as if she was ashamed of her reputation. "It's nice to meet you. Please forgive me for not knowing who you are. I have been in seclusion for quite some time. I have heard that you have been chosen by Odin to help keep order in this chaotic new world we live in. I think that we are lucky that this true God finally took over and retired us. I'm afraid our own vanity caused so much dissention among the gods and deities after all that it was we who were leading the world to destruction. If it was not for the true God I would never have been given a chance to assimilate back into the world of my peers. Is it not strange that now it is human leaders who want to control and take over the world just as the god's of old had done?"

Ole: "It is strange. Hopefully the true God will step in as necessary to stop the evil in this world. Although, if my knowledge of the bible is correct he is giving humans a chance to choose between good and evil and when the time comes we will be judged by our individual acts. One God for all of us is as you said a good thing."

Krympe made our apologies about having to take our leave so quickly. She explained to Medusa that as the guests of honor we needed to mingle with the other guests as quickly as possible for Odin would soon be making an important announcement. Ole and I told Medusa it was nice to meet her and then we moved on with Krympe who was making sure we greeted all the individuals and creatures that we needed to.

One large bodied couple I found extremely interesting. The male was close to nine-feet tall and his wife was closer to the eight-foot tall mark. He had very dark fur covering him from head to toe. She had reddish blonde fur that covered her from top to bottom. Both had faces that were somewhere between simian and human. Long arms and super large feet set them apart from most the other guests. His name was Sequoia and hers was Pinecone. They are Sasquatches. Krympe made a point to tell us before introducing us that they would find it offensive if we referred to them as Bigfoot.

After we met them I was super excited. "See Ole, they are real. All this time people doubted their existence. This is great. We met two Sasquatch and Medusa all on the same night."

Ole: "Sven. Look around. Every legend and myth we have ever heard of is here at this party. There's a group of leprechauns over there, and there is Wendigo from the American Indian legends, way back in the corner is Paul Bunyan and Babe the blue ox."

"Bow-wow! Babe the blue ox, we've gotta meet Babe. Never in my wildest dreams did I ever think I'd see Babe the blue ox!"

Krympe gave us a few minutes of time for a quick introduction to Paul Bunyan and Babe. Paul and Ole made some small talk. I stood tongue-tied staring at Babe, who gave me a bellowed out, "helloo, nice to meet you." Best I could do was slobber out a weak "hi"

As we made our way back into the crowd I said. "Babe, Sasquatch and Medusa, all in one night. I wish I could tell someone."

Krympe: "Sven, be sensible. You know you can never tell anyone what or who you have seen here or on your travels for Odin. If you did it would not bode well for your or Ole."

Ole: "Even if you did tell someone they would think you were crazy and lock you up in an insane asylum."

Krympe: "Sven, no need to worry about humans thinking you are crazy. If they knew you were a talking dog they would lock you up and run experiments on you until you died. It would be like putting you in a doggie concentration camp."

Well, both Krympe and Ole made a good point. Guess I'll just keep things to myself and Ole. What a 'cat' astrophe get it? A little nasty cat reference there 'catastrophe.'

The party was in full swing. Parkurkarkus was in charge of entertainment and with the help of who knows what deity he had recruited none other than Roy Orbison from the future with his band to perform. Roy was wooing the crowd with songs like Mean Woman Blues, Blue Bayou, Claudette and many others. Aegir went to the stage and requested one of his favorites which Roy gladly obliged. Leah was sung for Aegir to satisfy his ocean minded desires, by this time almost all in attendance were swaying or dancing to the music. Krympe went up to the stage and made her own request, she then returned to Ole's side with a mischievous little smile on her face.

She nudged Ole in the ribs and whispered to him as she pointed at Medusa. "Ole, she's so lonely and shy, ask her to dance."

Roy started singing She's a Mystery to me. Reluctantly Ole did as Krympe suggested. He knew what it was like to be an outcast from his own school days and it was not a feeling he would wish on anyone. It was quite a sight to see, Ole leading Medusa through the dance with her serpents tail swaying in joy. I just hoped they didn't get so active that Medusa's sun glasses might fall off and turn my partner to stone. One thing I had to admit the song was certainly fitting for Medusa.

Roy finished his performance singing Pretty Woman to a room filled with applause. He looked over the audience and made a brief thank you speech. "Folks, at least I hope it's all right to address you as folks as I'm not sure what other term to use and I surely do not wish to offend anyone. I'm not quite sure how I got here. In fact I'm not really sure I am here. It might just be a dream. If it is a dream it's by far the most unusual one I've ever had. I wish to thank you all for having me and my band, now I really need to wake up or else someone is going to have to tell me how we can get back home. There was a huge puff of smoke on the stage and as it dissipated Roy and the band disappeared

Once the band was gone the place got pretty quiet. Odin pounded the butt end of his sword on the ground to get everyone's attention.

Odin: "We are out of music and more importantly we are now out of grog. Thank you all for coming. The party is officially over. It is time for everyone to leave except for Asil, Einer, Sven, Ole, Parkurkarkus and Krympe.

CHAPTER 2

It was amazing how quickly a party filled with unusual beings can disappear so fast. Then again, when those beings are retired deities, myths and legends they have abilities to transport themselves well beyond the comprehension of us canines and mere mortal humans.

Once the cavern was emptied of guests we made our way over to Odin who sat wobbling on his throne. No doubt a case of a little over indulgence of grog.

Odin: "I know this celebration was held to commend you for a job well done in the future America. I'm sure you figured this was your last quest."

Odin burped, wiped some excess grog from his beard and licked some of the spilled grog from his hand. He leaned forward with his hands on his knees as he looked at us. His one unpatched eye bloodshot from too much partying, eating and especially drinking.

Odin: "Well, you figured wrong my Viking warriors. The one true God has one last assignment for you. When I say last I mean last, this is the end, the final chapter in your saga. He told me himself, once this mission is completed it will be the end of the chronicles of Asil and her Drogon Einer. Asil and Einer will be able to retire in peace. She can settle down, maybe find a man that is fitting to her position as a Princess of the Drogon. Now, I bet you would like to know what the final quest is all about?"

I for one was a bit worried about one of the things Odin had just mentioned. I looked at Ole and I knew he heard what I heard. Asil should settle down and find a partner that would be fitting of her position in the world of the Norse legends. In my own mind and probably in Ole's too there was serious doubts that my partner was to be that man.

By this time Odin was getting drossy and having trouble concentrating.

Odin: "Any guesses as to your next assignment? No? All right then, I'll tell you. As all of you are probably aware the Germans have finally surrendered and officially the war in Europe is over. Well, sort of over if you don't count the mess the Allies are going to have with the Soviets. Also, the mess the rest of the world is left in with the major world powers having to deal with colonies and countries who want the freedoms promised them if they sided with the allies or kept their neutrality during the conflict. Anyways it is going to be a major snafu as the military would call it for a very long time. However, that's not the problem we are currently worried about. Those doggone Germans, sorry Einer and Sven no offense meant. Back to my point, the Germans aren't ones to just walk away with their tails between their legs and go sulk off in a corner somewhere."

Einer and I looked at each other wondering if the tail between the legs, sulking off comment was another dog reference. We shrugged our shoulders and thought it best to ignore it as another slip of the tongue. After all, Odin was pretty well soused and his mind seemed a bit blurred.

Odin: "It seems some of the Nazi's, wait, let me rephrase that. Some of the dissidents that were loyal Germans because of their heritage, some from the military, some who were in the Nazi party and god-forbid possibly some of the non-military SS that ran the genocide programs have decided to continue to work on putting Germany back into a position of power as if their country had never admitted defeat. We know approximately where they are and a bit of what they are up to. Your mission, should you decide to accept it."

Odin chuckled to himself as his belly shook and he spilled some grog from his drinking horn.

Odin: "I heard that phrase, 'your mission if you should decide to accept it' from a thing they call a television show that Parkurkarkus told me about. Something from the future. I checked it out and he was right, there is such a thing. I marveled how they can find all those little people to put on those big flat screens so we can watch them act out their parts. I would have thought it was black magic if the one true God hadn't explained to me that it is something they now call technology."

I think we were all hoping Odin would get to the point pretty soon as he was looking drowsy and had to keep grabbing the arms of his throne and pushing himself back into an upright position. Odin took another swig of grog and then looked unhappily into his drinking horn. He took his finger and ran it around the inside of his drinking horn, stuck his finger into his mouth and sucked off the few remaining golden droplets of grog. Then he turned his drinking horn upside down. He looked sadly at us as he said. "Empty as my mother-in-law's heart."

Odin: "Well, let's get back to business. I suppose you are wondering why I called you all together. Wait, did I say that before? Oh well, no matter. I am sending you on one last assignment. You are to go to the Antarctic and find out what our German friends are up to. Rumor has it that they have some new technology and that if they get it up and running it will probably not be good for the rest of the world. Your job will be to stop them. God, our boss added in that it would be nice to do so with as little bloodshed as necessary. There is a truck with skis outside the rear entrance to the caverns and there will be a ship waiting for you at Hammerfest harbor to take you to the Svalbard airport where a plane and supplies will be made available for you to continue your journey. There was be more information I was supposed to tell you, but I'm too tired and drunk to remember what it was. You'll figure it out on your own, you always do. I think the ship's captain might be able to shed some light as to the next step in your journey. Time for me to go to bed. Good luck."

Asil: "Odin, just a minute. Just how many of us are going on this quest?"

Odin: "Oh, ah, yes. Umm…let's see. I know the answer. You Asil, Einer, Sven, Ole and Parkurkarkus. Might have been someone else, I can't be sure, just don't remember if there was or not. Oh well, if there is they will show up sooner or later."

Odin never made it to bed. He passed out on his throne snoring like thunder. We looked at each other and Parkurkarkus suggested we best be going.

We quietly made our way out to the back entrance of the cavern so as not to disturb Odin. Winter gear was awaiting us at the exit of the cavern. We bundled up in heavy parkas, boots, mittens and face masks. Krympe was not to be included in our mission but she was here to help us get ready to venture out into the cold. It was a sad and tearful goodbye between her and Asil as we left.

We trudged through knee deep snow with the wind blasting and snow swirling about us. In the distance we could make out the shape of what appeared to be a vehicle. We finally got near enough to see that Odin had supplied us with a bus equipped with tracks on the rear and skis on the front. Parkurkarkus pulled open the driver's door and crawled inside. Ole opened the rear door for Einer and me to hop inside and get out of the storm that was raging around us. As soon as we were inside Asil and Ole did their best to clear the vehicle of snow and scrap off the driver's windshield. There were blankets, food and water inside the vehicle along with shovels and pick axes to help us out if we should get stuck. The vehicle appeared to be a small six person bus converted for snow travel. Not so unusual for a vehicle in Norway. Once the snow was cleared from the outside of the vehicle Ole took a seat up front next to Parkurkarkus. Asil sat between Einer and I and the three of us cuddled up next to each other for warmth as Asil pulled a blanket over us.

Parkurkarkus pulled the engines choke and tried the starter. It took a few tries as the engine would slowly cough to life and then die. After the fourth try the engine sputtered to life as Parkurkarkus played with the choke and foot throttle until the cold engine finally kept enough life giving gas in its system to run on its own.

Parkurkakus and the rest of us breathed a sigh of relief all congratulating him on getting the vehicle running. He sucked in his breath and then admonished us all. "Everyone, try not to breath any more than necessary. You're fogging up the windows and it may take quite some time before this old truck warms up enough for the defrosters to work. If I can't see out the windows we aren't going anywhere and we need to get moving as soon as possible if we hope to be off this mountain before nightfall. Crack your windows a bit and exhale your breath outside."

Once the engine settled into a nice purr and Parkurkarkus had wiped the condensation from the windshield so he could see he tried to work the truck into gear. This was no easy task as the cold had stiffened the lubricant for the gears into the consistency of molasses in the winter. After much cajoling and grinding of gears the truck finally slipped into first gear. Parkurkarkus pushed down on the gas pedal and the truck shook as if it was in an earthquake as it made every effort to break the frozen tracks from the ice that had hardened around them. Parkurkarkus explained that when the truck had been parked the tracks were probably warm enough from the trip here that they had melted the snow around them and then it froze them to the ground locking them in place. Who had left it here or how long ago we had no idea, although it must have been recently or we would have never got it started.

Parkurkarkus had transversed these mountains many times in his days of being a scoundrel, and also as a guide, hunter, and trader. He knew the area like the back of his hand. Many years of questionable activities in the area had taught him all the tricks of survival we would be needing to survive in the cold and the wilderness. With the time we had all spent together trust in one another was never in doubt. Parkurkarkus was by far the best choice and the best hope of getting us to the nearest port alive and in one piece.

The first leg of our journey was smooth riding. Not too many rock outcroppings or steep grades to climb. The trucks heater was adequate enough for us to remove or mittens and parkas and settle in. Lots of small talk about our past adventures but no one cared to speculate about our upcoming assignment.

Parkurkarkus: "We'll have to find a different route then I usually take. I'm not sure what route was used to get this truck up here, knowing Odin it might have been done with magic. Either way there are no tracks for us to follow. The trail I usually use is too narrow in places for this thing. If we tried using it we would most likely go over a cliff and spend eternity in some chasm. The only other trail I can think of is pretty steep, great if we were on skis. Might be rather questionable with a tracked vehicle."

Ole: "Gee, that does sound inviting."

Asil: "Don't let Parky scare you. He knows what he is doing. He just wants to show off so we appreciate him more than we should."

Parkurkarkus smiled a big smile as he down shifted the truck to transverse some rock outcroppings. We were making good time and soon we came to the mountain slopes that would lead us down to the sea. We stopped and looked over the situation. We were on a precipice at the edge of a steep downhill slope. If we were on skis it would be one heck of a ride down to the bottom. In a truck with tracks, well, I guess we were about to find out.

Parkurkarkus: "This is it. If we are going down this is the only place I know of for a vehicle of this size. I suggest everyone hang on and get ready for one hell of a ride."

Parky slipped the truck into first gear and slowly inched forward. There was a drift right ahead of us and the trucks front skis went three-quarters of the way over the edge of the drift before the weight of the truck broke it away and we started down.

Parkurkarkus kept the truck in first gear as long as possible to slow our assent. Before long the tracks began to slide sideways as the truck gained speed. Parky shifted into second in hopes of keeping control. We kept picking up speed and soon the tracks were sliding again. The truck only had three gears and we were now in third to no avail. The speedometer showed us at 60 kilometers per hour and that was probably the fastest this old truck had ever went, much too fast for the tracks to keep up with when you consider with the tracks mounted this old jalopy was probably lucky to hit 30 kilometers.

The rear end of the truck started sliding sideways. With the weight of the tracks there was no way that the skis up front would be able to counter steer the rear end and with the throttle to the floor there were no other options. We were in big trouble and only three-quarters of the way down the slope. It did not take long before the rear end of the truck was now perpendicular to the front. As we continued our descent with the truck sliding sideways we all knew that the worst was soon to happen, and it did.

Sliding sideways as we were the truck soon started to tip. I'm not sure who yelled out or if all we did at the same time. "We're going over, hang on!" With a sickening thud the truck tipped onto its side as we all tumbled onto each other in a jumble of legs and paws. Laying on top of the side windows all we could see below us was white snow as the truck slid along moving in a slowly revolving circle and acting as if anytime it would start rolling end to end at any moment which would mean the worse for all of us.

Whether it was luck or fate or a helping hand from above I'm not sure. We continued our slide down the mountain slope as we were jostled, shaken and bruised up and even though the tracks dug in and lifted a bit the truck managed to stay on its side. Finally we came to a sudden stop as the roof of the truck slammed into an ice hardened pile of snow.

The jolt of hitting the hard pile of snow rolled Asil, Einer and I into a pile of bodies, luckily none of us was really hurt, but we were certainly shaken up a bit.

Parky and Ole stood up and pushed the door open on the upside of the truck. Parky gave Ole a leg up as he scrambled out the door. Ole reached back in and gave Parky his hand and helped pull him out. Ole stood on the side of the truck and opened the back door for us. Asil handed me up first and I was passed on to Parky who was waiting on the ground. Einer was next up. Ole then locked hands with Asil and pulled her out. Ole was about to give Asil a big hug but she backed away, something strange about that, but this was no time to ponder it.

While Parky and Ole looked the truck over for damage. Asil, Einer and I climbed to the top of the snowbank that had so unceremoniously brought us to such an abrupt stop.

Asil: "Hey fella's, you aren't going to believe this. There's a plowed road right here and there is an opening in the snowbank about a hundred yards from here. The truck should fit through it. That is if it's still in running condition."

Parkurkakus: "Asil come down here and help Ole and I push the truck upright. Luckily the truck had come to rest against the snowbank at an angle so that with one track embedded in the snow and the other track a few feet off the ground it was fairly easy for the three of them to put their backs against the roof of the truck and pushing with their legs against the hardened snowbank they soon had the truck flopping back down on its tracks and skis.

The big question now was if the truck would start. It had quit running on our downhill slide. Parky opened the hood and started brushing away the accumulated snow from the engine. Two of the spark plug caps had come loose but at least they were still there.

Parky reconnected them and was satisfied that things looked normal.

Parky: "Ole get in and turn it over, let's see what happens." The trucks engine shook and sputtered. "I think it's flooded. Hang on for a minute, I'm going to take off the air cleaner and hold the carburetor open. Ok, try it again with no choke."

Ole tried again, excess gas in the carburetor shot in golden droplets into the air. The engine sputtered and shook. "Hold the throttle to the floor" hollered Parky The engine kept sputtering and then it coughed on two cylinders, shaking and rattling like it was about to break loose from the frame. The third and fourth cylinders finally sputtered to life. For about two minute the engine ran as if it was in extreme pain. We all crossed our fingers and held our breath.

If it hadn't stayed running it might be a long time before any vehicles came along to help us and an even longer walk to the nearest village. The wind was still blowing but much less so then it had been higher up the mountain and the snow had stopped. It was still cloudy and maybe zero degrees so if the truck wasn't going anywhere we probably wouldn't be either. After another five minutes the trucks engine was purring again like it was supposed to. So far so good.

Asil: "Let's pile in and get moving. Parky, do you have any idea which direction we should be going?"

Parkurkakus: "I do. Call it a sixth sense. However, we best see if this old truck can still move under its own power. Ole and my visual inspection didn't find any serious damage we could see but we'll know more once we put it in gear and start moving. That was a rather nasty trip it made down the mountainside. Could be some unseen internal damage."

Parky slipped the truck into first gear with barley a grinding noise to be heard. Certainly a good sign. Once we started to move it was a different story. The rear of the truck went up on one side and came down with a thump that almost tossed us off our seats.

Ole: "Well, that doesn't feel right. Hold on, I'll get out and take a look."

Ole went behind the truck and laying on his back he pushed himself under it. "Sven, come here, you're smaller than me. I want you to take a look at the connection rod to the track on this side."

I jumped out the door and joined my partner. I got down on my belly and crawled under the truck. I managed to get an up close look at what Ole was talking about. I came out from under the truck and Ole and I got back inside out of the cold. I told everyone that the rod was bent. Parky said there was no way we could fix it in this bitter cold. If we were to try and pound it straight it would be so brittle that it would most likely break. All we could do was to go slow and limp the truck to the nearest village and hope we would make it before the rod broke.

We slowly made our way to the opening of the snowbank and drove onto the main road. Once we were on the road we began to ka-thump, ka-thump our way along at about five to seven kilometers per hour. We were running low on petrol but luckily our benefactor who had supplied us with the truck had seen fit to have jerry-cans of petrol strapped on the outside back of the truck. We stopped to fill the petrol tanks after about an hour of driving. This stop was a welcome reprieve for all of us to get out and stretch our legs and our aching backs from the rough ride. So far we had not seen so much as a vehicle or building anywhere. Asil climbed on top of the truck to look around.

Asil: "Good news fellas. I can see a village ahead and a sign that says Hammerfest Harbor two kilometers."

Parky and Ole finished filling the truck with petrol and we were soon back on the road. The village was now in sight which was a good thing as the old truck was slowing down. The radiator must have been damaged and probably had a slow leak, it was now low on water and the engine was overheating. Smoke and steam were wafting out of the engines hood as we ka-thumped into the village. Our poor old workhorse of a truck finally clunked to a stop in front of the One Horned Viking Pub. We got out of the truck and Parky rushed over and tossed open the engines hood to make sure it wasn't going to burst into flames. He hollered at Ole for some help and they proceeded to toss handfuls of snow on the engine to cool it down. Steam filled the air but there was no fire and soon things seemed to be under control. Everyone was safe and sound except for our mode of transportation. Parky sadly told us the engine was most likely shot and would have to be replaced. However we were in a village and near the harbor and as far as we could tell this was our destination to the next leg of our journey,

Parky and Ole joined the rest of us on the cobblestone sidewalk. We looked up at the sign jutting out from the front of the building as it swayed in the wind, the chains holding it in place creaking in the breeze. The oval sign was painted with the words One Horned on the top and Viking on the bottom. In the center was the face of an inebriated Viking with a one horned helmet slightly askew on his head.

It was still bitter cold so Parky quickly suggested. "What are we standing around for? Say your prayers for the old jalopy 'cause it's dead and ready to be scrapped or get an engine and rear end transplant. As for me I'm starving and my thirst needs quenching."

We went into the pub, it was a bit on the dark side. A few lights shone down from the ceiling casting weird shadows on the floor from the tables, chairs and especially from some rather comical Viking characters that were carved of wood and jutted out from the wall like the masthead figures used on old sailing ships. Each character had an inebriated look on his face and a one horned helmet on his head. Some at a tilt, some askew and some backwards.

We approached the highly polished wood bar along one side of this rather narrow little establishment. A rather robust lady with puffy red cheeks and long blonde braided hair hanging in pigtails was behind the bar and spoke to us in Norwegian.

Luckily, Asil, Parky and Einer understood her. Of course Einer couldn't say anything. Ole and I had no idea what was being said but we assumed things were going well as Asil led us to one of the tables near the back of the room. Parky soon came over with a tray filled with beer, large pint mugs for the humans and two bowls, one for Einer and one for me.

Parky: "I hope you don't mind but I took the liberty to order food for all of us. The Barmaid said she just got in a shipment of deep-water Prawn from one of the local fishermen. She's going to cook some up for us along with chips"

That seemed to be fine with Asil and Einer and certainly with Ole and I as we had no idea what was going on around us with the language barrier. However, whenever someone made mention of fish we were fair game to try anything.

Parky: "I mentioned to her that we were here to meet a ship to take us to Longyearbyen. She said the captain was a regular customer and had told her to keep an eye out for us. Seems he had heard mention that I was one of those who would be traveling with him. I'm not sure why but he seemed to figure I would be stopping here as soon as I arrived, it being the only pub in town. She is going to make a phone call so that someone can fetch him here. From what she told me he is the Captain of a puffer."

Ole: "I hate to seem dumb. What the heck is a puffer?"

Parky: "A puffer? Really, you have never heard of a puffer?"

Asil: "Me either. Exactly what is a puffer? Is it the same as a blowfish?"

Parky: "It's not a fish. It's a ship. They started building them in the 1850's right up until 1939. In the beginning they referred to them as Clyde Puffers because originally they were built to transverse the Clyde Canal. As they ventured into more areas and different canals the name was shortened to just puffers. Originally they were designed to traverse the locks around Scotland and the British Isles. There flat bottoms and narrow hulls made them ideal for carrying freight in narrow canals that were the main means of moving freight in the mid to late 1800's right up until today. They mostly kept to fresh water areas as they used coal powered steam engines that made a distinctive puffing sound and hence the name. The early steam engine puffers drew fresh water from the canals so they did not venture into salt water as it would ruin their boilers. Later models either converted to or started out with diesel engines so they had no need for a fresh water supply and could start venturing out into salt water travel. There one disadvantage to sea or ocean travel is their flat bottoms can make for a harsh ride in rough seas. On the plus side they can get into shallow harbors and they tend to be tough as nails"

We were just finishing a very satisfying meal when a tattered looking man with a grizzled beard, short in stature and a captain's hat came through the door of the pub. The woman behind the bar greeted him with "Hello Captain, I assume you want your regular?" Of course she said it in Norwegian but I got the drift.

Captain: "Yah, you best make it two and some of today's special. Where's the folks that been waiting for me?"

She pointed at us and the Captain made his way to our table. He removed his hat and took Asil's hand and kissed it. "I'm your Captain folks. I never dreamed that one of my passengers would be so beautiful. May I ask you name pretty lady?"

Asil blushed as she answered: "My name is Asil. My companions are Parkurkarkus, Ole, Einer and Sven. Please join us Captain. Do you speak English, if so please do so as Ole does not understand Norwegian."

Captain: "I do. I do not speak English so well, but I can get by. My crew Lars and Diesel they also speak English so we will all do our best to accommodate your request. I was told you wish to go to Longyearbyen is that correct?"

Asil: "It is. How soon can you have your ship ready?"

Captain: "Who is in charge of your group? I have an envelope on board the ship in my safe. It is to be given to the one in charge just before we reach Longyearbyen. I need to know the person's name and if it matches the name on the envelope and you have papers proving your identity we can set out as soon as the tide comes in."

Asil looked at the rest of us. We had never really picked anyone to be in charge. Einer and I knew we were not candidates. Ole and Parkurkarkus both pointed at Asil.

Asil: "I am in charge." She pulled out her identification papers which all our human partners had been issued at the very start of our adventures together. They were a bit tattered and worn but still legible.

The Captain looked them over and compared the photo and description of Asil. "Looks to be in order. I was told there would be three of you and two dogs so I guess you meet the criteria."

The Captains food came and we all ordered more beers to make things a bit more sociable The Captain and Parky seemed to be in a bit of a contest as they consumed beers at a rate of 3 to 1 compared to the rest of us. Although Ole was doing his darndest to keep up with them.

Ole: "Captain. I heard your ship is a Clyde Puffer. Is that true?"

Captain: "Aye, it is. Diesel powered she is, can do 6 knots steady on a most days. On calm seas she may even be able to reach 10 knots. She's called the Carolsea and a finer vessel has never sailed from this port."

Asil: "Captain. It's quite a distance from here to Longyearbyen. How long do you think it will take us to get there?"

Captain: "Right you are Missy, it is a fair ways away, about 1046 kilometers or close to 650 miles as your American friend there would say. I've made the run many a times before and during the war. A shortage of cargo ships put a lot of strain on the few of us that could ply the oceans and avoid being sunk. I would say if we have fair weather and smooth sailing we should make port in 8 days, 9 at the most."

Ole: "You would have thought that we would have been supplied with air transport. We could have been there in a matter of hours."

Captain: "Air transport. No way that would or could happen. With the shortage of planes and aviation fuel and the fact that most of Norway and the Svalbard Airport near Longyearbyen are still under military control there is not a chance of civilians flying anywhere. You have me and only me that was even willing to take passengers on board. If the man that made your arrangements hadn't paid me in gold and gotten me well-oiled with beer you would be stranded here. I got plenty of cargo on board and it pays well and the people of Longyearbyen are depending on me to deliver.

Parky: "Just what did the man look like that paid our passage?"

Captain: "Not many things scare or impress me, this fellow did both. He was a big man. Close to seven foot tall with long hair and a long beard. Had the way of a man of the sea if you know what I mean. From our drinking discussions I have the feeling this fellow traveled more oceans and sea voyages then I even knew existed. I noticed the gold jewelry he wore around his neck and wrists and the only place I have ever seen gold designs like that were in pictures of long lost treasure ships. When he tossed a leather bag of ancient gold coins in front of me I almost sobered up on the spot. I took out one coin and looked it over, it was worth the passage for all of you. He looked at me and asked what I was doing. I sheepishly returned the coin to the bag. He laughed and downed a whole pint of lager in one gulp. He motioned me to do the same, so I did my best. Then he said, the bag of gold is yours providing you follow my instructions. He told me what to do and handed me an envelope. If you do not fulfill your commitment he said, I will have your ship, the gold, your crew and you as my guests in the briny deep of the deepest of oceans, and there you will toll for eternity in Davey Jones locker. Needless to say, I will do all in my power to fulfill his wishes."

All of us sat wide eyed and bushy tailed, well, Einer and I were bushy tailed. It sounds like Aegir was still on the job of looking after us.

The Captain finished his meal and Asil suggested we best be on our way. However the Captain had other ideas.

Captain: "Wait just a minute. No big rush matey's. High tide won't be for another hour and the Carolsea is still resting on her bottom in the cove. How about we have a few more beers and play some darts?"

Parky: "Sounds like a fine plan to me."

I could see Asil was not too pleased but what could she say? She played a few rounds of darts with the men and then joined Einer and me back at the table. Our three male members were drinking heavily and it was becoming doubtful as to their usefulness when we set sail. For Parky and Ole that was not a problem. For the Captain of our ship it might prove to be a detriment. After an hour had passed Asil quickly put an end to the dart playing and the drinking.

Asil: "Tides in boys, time for us to sail."

Barmaid: "Captain, time to pay you bill you old bilge rat. No sneaking out like you usually do. I can't be waiting a month of Sunday's for you to settle up your accounts."

The Captain drunkenly answered. "I believe Asil is in charge this voyage. She'll settle up for me and her crew."

Asil decided it best not to argue with the Captain's logic. She paid our bill and ushered her three drunken charges out the door. "How far to the ship Captain?" She asked.

Captain: "Not far, just a short walk from here. You just follow me and my two new friends Parky and Ole"

With the Captain in the center and Parky on one side and Ole on the other they soon had their arms around each other's shoulders to help keep the three of them from falling over. Asil grabbed a big stick off the ground that she used to prod her drunken campions along.

Soon the three of them were singing a rousing chorus of. 'What will we do with a drunken sailor?'

'What will we do with a drunken sailor? What will we do with a drunken sailor? Early in the morning. Way hay and up she rises, way hay and up she rises, early in the morning. Shave his belly with a rusty razor, shave his belly with a rusty razor.' Well, you get the point. The three of them were well lubricated and inebriated to the point you could almost hear the beer sloshing about in their bellies.

We finally arrived at the pier. A young man about sixteen years of age was sitting on the edge of an empty wooden crate waiting for us. He jumped to his feet when he saw us approaching. He rushed over to the Captain and said. "Captain, you promised me you wouldn't get drunk. I knew you would be like this. I could hear you and your companions singing about the drunken sailor five minutes ago. Look at you Captain, you are the drunken sailor you've been singing about."

Captain: "Hold your tongue boy. That's no way to speak to your captain. Where's the dingy?"

The lad looked at Parky and Ole and seeing the condition they were in he decided to address himself to Asil. "My name is Lars me lady. I'm first mate on the Carolsea. Please accept my apologies for the Captain. He's a fine sailor and you can trust him even in the roughest of seas. However, he sometimes goes a bit overboard with his drinking if you know what I mean."

Captain: "Don't you go apologizing for me boy. I asked where the dingy was."

Lars: "It's at the end of pier Captain. You'll have to go down the ladder to board it. I'll go first and you can follow so I can make sure you don't fall in the water like the last time you were drinking."

Captain: "I didn't fall in, I jumped in. I was in the mood for a swim."

Lars looked at Asil, Einer and I and he mouthed the words. "He was drunk, he fell in."

Lars: "Yes Sir, Captain. Best not to go in swimming today. The water is mighty cold. Once you are on board the dingy I'll go back up the ladder and help your friends down. We certainly don't want any of them falling or jumping into the water."

Asil held Parky and Ole back so that they would not attempt the trip down the ladder on their own. "That sounds like a good idea Lars. These are your other passengers, Parkurkarkus, we call him Parky and the other one is Ole. I'm sure they are not in the mood for a swim either, although it might do them some good and the gods only know they should be taught a lesson. If it's all right with you maybe I could hand our canine companions Einer and Sven down to you when you're ready."

Einer would have preferred to fly down to the dingy on his own but of course he knew that wasn't permissible to let anyone see him flying about.

Lars: "That sounds like a good idea Miss Asil."

Once Lars had everyone situated in the dingy he grabbed the oars and rowed us out to deeper water where the tide had lifted the Carolsea to floating level. The Captain, Parky and Ole once again broke into a chorus of 'What do you do with a drunken sailor,' so there was no doubt that the remaining crew of the Carolsea would be expecting us.

Once we were alongside the Carolsea a man on board the ship stood waiting at the decks railing. He dropped a rope ladder down to us.

Lars looked up at the older man and hollered. "Got the Captain and three passengers plus two dogs. Requesting permission to come aboard ship."

The man looked down at us as he answered. "Lars you idiot. Don't act so formal this ain't the Navy. Looks to me as if the Captain has had a snoot full again."

Lars: "Aye, he has, as have our two male passengers. I'll steady the ladder down here, you get ready to help them aboard. I also have a female guest and two dogs to board. Can you send down a wooden crate with a rope attached for me to put the dogs in so you can hoist them aboard?"

"No problem Lars." He answered.

Once we were all on board the older man who was the ships engineer we learned was called Diesel. He led the Captain to his quarters for a needed rest and sobering up period. Lars helped Asil take Parky and Ole to the crew's quarters and put them to bed. Asil volunteered to stay with them as did Einer and I. There were four bunks in the crew's quarters. Two on each of the longer walls. Parky and Ole were put into the bottom bunks so that if they fell out it wouldn't be so far to the floor. Asil put Einer and me on one of the top bunks and she took the other. The bunks were narrow, one person per bunk was maximum or two dogs per bunk was all right. It had been a long tiring day fraught with thrills and dangers that had tired us out. I vaguely heard the rumble of the diesel engine of the ship and felt the smooth movement we made as the ship started us on the next leg of our journey. I was soon fast asleep next to Einer who was twice my size and I appreciated his warm body close to mine to keep the chill of the night from my bones.

There was a bright light, then a shadow, light and shadow, moving past my closed eyelids. I opened one eye and noticed it was a streak of bright sunshine, than shadow. The Sun was just coming over the horizon and the undulating of waves was moving the ship slowly up and down just enough to let the sun have its brief moments of brightness enter the porthole near our bed. I raised my head and could see daylight was upon us. I nudged Einer. "Time to get up and greet the day buddy."

He rolled on his back and wagged his tail as he looked at me. "Nice to be at sea again. I'll glide over to Asil's bunk and wake her up."

He had a definite advantage over me as our bunk was way too high for me to safely jump down without risking injury to myself. He woke Asil up with a few well-placed doggie kisses to her cheek. She climbed down from her bunk and came over and helped me to the floor. Parky and Ole were still sound asleep and each was making a combination of gurgling and snoring sounds. Asil looked at Einer and me and said. "You two wake them up and don't be gentle about it."

Einer took Parky and I got Ole. We both jumped on top of their bellies as they let out a startled grunt like the pigs that they had been last night. Next we started licking and slobbering on their faces until they tried to shoo us away with their hands. We finally got both of them sitting up on the edge of their bunks trying to avoid us. They coughed and hacked like drunks often due for a few minutes as they forced their blood shot eyes to stay open.

 Parky: "Ole, is that you? You look a bit blurry."

Ole: "Yeah, it's me. You don't look any better. Where are we?"

Asil: "You both look like dragon poop on a warm day if that's any consolation. As to where we are. We're on the puffer ship the Carolsea heading to Longyearbyen. You two and the Captain hung one on last night. I suggest you get cleaned up and head up on deck so you can sober up. Sven, Einer and I are going to go to the galley and make some breakfast after we check in with the Captain. Hopefully he's in better shape than you two. When you feel up to it you can join us, providing you aren't smelling like stale beer and you look presentable."

The Captain was in the wheel house when we stopped by to say good morning. He was chipper and looked the same as we did when we first met him, unshaven, a bit old, grizzled and decrepit looking. Also, amazingly enough he did not look any the worse for wear after a night of drinking.

Asil: "Morning Captain. How are you feeling today?"

Captain: "Good morning Asil, Einer and Sven. It's a beautiful day, blue skies, hardly a cloud in sight and calm seas. Not good weather for a ship with sails but for the Carolsea this is perfect conditions. By the way, how are your friends feeling this fine morning?"

Asil: "They could be better."

Captain: "Aye, I noticed last night that they seemed a bit under the weather shall we say. You might want to curb their drinking in the future. I don't think they have the constitution for it."

Asil: "I'm afraid you're right. Do you have a cook on board?"

Captain: "Not a full time cook this voyage. It's just Lars my first mate, he doubles as the cook and to be honest his culinary skills leave a bit to be desired. A boat our size should really have a crew of four, but with the war and the shortage of able bodied seamen we have to get by with just the three of us. Better Lars as cook then my engineer Diesel or me. If you want I can have Lars whip something up for you and your friends.

Asil: "Would it be all right with you and your crew if I volunteered to take over the galley as cook for the rest of our voyage? I'm sure once they are feeling better that Parky and Ole will be more than happy to volunteer as deckhands."

Captain: "Aye, Asil you warm an old man's heart. To have a real cook in the galley and some extra hands 'board ship is a Captain's dream."

Einer and I and the rest of the crew including the Captain had our breakfast long before Parky and Ole stumbled into the galley. It was a good thing they were late as the galley was small and maximum capacity was four humans and Parky took up space for two. Asil looked Parky and Ole over with an incriminating eye.

Asil: "Well, you both look like humans again instead of gutter trash. Shaved and washed I see. Eyes are still bloodshot and red.

As soon as you finish your breakfast you can report to Lars the first mate on deck. You both volunteered as deck hands for the rest of our journey."

Ole: "I don't remember any mention of us working our way across the ocean."

Parky: "Me either, I sure as heck didn't volunteer as a deck hand, did you Ole?"

Ole: "Not me. Just who do you suppose volunteered us?"

Asil: "I did. Any complaints?"

Ole and Parky answered in unison. "Nope, no complaints."

Once the boys had finished their breakfast Asil hurried them along to the deck of the ship and told them to report to Lars.

Lars: "The Captain told me I was getting two new deckhands. Welcome aboard swabbies. There are buckets over there. Fill them with water and grab some brushes and soap and start scrubbing the decks. Nothing cures a hangover better than a day of sailing on the water and scrubbing decks under a hot sun."

Parky whispered over to Ole. "This might not be so bad except the first mate is a sixteen year kid still wet under the ears and he's are boss."

Ole whispered back. "Like Laurel and Hardy, this is one revolting predicament you've gotten us into Parky."

Parky: "Me. I believe it's all your fault."

Lars: "Enough chit-chat gentlemen. Less talk and more scrubbing if you don't mind."

Ole: "Just one question Lars. What about the Captain? How's he feeling this morning?"

Lars: "The Captain? Why he's been up since the crack of dawn. Feeling chipper as can be for a grumpy old Captain."

Parky: "He's not hung over?"

Lars: "The Captain hung over? I see you don't know him. That man could drink a bathtub full of beer before bed and wake up sober as a minster on a Sunday morning."

The next few days Parky and Ole were assigned menial jobs like scrubbing the decks, polishing brass, scrapping and repainting wood, cleaning windows, mending torn canvas tarps and even helping Diesel in the engine room. I heard Parky say it was a good thing the trip was winding down as he had just stripped the old paint off the diesel engine and then he had to repaint the block grey and the top section red to satisfy Diesel the ships engineer that everything was now ship shape just like the Norwegian Navy.

As for Einer and me, we just lay on the deck most of the time soaking up the sun's rays and swapping doggie tails, or is it doggie tales? Whichever it was we reminisced about our past adventures and relaxed.

The ocean had treated us kindly. No rough seas and the swells had been at a minimum. However, we did notice that a flat bottomed puffer ship was affected more by the ocean swells then our Viking longboat which had a nice v-shaped hull that sliced through the swells like a hot knife through butter.

It was our last night at sea. The moon was just a sliver in a sky filled with the twinkling of stars. Not a cloud in sight to obstruct the view of one of Gods perfect nighttime murals. The Captain had just turned over the night watch to Lars. Asil, Diesel, Parky, Ole, Einer and I were relaxing on deck enjoying the cool breeze and the smell of salt in the air.

We saw the Captain step out of the deckhouse and stop. A flash of light illuminated his face as he lit his pipe. He sort of reminded me of the cartoon character Popeye, sans the muscles. He came down the stairs from the deckhouse to join us.

Captain: "She's a beautiful night, eh matey's." Tomorrow we will be in Longyearbyen. Aye, and it will be our last night together on a perfect voyage. I do believe we should celebrate."

Asil: "Celebrate how, Captain?"

Parky: "I bet our old sea-dog has a bottle or two of spirits in his cabin."

Captain: "Aye, I do. But it is for medicinal purposes only. However, remember when I told you back at port that I had a valuable cargo to deliver to Longyearbyen?'

Ole: "I'm sure we all remember that."

Captain: "Well, I never told you just how important it was to a bunch of folks on an island in the middle of nowhere. Below this very deck you are standing on there are five-hundred cases of beer. I have the feeling that the good folks of Longyearbyen won't miss a case or two. Diesel and Parky, how about you two fetch us up a couple of cases and we'll celebrate the end of our journey together."

Asil: "Captain, Ole and you too Parky. Remember what happened the last time you three had a few beers together."

Captain: "Asil, don't be throwing a wet blanket on our little celebration. I insist you join us this time. If anyone is feeling a bit tipsy they are welcome to go to their bunks and sleep it off."

Einer added in his comment of course only heard by us that were in the privy to understanding him. "Come on Asil, for once in your life let your hair down and join in on the fun."

Everyone looked at Asil and put a guilt trip on her that she dared not refuse. After all, once we reached Longyearbyen and started on the next leg of our journey we might just be heading into the jaws of death.

Asil: "All right, I'll join you but just for a little while."

Diesel pried open one of the wood cases filled with beer. He popped open the bottles and passed them around. Ole retrieved two bowls from the galley for Einer and me so we could share in the bounty of freshly poured beer.

Parky: "Captain, why don't you tell us of some of your adventures with the Carolsea?"

Captain: "Aye, my adventures. I'm afraid to tell of them all or the poor old Carolsea would have to navigate the globe a half-dozen times over before I could finish telling of all my adventures. Diesel there has been at my side since we was both lads and oh the adventures we two have shared. Everything from battling land pirates, canal pirates, sea pirates, Nazi's, Russians, you name it we've fought 'em."

Diesel: "That we have. And we bested them all didn't we Captain."

Captain: "That we did, let's raise a toast to surviving as long as we have."

The Captain and Diesel started to tell us of their adventures and at all the high points where the two of them bested their opponents we made another toast.

Around about midnight all of us were well past being sober. It was Asil who temporally broke the mood of revelry.

Asil: "Captain, may I ask how Lars came to be with you. He seems like such a nice young lad to be spending his life on a ship with two old sea-dogs. Shouldn't he be at his home attending school and chasing after pretty girls?"

The Captain finished off his beer stood up grabbed another bottle and said. "I think I'll take a brief stroll around the deck."

As soon as he was out of earshot Diesel spoke up. "Lars is a might touchy point with the Captain. You see the Captain had a daughter that married a British Naval officer. He was killed on the HMS Hood when it was sunk by the Bismarck. She died in the London blitz. Lars had been sent to the country during the blitz for his own safety. He was their only child, the other relatives didn't want to keep him permanently so other than the Captain he had no place to go. That was almost five years ago. The Captain being the lad's only other living relative took the boy under his wing. Lars worships that old man and although he will never admit it the old man feels the same about the boy."

The Captain returned to our little group with an empty beer bottle in his hand, he dropped the empty into one of the wood crates and took out a full one to replace it.

Captain: "Time for some singing matey's. Diesel, you grab your squeezebox from your cabin and give us some music to sing by."

Diesel: "Aye, aye Captain."

Diesel quickly returned and played My Bonnie lies over the ocean and Blow the man down as we all sang along.

Everyone seemed to be feeling the effects of the beer and we were all have a rousing good time. We heard Lars ring the bell to indicate it was two o'clock in the morning.

Asil: "It's going to be a long day for me and my boys tomorrow Captain. Once we reach port we will have to go ashore and get ready for the next step of our journey. Might I suggest we all retire for the evening?"

Captain: "Aye, the morning will soon be creeping up on us. May I suggest one more appropriate tune to close out our little celebration?"

It was obvious we really didn't have a choice. After all he was the Captain and we surely must follow the Captain's orders. At least that's how I looked at it.

Captain: "Let's end our last evening of partying together with the same song that brought us together for this voyage. Diesel. Squeeze us out the music for: What do you do with a drunken sailor."

It certainly seemed appropriate to me and seeing you have all heard the beginning of the song before we'll let you join in on the second verse.

Here we go, everyone sing:

What do you do with a drunken sailor? What do you do with a drunken sailor? What do you do with a drunken sailor? Early in the morning!

Way hay and up she rises, way hay and up she rises, way hay and up she rises. Early in the morning!

Put him in a long boat till he's sober, put him in a long boat till he's sober, put him in a longboat till he's sober. Early in the morning!

Way hay and up she rises, way hay and up she rises, way hay and up she rises. Early in the morning!

Stick him in a scupper with a hosepipe bottom, stick him in a scupper with a hosepipe bottom, stick him in a scupper with a hosepipe bottom. Early in the morning!

Way hay and up she rises, way hay and up she rises, way hay and up she rises. Early in the morning!

Put him in the bed with the captain's daughter, put him in the bed with the captain's daughter, put him in the bed with the captain's daughter. Early in the morning!

Way hay and up she rises, way hay and up she rises, way hay and up she rises. Early in the morning!

That's what we do with a drunken sailor, that's what we do with a drunken sailor, that's what we do with a drunken sailor. Early in the morning!

We finished the song and it was time for all of us drunken sailors to hit the hay.

Even Asil, Viking princess warrior she is, was feeling a bit tipsy. Humans and canines alike stumbled off to bed and soon we were all fast asleep.

We woke up all a bit the worse for wear to another bright sun shining day. Squinting to keep our heads from aching we had breakfast and went back up on deck. We could see the Captain in the wheel house and he was whistling a tune and once again looked and acted to be sober as a judge in court.

Around noon the Captain gave Lars orders to lower the Norwegian flag and to hoist up the German Provisional Ensign flag that had been ordered into usage at the wars end. The German Ensign flag was done in the colors of the allied countries that had fought them into submission. To say the least it was not well accepted or liked by the German merchant fleet.

Parky: "Lars, what's up with flying the German Ensign flag?"

Lars: "The Captain said he had orders from the person that hired us to take you to Longyearbyen to fly this flag so that anyone who sees us entering port will think that our ship is carrying a German crew and passengers."

Coming towards the end of our voyage it was time for the Captain to open his safe and give Asil the envelope that had been left for her. The Captain insisted that no one was to be allowed in his cabin other than Asil and himself as his orders were very specific. Asil and only Asil was to be given the envelope in strict privacy.

Parky: "Well, ain't that just like some demi-god, figuring us mortals ain't trustworthy of his confidence, and after all we've done for them. Risking our lives on every assignment we've been given. I feel just like I've gotten a demi-god fart right in my face."

We were standing on the deck when Parky made his comment. As soon as he said it black clouds rolled across the sky, thunder cracked and a lightning bolt streaked in front of Parky and touched down about a foot in front of him. A large black circle was burned into the ships wooden deck which sat smoldering as we all shook in fear.

Parky stuttered out. "I'm sorry. I didn't mean any offence to the retired deities. Really I didn't."

The sky quickly cleared back to blue with the sun once again shining.

Ole quietly whispered to Parky. "I think they heard your fart in the face comment."

Parky whispered back. "You think so? No doubt in my mind. I'm just glad they heard my apology."

I quietly commented. "I'm just glad they only sent a warning to watch your tongue or we might have had lightening fried Parkurkarkus on tonight's menu."

Ole looked at me and said. "You're lucky Parky didn't hear that. He might not have seen the humor in your comment. Although it was pretty funny."

Lars came rushing over from the other side of the ship and quickly grabbed a fire extinguisher to keep the smoldering deck from bursting into flames. Diesel came up from the engine room and looked the situation over with nary a comment. He wiped his hands on a greasy rag he took from his back pocket shook his head and returned to his engine room. The Captain leaned out the deck house window to see what all the commotion was about.

Captain: "Lars! What the hell's going on down there?"

Lars: "Nothing to worry about Captain. We were struck by a bolt of lightning."

 Captain: "Lightening you say. Look at the sky you little barnacle. You see any clouds? Lightening my foot. What's that I see on my wood deck? Is that a burn mark? If it is you better pull up the wood and replace it before I finish my watch and you take over. If it's not repaired by then they'll be lightening on the tip of boot making contact with your behind."

Lars looked at Parky and Ole with a bit of worry and a glint of evil in his eyes. "You two heard the captain. You best go see Diesel and get the tools and some new wood to fix that burn spot on the deck. Don't just stand there, hop to it swabbies!"

Lars might have been just sixteen years of age but he was first mate and he decided it was time to take charge.

Parky went to the engine room to get the tools and supplies to fix the deck. Ole and I looked over the burned spot and contemplated the best way to go about fixing it. Once Parky came back with the supplies he and Ole started their project. They drilled a few holes to create a template and then using a small hand saw they cut out the burnt section of deck which consisted of 3 blanks. Using a long board of decking that Diesel kept for deck repair they cut out three new boards to replace the damaged ones. A few wood pegs were pounded into holes to secure the deck and a bit of sanding soon had the deck, as they say looking ship-shape. The only way you could tell it had been repaired was that it was shining new wood and not weathered like the rest of the deck. Lars brought out a can of marine varnish and told the boys to seal it up. A few weeks of sun and salt water weather would soon age it to look like the rest of the decking.

The Captain showed up after Lars relieved him from the deckhouse. He sauntered over to Parky and Ole and looked over the deck. "The repairs look acceptable boys. Now you want to tell me again how you burned my deck?"

Ole: "We didn't burn it sir. It was a lightning strike."

Parky: "Honest sir, it's just as Ole said, a freak lightning strike. It just came out of nowhere. Most likely static electricity built up in the air."

Captain: "I may look old and senile to you two, but I'm not. The skies are blue and not a cloud in sight. I've sailed these seas since you two were sea-pups. I'm not so gullible as to think there was a lightning strike on a day like this. Even if there was it would have hit the lightening rod attached to the mast and would have been diverted from doing any damage to the ship. The only other explanation is that you two pissed off the gods of the deep and they tried to strike you dead with a lightning bolt. Now that's funny boys, how come you're not laughing?"

Parky and Ole quickly started laughing. They knew that was by far a lot better thing to do then to try to convince the Captain that Parky had actually ticked off one of the demi-gods.

Captain: "I left Asil in my cabin to check out the contents of the envelope that was left for her. We should be docking in Longyearbyen in a few hours."

Diesel joined us on deck and we lounged around as there was not much else to do. It wasn't long before Asil joined us. With Diesel present she couldn't say anything about what she read in the envelope. She was leaning on the rail of the ship as she slowly shredded the contents of the envelope and let the wind take the pieces where they would be swallowed up by the sea and dissolve on their way to the bottom of the ocean.

It was early evening before we docked at Longyearbyen. The Captain, Lars and Diesel all came on deck to wish us farewell.

Captain: "We're going to miss the five of you. I must admit I was a bit leery of taking on passengers as most of those that have travelled with us have been stuffed shirts who figured they were better than me and my crew. Certainly not the case with you five. Asil you made a first class galley cook. Parky and Ole you two were top notch mates. Einer and Sven, well, what can I say, as good of sea-dogs as have ever graced the decks of the Carolsea."

Asil, Parky and Ole thanked the Captain and the crew for taking us on a pleasant voyage and the company we all shared. Einer and I gave a tail wag goodbye as each of the crew patted us on our heads and sent us on our way down the gangplank. Parky looked back at the Captain and hollered. "Captain, till the next time we meet, more beer and song will be mandatory."

Captain: "Aye it will be my friends. Safe journeys to all of you."

Asil gave Parky a sideways glance of disapproval but as usual he ignored her.

CHAPTER 3

We were still in view of the Carolsea when a young man approached us. He had on a blue blazer with a patch on it that had a German Eagle crest above the left breast pocket.

"Pardon me folks, would you happen to be the Asil party?"

Ole: "We might be. Why do you ask?"

"I saw you come off the ship flying the German Ensign. I was told to keep an eye out for you and if you are in fact the party I just mentioned I am here to greet you and to be your guide."

"My name is Lancelot Algernon. You may call me Lance. I am from the German Consulate."

My first thought about this young man was why would his parents ever stick him with such a moniker.

Asil: "I'm Asil and these are my associates Parkurkarkus, Ole and the dogs are Einer and Sven."

Lance: "Nice to meet all of you. I have a car waiting. I'm to take you to the Svalbard Airport."

Asil: "Lance, if you don't mind could I have a word alone with my associates?"

Lance: "Of course, take all the time you need."

Asil, Parky and Ole went into a circle sort of like football players in a huddle, Einer and I sat in the middle, hopefully not like footballs waiting to be kicked. Hee, hee, just a little pigskin humor there.

Asil: "Ok guys, about the envelope. It didn't say much other than we would be met by a German representative at the docks and he would be taking us to the next leg of our journey. So far as I can tell everything is going along as planned. We just need to let Lance take us to whatever destination he's been ordered to and everything should be all right. We're to act like German nationals so just play along. I speak acceptable German and Parky is fluid in the language. Ole, you best keep your mouth shut."

Lance led us to a waiting Mercedes-Benz 770 touring car. Ole whispered to me. "Wow, that's the same type of car used by most of the German Dignitaries and elite Military leaders. Whatever we're getting ourselves into it must be something important. A representative from the German Consulate, a German limousine and our arrival in port flying a German ensign on the Carolsea. This certainly is getting interesting."

"Or, something really dangerous." I added.

Lance held the front door open for Asil and then he ushered the rest of us into the back seat. Lance took his place behind the wheel and made sure everyone was comfortable before he started the car and pulled out onto the road.

Asil: "Pardon me Lance can you tell us where we are going?"

Lance: "I have orders to drive you to the Svalbard Airport. There will be someone there to give you further instructions."

Parky: "Just how far is the airport from here?"

Lance: "Not far. About five kilometers."

Parky: "I was under the impression that most of the airports were still under military control, and all things considered I wouldn't think too much of that control would be German."

Lance: "You are correct, although, we may have lost the war that does not meant that life as we used to know it has completely ended. Planes still need to fly and ships need to ply the seas and trucks and automobiles need to travel the roadways. People and goods still need to get from place to place. Even though the German people are under constant surveillance we still need to do our jobs and work with the allies as needed. I do my job as I am sure you are here to do yours."

Lance pulled into the airport where we were stopped at the main gate by the Norwegian Military. They checked Lance's documents and then ours. It took a few minutes and Einer relayed to me   that the guards had talked amongst themselves and we seemed to somehow gained priority clearance to continue on our way to one of the hangers that was off limits to most of the airport personal.

One of the guards returned our documents as the other guard raised the gate and motioned us on. Lance was perspiring and looked relieved once we were on the move.

Lance: "It always makes me a bit nervous when they check our documents. Scrutiny of anyone that is German is always quite meticulous. I have been here before so I was not too worried. However, I wasn't so sure about you three. If anything would have been amiss all of us including me would have been taken to the guardhouse and held for questioning. I don't know who you three are but you must have connections in high places. The hanger we are going to is off limits to almost everyone. The rumor is that there is top secret things going on there that were brought here from Germany when it looked as if the war was lost. Some say that they were smuggling things out of Germany by the beginning of 1944. I'll be dropping you off at the side door of the hanger. That's all the farther I am allowed to go. I've never actually been inside. Once I drop you off you are on your own."

Lance pulled up to the hanger and stopped the car. He got out and opened the doors for us. Once we were all out of the car he walked back to the driver's side and pointed at the hanger's small side door as he said. "Good luck, I hope all goes well." He got into the car and accelerated so quickly that the rear tires spun in the dirt.

Parky: "Looks like the boy was a bit scared of something. You suppose there's something evil in that hanger?"

Ole: "It's the German's Parky. Might be monsters in there for all we know."

Asil: "Monsters, evil, you two are idiots. Why did Odin saddle me with two goof offs like you? Come on, let's go see what's in the hanger."

Parky: "Asil, you know as well as we do that some of the Nazi's were evil so calling them monsters isn't so far-fetched."

Asil: "Yes, I would have to agree with you two on that one."

We walked over to the side door of the hanger and stopped.

Ole: "You suppose we should knock before we go in?"

Parky: "Let me think about that for a minute. We are in a highly restricted area. The hanger has probably got German military personal inside and being a restricted area we can presume they have guns. Yes, I think it's probably a good idea if we knock."

Asil: "You two do know the war is over? I don't think anyone inside the hanger will shoot us without seeing who we are and what we want."

Parky: "I agree with Asil. Knocking is probably the safest thing to do."

Asil: "You two are something else. Safe or not, it's actually the polite and proper thing to do."

Asil knocked on the door. We waited for a moment and then we saw a small peephole in the door open and an eye was staring at us. We heard a deadbolt lock unlatch and the door handle turned. The door opened and a young mechanic probably in his early twenties wearing clean gray coveralls motioned us inside.

Mechanic: "We've been expecting you. Follow me, the Generalleuntnant is waiting for you in his office."

Well I knew just enough German to know we were going to see a Lieutenant General in any man's army and it was a rank to be reckoned with.

We followed the mechanic past an immaculate Junkers Ju-52 with skis attached to the wheels and it was still bearing German Military markings. The office was a small room in the far corner of the hanger. Two other mechanics were sitting at a table playing cards, German luger handguns were on the table and easily within their reach. They warily watched us as we walked past them. I noticed that as per the scuttlebutt we had heard about German efficiency that all the mechanics tools were clean and shiny as were their coveralls. Their lugers were black and lethal looking.

If their well-kept tools and work station were any indication to their efficiency and those two had been working on the plane it was probably in immaculate working condition inside and out. With a high ranking German officer on the premises I would have to figure all my assumptions up to this point were correct.

The office we were escorted to had a large window in the front so that most of the hanger was visible to the officer in charge. As for the hanger itself there were no side windows although there was a large skylight in the roof that brought in the days brightness. I did notice that there was a mechanical panel that at the push of a button could be used to block out the incoming light from the skylight. Most likely it was used in conditions when prying eyes from overhead planes might be a detriment to the activities inside the hanger.

The mechanic knocked on the office door and we waited for an answer. We could see a rather large man sitting at the office desk. His chair was turned towards the wall so that his back was towards us.

We heard the Officer inside say: "You may enter."

Mechanic: "Excuse me Herr Generalleuntnant. I have the three guests and there, um, well, ah, they happen to have two canine companions with them."

Generalleuntnant: "That's fine. Let them in and ask them to be seated. I'll be with them in a minute. That will be all for you, please double check the plane and make sure it is ready for takeoff."

Asil and Ole slowly occupied the two chairs at the front of the desk. Parky, Einer and I took our place on a couch that was below the window that looked out into the hanger. It was quiet enough in that office that you could have heard a cat licking its whiskers. 'Sorry, I just had to slip in a bit of feline humor.' Might help to ease the tension we were all feeling as our host kept his back towards us and heightened the suspense of our surroundings.

Slowly the officer behind the desk swiveled his chair to face us. As he did so he removed his hat and his long hair cascaded out and fell about his shoulders. He smiled as his pearly white teeth twinkled from the overhead lights. His long beard fell across his chest. It didn't take a rocket scientist to realize this particular officer was none other than Aegir disguising himself as a high ranking German Officer.

Ole: "Aegir! You. You're the German Officer in charge of this hanger?"

Aegir let out a laugh as only a Norwegian demi-god could do. It shook the windows of the tiny office. A quick glance out the window showed the three mechanics were rather surprised and shocked that a German Officer could let out with so much mirth.

Aegir: "Of course it's me. Who were you expecting? Maybe Adolf Hitler. No, couldn't be him he's dead and cremated in a hole dug in the ground and doused with petrol. I guess that's one way to be cremated, but if I have to go give me a Viking funeral where they lay your body in a long boat set it off to sea and then shoot it full of flaming arrows. Now that's a funeral fit for someone of my status."

"Now, as far as how I got here. I gave the acting Officer that was in charge a leave of absence so he could go back to Germany and visit his family. I didn't want to leave anything to chance. This mission is very important and Odin sent me to make sure that there was to be no snags as you continue your journey. Of course there was the added bonus for me of getting to see Asil one more time before she has to risk her life to save mortal mankind from another threat by the Germans."

Asil smiled at Aegir and blushed, something I had seldom seen her do. I didn't much like it and looking at Ole I could see he was none too happy at this unexpected turn of events. Things between him and Asil had been cooling down for some time and right now they were about as cold and frosty as the conditions would be when we arrived at our next destination in the frozen north.

Ole: "All right. Enough chit-chat. What's up Aegir? Why don't you demi-gods just handle this problem yourselves?"

Aegir: "Ole, by now you should know we have been retired, the True God will let us help out a bit but we can't directly interfere in the matters of mortals anymore. It's a job for you humans to take care of your own problems. Asil and Einer are allowed to take part as she was never considered a God or in her case a Goddess.'

Ole: "All right, enough of your retired-god politics. You here to give us instructions on the next leg of our journey or are you just here to flirt with Asil?"

The little office got suddenly warm as Aegir's eyes gave Ole a look that could melt a glacier.

Aegir: "Listen to me mortal. I may be a retired god but I still have the power to turn you into a toad and send you off to the jungle swamps to become a tasty morsel for a nice hungry crocodile. So you best keep that jealous little human heart of yours under control."

Asil: "Aegir, Ole didn't mean anything by what he said. It's just that he and I have been working together for some time. He's a little protective of me is all."

Well, if that don't beat all. I felt really bad for Ole, this certainly looked like the big brush off from Asil. I figured that Odin had been right all along and Ole wasn't about to accept the fact that there could be no future for a mortal and a Norse Princess of the Drogon. As for me, well, you don't need to hit me in the head with a dead cat for the point to sink in. Of course as I looked at Ole I could see his heart was breaking and there was nothing I could do or say to mend it.

Ole was all primed to start an argument but Aegir had anticipated that and as Ole opened his mouth and started to speak the only sound that came from his mouth was "ribbit, ribbit, ribbit." To say the very least he sat back with a very surprised, dejected look on his face and embarrassment beyond belief filled him from head to toe.

Parky quickly got up from the couch and helped Ole to his feet as he led him from his chair to Parky's spot on the couch. Once Parky had Ole seated between Einer and me he took Ole's place next to Asil.

Asil: "Aegir. That was not very nice. You restore Ole's voice right this instant or else you will need to find a new crew for this mission."

Aegir: "All right, as you wish. I was just having a bit of fun with the mortal. His voice is restored, however I sort of preferred him when he could speak frog. Now, let's get back to business."

Ole looked at me and whispered. "Sven, can you understand me?" I answered in the affirmative and I put my paw on his leg to reassure him that I was still his partner and always would be. Dogs are always loyal to their human partners no matter what language they speak. Women, no matter how much you love them can be fickle as a cat. It may be a sad state of affairs but in most cases it's true.

I did my best to make Ole smile as I said. "Well partner, just be grateful you only said 'ribbit' and didn't crook." For some strange reason all I got was a dirty look. I guess it was still too soon for frog humor.

Parky figured he was now in the best position at the moment to deal with Aegir so he took charge.

Parky: "Aegir, looks like you are to be our contact to get us moving along on our quest. What's the next step?"

I could see by the look on Asil's face as she stared down Aegir that he figured it was best to get back to business and try to appease Asil's anger at him for toying with Ole.

Aegir: "It's time for the next leg of your journey to stop the Germans from whatever they have planned. Have no doubts this next part is not like the little pleasure cruise you made across the ocean from Norway. Parky, if I have been informed correctly you are a capable airplane pilot and navigator. Is that correct?"

Parky smiled as he always did when someone gave him some praise. "Right you are. Just one of my many talents."

One thing about Parky, he has lots of different talents but modesty is not one of them.

Aegir: "I'm glad to hear it. If you'll take notice that the Junkers Ju-52 sitting in the hanger is equipped with ski's attached to the wheels. There is an opening below each ski to allow the wheels to jut through. A hydraulic system is attached to the wheels so they can be lifted above the skies once you have taken off from the runway. Your destination is the Arctic Circle and you will of course need those skis to land on the ice pack. The coordinates for your trip are in the cockpit of the plane. Under the circumstances you should have a co-pilot and I feel Asil and Einer would be best to fit that position. You can teach her what she needs to know along the way. Einer, Sven and Ole can ride in the cargo bay and make sure everything is ready for the next step of your journey when you land. The cargo bay has a full supply of cold weather gear, food, guns and ammunition. For transportation on the ice pack there is a NSU Kettenkrad tracked motorcycle with a ski attached under the front wheel. The Kettenkrad has two jerry cans of petrol attached to its side in case you need them."

Parky: "Just how far is it to our destination and why do you think we will need the Kettenkrad?"

Aegir: "Best as we can ascertain it's about 650 miles from here as the Americans would say. So it should take you about five to six hours depending on your air speed and if you pick up a good tail wind. The coordinates I gave you should put you close to your destination, however, depending on the terrain and if there happens to be ice ridges you may have to land slightly off course. If that's the case, you will have to continue your journey using the Kettenkrad."

Parky: "Assuming we get that far, just what are we looking for?"

Aegir: "Somewhere in that frozen wasteland there is a German base. To the best of our knowledge it is not on top of the ice pack or the allies would have flown over the area and discovered it. So, the only other answer is that it is somewhere hidden below the ice pack. The Germans tend to be rather ingenious at hiding and camouflaging things as they proved when they dug out tunnels to hide their V-rocket assembly and launch pads. We have to assume they have figured out how to carve out a base of operations under the ice and totally out of sight from the air patrols. Your job is to find it, infiltrate it and to figure out what they are up to. If they are planning anything that may adversely affect the human race, well, you know your mission. Stop them at all costs."

Parky: "I think we all understand the mission. Only one thing may put a crimp in the plan."

Aegir: "Just what might that be? The fact you may all die trying to save the world?"

Parky: "Yeah, the may die thing would certainly be a detriment. However, I was thinking about something else. Something not quite as serious as the dying part. Asil and I speak German well enough to get by. Ole on the other hand, well, he's a lost cause when it comes to the German language. He likes sauerkraut and he knows a few words of German but not enough to fool anybody. I was just thinking. You got Ole to speak frog, maybe you could toss a spell or whatever is that you do and get Ole to speak fluent German."

Aegir: "No more said than done. I'll even make sure that Einer and Sven are also fluent in German too, that way all of you will fit right in. Ole, sorry if I offended you before. You have no need to worry, you will be able to understand and speak German as if it was your native tongue. When your mission is finished you will revert back to you English speaking self."

Asil: "What about our outfits? Are we going in as German civilians?"

Aegir: "Good point. I almost forgot to tell you. There are German military outfits in the plane's cargo hold. Make sure you change into them when you are on your way. You must, and this is extremely important. You must toss your old clothing out of the plane as soon as you take off. There can be no trace of your former identities just in case the German's may send out a search party and find the plane. Your identification papers will be left here with me. New identity documents will be with your new clothing in the cargo hold. Parky, you will be given the identity and rank of a Captain and Asil shall hold the rank of Corporal. She be your assistant. Ole, you will be a Sergeant. By the way once you assume your new identities it is felt that Parkurkarkus and Asil can continue to use their names. Sergeant Ole will need to pass himself off as a Norwegian volunteer from the German Nordland division and seeing you have spent some time in Russia where that division did a lot of fighting you should be a welcome addition to our little band of refuges looking to make a new Germany. If of course that is what they are up to."

I could tell by the look on Ole's face he was disappointed that Aegir had teamed up Parky and Asil together. In the back of my mind and I'm sure in Ole's too we both knew that not only was this to be our last mission together as a group but it was also the end of any romantic involvement between Asil and Ole. As we were warned long ago. Mortals and Norse legends can never truly find love together.

Parky: "I have one more question. What happens if we cannot locate the German base of operations? It sounds to me that it is well hidden in a land that is not hospitable to human survival."

Aegir: "That is not really an option. Your mission is to find it, figure out what they are up to and if deemed necessary destroy the base and all those involved in its operation."

Ole finally decided to speak up. "So, if we don't find it we will be left to freeze to death?"

Aegir: "Ole, maybe you are smarter than I gave you credit for. You are absolutely right. This is a do or die mission. You five have been on missions before. I am quite confident you will figure it out and do whatever it takes to complete your mission in one piece. There is also a strong possibility with the Germans expertise in reconnaissance that they most likely will see your plane and its German markings. If you have to resort to using the Kettenkrad They will most likely monitor that and once again once it becomes apparent to them that you are Germans and the only reason for your being there is that you know of their existence and are hoping to join them it should be to your advantage."

Asil: "Seems we will be trusting a lot on luck."

I saw Ole opening his mouth and I quickly put a stop to it as I admonished him. "Ole, if you know what's good for you and probably me to as I'm your partner I would strongly suggest you keep your thoughts to yourself." Wait. Let me rephrase that. Keep your mouth shut and don't say a word until we are in the plane, off the ground and at least one-hundred miles from here. Then, remember what happened when Parky dared to bad mouth the demi-gods. I don't think an airplane will fair nearly as well from a lightning strike as the Carolsea did. We would probably have survived being knocked into the ocean by that lightning strike. Falling from thousands of feet in the air from an airplane would give us a lot less chance of survival."

Ole sat back and I think he had to bite his tongue almost to the point of bleeding as he held back his comments.

Aegir: "If there are no more questions let's get this show on the road or in the air as the case may be. Your plane awaits."

Aegir stood up, tucked his long hair under his officer's cap and opened the office door letting Asil go first. Einer was next, then Parky, Ole and me. We walked past the mechanics who warily eyed us but made no movements or sounds. They were almost like robots just doing as they were ordered.

Aegir walked us around the plane and showed us how the ski conversion would work. He said the fuel mixture and engine settings were set up for cold weather travel and had been well tested on previous Junkers airplanes in Russia during the ill-fated battles that had raged around Stalingrad.

Aegir: "The Planes ready to go. Parky, since you're the pilot any questions?"

Parky: "No, I figure I know all I need to know. Let's board up and take off."

CHAPTER 4

As we boarded the plane Aegir had the mechanics open the hanger doors and then the four of them pushed the Junkers outside. The runway we were to use was right in front of us so no need to taxi to another area. Ole and I settled into some side facing seats in the cargo hold. Parky, Asil and Einer took their places in the cockpit.

We heard the three BMW engines turn over and start up. A slight shudder went through the plane. Once Parky had the engines feathered out the vibration ceased. We felt the plane moving forward as it picked up speed. I was looking out one of the side windows as the trees outside moved quickly by. Soon the sound of the wheels on the runway under us disappeared and we were airborne.

My keen canine hearing picked up Parky's comments about the takeoff to Asil. "I'm not so sure those mechanics had the ski system fully worked out. The skis must have been a bit to long for a regular wheel takeoff. I could feel the back end of the skis dragging on the runway as we started our lift off. It slowed our ascent a bit. Hopefully the skis didn't bend or break off or we may be in quite a frozen pickle when it comes time to land."

Ole is not the best of passengers when it comes to air travel so I decided not to mention our possible predicament. For the time being we were in the air safe and sound. That was the most important thing for now.

I was keeping a close eye on Ole. He had beads of sweat on his brow and was breathing heavily which I knew from our past was a sure sign to his nervousness of flying. I could have waited him out, however, I knew that would mean he would eventually vomit and the stench of that would not be good for any of us. With that in mind I made my move and decided to keep him occupied which would hopefully take his mind off his flying phobia.

"Ole, look at the back of the plane. What do you see?"

Ole: "Looks like the front end of a motorcycle."

"It's the Kettenkrad we are supposed to use if needed. You love motorcycles. Let's check it out before we land so you can familiarize yourself with the controls. Parky might be an airplane pilot but he's no match for you when it comes to handling a motorcycle." I knew stroking Ole's ego would be a big plus. Something us canines learned from past experience is that humans have huge egos.

We walked to the back of the plane and looked over the Kettenkrad. It had been painted white to blend in with the terrain we would be traversing. There were three white German helmets on the rear facing back seat. Also laying on the back seat were three winter great coats, mittens, boots and googles for extra protection from the cold. Of course I had to think that Aegir had arranged nicely for the warmth and protection of the human members of our group but he had totally forgotten the canine members. Einer being an ice breathing Drogon was used to the cold and I sometimes think he had ice in his veins when it came time to do battle or protect Asil. Me, on the other hand am more of a warm weather dog.

We did a walk around of the Kettenkrad. Jerry cans of extra petrol were mounted on one side. Picks and shovels along with some spare track parts were mounted on the other side. Rubber cleats on the tracks should give us good traction on snow or ice. The four cylinder Opel engine would supply more than enough power. The seat facing the open back had room for two people. If needed it would allow for a quick escape to defend us against possible enemy attack, or, in a dire situation a quick escape from an open lead of water if Ole was unable to avoid it. In that case I had grave doubts that my partner would be able to get out and survive.

Ole climbed into the driver's compartment to familiarize himself with the controls. There was a six-speed floor mounted shifter similar to that of an automobile or truck. There was a lever to allow the gearbox to be shifted into low or high depending on the conditions. An automotive foot clutch on the floor for shifting. Steering was done with a conventional style motorcycle handlebar mounted to a girder style motorcycle fork. Ole found an owner's manual and learned that the front wheel assembly was to light to turn the Kettenkrad like a motorcycle. Instead, when the handlebars were turned they would stop one of the tracks which would cause the unit to make a turn in the desired direction. It was the same principle as applied to other track equipped vehicles currently in production.

Sitting in the Kettenkrad with his seat on the saddle and his hands on the handlebar grips brought a smile to Ole's face. Of course the grin on his face would soon be frozen in place once we unloaded the tracked motorcycle from the plane and started travelling across the frozen landscape.

Once we had finished checking out the Kettenkrad it was time to investigate the supplies that Aegir had told us about. There were two flat topped steamer trunks strapped to the wall which we figured must contain our cache of goodies.

Ole opened the first trunk which was filled with German uniforms and even German made underclothing, watches, currency and other small items that a typical German military person might be carrying. Including the correct identification papers. Everything was of authentic German manufacture.

To my surprise there were even German made doggie jackets, boots, caps and goggles for Einer and me. I dared not say it to Ole but Aegir or whoever he had assigned to the duty of packing our gear certainly bespoke of German efficiency.

Ole found the sergeants outfit and stripping down to his birthday suit he quickly got changed into the appropriate outfit of a German soldier.

Upon opening the second trunk we discovered it was filled with German weapons and ammunition.

I suggested that before we dig into the weapons supply it might be a good idea for Asil and Parky to get changed into their German uniforms. After all, Aegir said we should get rid of our old clothing as soon as we were airborne.

Ole and I went to the cockpit where Ole proudly showed off his new rank as a sergeant. Asil told Ole to take her place in the co-pilots seat while she went to the cargo area to change clothes. She looked at me and suggested that being a male I should remain in the cockpit with Ole. Parky offered to go with Asil and change into his uniform at the same time. Of course Asil quickly shot him down.

Asil: "Parky you old pervert. What makes you think I would let you watch me change when I just stopped Ole and Sven from doing so? Einer, you stay here and stand watch. If any of them so much as tries to sneak a peek you have my permission to freeze their eyeballs like too ice cubes in a glass of cold water."

Asil changed places with Ole and you never saw three guys like Parky, Ole and me keep their eyes looking straight ahead with the conviction of a cat stalking a mouse. 'Whoops, just another cat reference that sort of slipped out on me.'

Asil finally reappeared. Aegir or his minions had done a good job with her outfit. Everything was as it should be for a Captains female aide except long pants had been substituted for a skirt. A much more sensible dress code under the circumstances seeing we were headed for the frozen north.

Parky switched the controls to auto-pilot so there was no need for Asil or Ole to do much other than sit there and make sure nothing went wrong. If it did, Parky was only a holler away and hopefully would be able to get back to the controls if needed.

Parky soon returned to the cockpit but before Ole could get up and change places with him the big-man stopped him. Parky had all of us turn around and look at him.

Parky: "Look me over crewmates. I make one impressive German Captain if I do say so myself. Of course you all agree. Don't you?"

We knew better than to argue with Parky. Considering he was the pilot and the only one capable of getting us to where were going. He was also the only one on board who could land the plane safely so we all readily agreed with his assumption of being a great looking Captain in the German officer corps.

Asil: "Ole, you should go back to the cargo hold and dispose of our old outfits as Aegir suggested. We are still over the ocean so there is little to no chance of anyone finding them, once you toss them out of the plane."

Ole cringed at the mention of Aegir's name but we did as we were instructed. Ole noticed a box of tools and took out the heaviest ones he could find. He rolled the tools up in the center of the clothing and using the cord from a parachute he tied it all together. Of course one of my thoughts was I sure hope we don't need that parachute. Once the bundle of our belongings hit the water it would sink like a rock. I have to give my partner credit. It was a great idea to sink the evidence to the bottom of the ocean. Knowing the Germans they might have trawlers looking for any evidence of spies and if this clandestine base was as thorough as the Germans were during the war it was best we not take any chances of having our cover broken.

Once our bundle was ready Ole went to the cockpit and asked Parky how he wanted to handle the disposal of our belongings.

Parky: "I could tell you to open the side door and toss it out but I'm afraid the wind might just suck you out with it. I noticed when I was changing clothes that there is a bomb-bay door in the floor. Most likely a left over from the plane's years in war service. Put the bundle in the center of the doors and let me know when you are done. The controls for the bomb bay doors are still in the cockpit. I'll open them and drop it like a payload of bombs when you two are safely up here with us."

Ole and went back to the cargo area and moved our bundle of goods to the bomb bay doors. Once we had finished we went back to the cockpit and told Parky the payload was in place and it was time for him to jettison the load. Ole and I stood with our backs to the cockpit so we could watch the load fall as Parky pushed the controls to open the bomb bay doors. We heard Parky holler out "Bombs away!"

The doors in the cargo bay floor opened as we felt a gush of wind rush at us from the cargo bay. We could hear the creaking of the metal that accompanied the bomb bay doors as they made their way back into the planes belly and clamped themselves shut with a loud clunk.

Ole and I returned to the cargo hold and did a quick check of the trunk that contained a stash of weapons. Three k98 Mauser rifles, two Walther P-38 pistols, one Walther PPK pistol and one Steyr submachine gun. There were also a half-dozen grenades or as Ole called them potato-mashers due to their unique shape. Also included in our cache of goodies were appropriate belts, holsters and plenty of ammunition. There was an officer's dagger for

Captain Parky, an enlisted man's dagger for Ole and for Asil there was a smaller size dagger that could be attached to her belt.

Ole and I decided to relax and took our seats in the cargo hold. There wasn't much to do other than to wait until we landed. Once we were safely on the ground we could help everyone get ready with their appropriate weapons and gear.

The plane droned on as we made our way to the frozen north. For some time when I looked out the window all I saw was the dark wave tossed water that was below us. That soon changed and the water had gone from my view. The world below us was now an expanse of white, cold and ice.

My ears felt stuffed up and I could feel the pressure in my sinuses as the plane started to descend. I shook my head a few times and I felt a popping in my ears which relieved the sinus buildup. Ole was not faring quite as well as I was. He gripped the edge of his seat as his knuckles turned white.

Looking out the window I could see a lot of ice ridges below us, they looked like some ice giants evil fingers waiting to grip the wings of our plane and tear it to shreds. I figured I best keep that thought to myself. No need to worry my already over anxious partner.

Parky kept the plane steady for some time looking for a place to land. Then I heard him holler back to us. "I see what looks like a safe spot to land between some low ice ridges. I'll need to make a sharp banking turn so hold on."

As the plane banked Ole held on to the edge of his seat and dug his heels into the floor to keep from sliding off and falling to the floor then tumbling to the other side of the plane. I dug my claws into the seat cushion and wondered why there no seatbelts to strap us in.

The plane leveled off and we could feel the quick descent as we came in for a landing. We bounced up and down a few times as Parky touched the planes skis down on the ice pack. It was a rough landing as there were small ridges of ice that came close to sending the plane into a nose dive. The bending of the skis at takeoff was certainly no help. When we finally came to a stop we all breathed a sigh of relief and more than a few prayers to the true God were sent aloft to thank him for a safe journey and a safe landing.

Parky turned off the engines. It seemed surreal to be sitting in total silence. Not a sound was to be heard anywhere. If there was a wind outside the planes metal body kept the noise at bay. It was some time before any of us moved or said anything. I think we were just relieved to be on the ground safe and sound.

Ole, who was probably the most relieved to have our flight over with was the first to speak.

Ole: "All right everybody. We made it this far, Asil or Parky did either of you see anything that looked like a base of operations?"

Parky: "We were both scanning the area, as far as we could tell there was nothing that stood out."

Ole: "So why did we land here?"

Asil: "The coordinates we have from Aegir indicate that we should be close. The Germans are masters at camouflage. Just because we can't see their base of operations doesn't necessarily mean it's not here."

Parky: "We have to figure that if we are close they know we are here. If they were tracking us or saw us land they will be more than curious about us. After all our plane has German military markings. They may be leery as to who we are but with us scouting the area in a German marked Kettenkrad and wearing German military winter outfits they will almost certainly take us prisoners to start with. We'll be interrogated and hopefully we can convince them that we are German Nationals who have heard about them and are only here to help. I suggest we gear up, unload the Kettenkrad and take a look around."

Asil stood up and came towards the cargo area. She looked at Ole and said. "You heard Parky, He's the Captain now so get used to taking orders. Help us gear up and then unstrap the Kettenkrad. There is to be no more contact as friends. We are soldiers doing our duty for the future of Germany."

I looked at Ole and I could tell he was hurt by the way Asil had snapped her commands at him. Whether it was meant to cool down his feelings towards her or was it that she had already immersed herself in the part of a German Captains assistant was hard to say.

Asil, Parky and Ole gathered around the trunk of weapons. Ole passed out the correct belts, holster and scabbards. Parky seemed familiar with how they went on. Asil on the other hand had seen them on occasion when we were in Germany, however we had not seen to many women in German uniforms so she was a bit confused as to the proper way to attach everything. Ole was about to help her when she stepped away and looked at Parky.

Asil: "Parky you always seem to know about everything. Would you mind helping me with my gear? It's very important we get everything absolutely correct. We can't leave anything to chance. If the Germans we are to be in contact with figured out how to build a base of operations here they certainly will be meticulous in checking us out."

Ole had finished getting ready and he headed back to release the chains that were holding the Kettenkrad in place. I followed him and quietly said. "Asil didn't mean anything by what she said. She's just playing the part we all have to play to be safe."

Ole: "Yeah, sure, I know. Now let's get to work and forgot about it."

Once everyone including Einer and I donned our cold weather gear we unloaded the Kettenkrad.

Parky: "Ole, you want me to drive. I have a map of the approximate coordinates."

Ole was still a bit testy about the Asil comments as he answered Parky. "No, I'll drive. You might know how to pilot a plane but when it comes to piloting a motorcycle that's my expertise. You read the map and give me directions, Captain."

The Kettenkrad was still warm from being in the plane and it fired right up. Within seconds the warm air from motors exhaust hitting the cold air created a telltale exhaust vaper that would certainly be visible if our friends at the German camp had scout's watching for anyone in the area. I had my doubts about that, I mean did the Germans really have to post guards and lookouts in this frozen land. Who in their right mind would be just roaming around? Then again I guess we were roaming around. However, just because we took this job and were here might cause some doubts on whether we were in our right minds.

CHAPTER 5

I was seated on Ole's lap. With my own insulated coat, cap, boots and googles I looked like I belonged to the 1908-1909 Robert Peary expedition to the North Pole. The big difference being I was riding in comfort on a motorized vehicle instead of being one of a pack of dogs pulling a sled filled with supplies. I must admit I really preferred my current situation over the dogs that were with Peary. Especially since if we were stranded or low on provisions I doubt my companions would eat me.

Luckily the snow was not deep and fluffy or we may have bogged down. It was more what you would expect at the North Pole. It was a mixture of snow and ice hardened by the wind. Almost perfect conditions for the Kettenkrad's rubber encased tracks and the front ski to help keep us gliding along at a good thirty to forty kilometers per hour.

A small flap on the side of my hat was pulled over and snapped at one side to cover my face. It was a good thing it was there as it was on all of my companion's faces or the cold would have made it almost impossible to breath. Moving at the speed we were it was nice that a windshield had been install to help break the wind. As we moved along and I looked over the landscape I realized that this frozen north was a white cold hearted mistress. Sort of like the impression that Asil had been giving to Ole.

Parky was keeping his eye on his compass and would holler out directions to Ole every so often. In this bleak white landscape with only occasional ice ridges breaking up the monotony. We really had no idea how Parky had any sense of direction. Then something came to me. I nudged Ole with my back leg to get his attention over the drone of the Kettenkrad engine.

"Ole, if we are truly near the North Pole how is it that Parky has a compass that actually works?"

I looked up at Ole as he looked down at me. I could see the worry in his eyes as he let off the throttle. With the tracks on the Kettenkrad we quickly coasted to a stop without the use of brakes.

Ole undid his face mask as he turned to look back at Parky. With the Kettenkrad at a dead stop Asil, Parky and Einer all turned their heads to look at Ole.

Asil: "Why are we stopping? Do you see something?"

Ole: "I don't see anything other than white. Parky. If my memory is correct and we are anywhere near the North Pole. I seem to recollect from my school days that we would be near the center of the earth's magnetic pole. If that is correct your compass would be totally useless here."

Asil: "Parky is that true?"

Parky: "Well, yes it's true. I didn't want you to think we were lost or that I didn't know what I was doing so telling you a little 'white' lie seemed like the right thing to do under the circumstances. Just a bit of humor there, did you four get it? White lie, everything around us is white. Come on, I can't see you smile with those face masks on so at least give a bit of a chuckle so I can hear you."

Asil: "I don't see the humor in it."

Ole: "Me either."

I looked at Einer he and I thought it was, well, not real funny, but cute.

Einer: "I could fly up and scout the area."

Asil: "What if you are seen. A flying dog would surely bring undo attention to us."

Parky: "Yes it would jeopardize our mission. Einer and you too Asil you have powers we may need to use when the time comes. If the Germans knew of your powers they would put you in prison and brain wash you so they could use your powers as a secret weapon. What you possess may be even greater then what they are working on."

Ole: "Let's get back to the subject at hand. What did you hope to achieve by deceiving us?"

Parky: "I wasn't really deceiving you. I was just trying to put you at ease. This is a dangerous land we are in and the calmer we all are the better off we will be. No need to get scared or nervous and maybe make some fatal mistake."

Maybe Parky had a point.

Parky: "The latitude and longitude from the reading I took in the airplane shows we are very near to the area Aegir told us about. The size of our plane and the noise from its engines would surely alert anyone in the area. Add in the noise the Kettenkrad makes and it should be just a matter of time before a German patrol locates us. I figure if we drove around it might just bring us closer to our destination."

Asil: "So what do we do now? Just keep driving around?"

Parky: "Not exactly around, I suggest we keep going straight ahead."

Ole: "Straight ahead? That just takes us farther from the airplane. If we don't find the German base or if they don't find us we could run out of petrol and be stranded in the cold. This is not a place I would chose to end my life,

Asil, Einer and I all agreed with Ole.

Parky: "No need to worry. Have I ever let you down? We have two extra jerry cans of petrol strapped to the side. If worse comes to worse we can tip the Kettenkrad upside down and use it as a shelter, piling loose snow around it will make it sort of a makeshift igloo. There are picks and shovels here with us and we can even cut blocks of ice to form a more permanent shelter should the need arise. I've been in lots of dire situations when the law was chasing me back in Norway, Sweden, and Finland."

None of us relished the prospect of shacking up on the ice but Parky was right about one thing, he had never yet let us down. We were a team and had trusted each other in many a life and death situation. Ole and I resumed our position as Ole started the Kettenkrad.

We headed due, will due somewhere. Without a compass none of us knew what direction we were headed.

Suddenly, about 400 yards straight ahead and flanking our sides we saw the snow lift up as if some mysterious underground activity had blown chunks of ice into the air. Each hole had a figure pop out of it. My first thought was we were about to be lunch for a bunch of Yeti.

Upon further examination the figures were not Yeti but men in white camouflage and each was brandishing a Steyr sub-machine gun.

Ole slowed the Kettenkrad down until he was within 10 yards of the man in front of us. The others quickly raced across the ice and surrounded us. Asil and Parky had already reached for their weapons and having to many targets to choose from they lowered them back down.

Surrender being the better part of valor as they say seemed to be the best option. This of course was just what we were hoping for, providing they didn't shoot us.

The soldier in front of us ordered us to halt and to lower our weapons and raise our hands in the air. Of course he spoke in German which we all now understand thanks to a bit of help from Aegir.

The soldiers approached us and ordered us to dismount the Kettenkrad and to keep our hands in the air. They relieved us of our visible weapons and then patted us down. Asil, Parky and Ole all had holstered weapons and daggers attached to their uniforms. The leader of the men told us to take off our snow gear.

Ole: "Are you crazy? We'll freeze to death. Anyways we can't access our weapons under our cold weather gear."

The leader raised his machine gun and smacked my partner in the side of his face with the butt of the gun. Ole went down like a falling brick and hit the ice. Blood oozed from his cheek bone and although he was dazed he got up on one elbow with hate in his eyes as he stared in defiance at the man who hit him.

Leader: "Get up swine! You will all do as you are told or we will shoot you here and now and leave your bodies for the polar bears to feast on."

Asil: "Yes sir. We will follow your orders. We are looking for a German encampment. We came as friends. I understand your reluctance in believing us. Anything you want us to do to put your minds at ease we will do. Parky, Ole, do as they ask."

Reluctantly, Ole and Parky did as they were told. Asil was more cooperative and as such the leader of the soldiers gave her the option of trust. He said that he would let her hand over her weapons voluntarily without the need for being searched and as soon as she had done so she could get back into her winter gear.

Parky and Ole on the other hand were treated rather harshly. They had to open their shirts, take off their boots and step out of their trousers. The soldiers went through their pockets and felt inside their boots for hidden weapons. Both of them were soon turning red with cold. The soldiers took their time and made sure Parky and Ole were two standing, shivering, ice cold prisoners. Finally, Asil had had enough and intervened.

Asil: "Sir, and I address you as such as I do not know your rank. I feel you have punished my comrades enough for their insolence. May they please be allowed to get dressed before they catch frost bite or die?"

Leader: "As you wish Fraulein. Let the men get dressed. By the way I am Colonel Kempler. I see you are in German uniform. A Corporal according to your insignia. May I ask your name?"

Asil: "You addressed me as Fraulein, do you assume I am not married?"

Kempler: "Pardon me. I may have addressed you as such in hope that you are single. I cannot image you would be married to the big hunk of flesh or that disrespectful swine that are standing there shivering from the dressing down my men gave them."

Asil: "Colonel Kempler I find your attitude and treatment of fellow German soldiers to be totally disrespectful. You are a disgrace to the uniform of a German Officer. You can see by our outfits and identification papers that Parky and I are German military and Ole is a Norwegian volunteer who fought with the German Nordland division. I suggest you take us to whoever is in charge."

Kempler: "Until I know more about you and your companions it will be necessary for us to keep your weapons and your identification papers. The three of you and your dogs may remount you Kettenkrad and follow us."

The Colonel and his men fell into a classic maneuver of one leading, two flanking each side as they led us towards what seemed to be more of nothing. Just straight ahead into the cold white landscape. After about three-hundred yards we stopped.

Kempler pulled something similar to a cigarette lighter from his pocket. We didn't see a flame as he flicked the top open, instead there were two small metal wires and a purple arc like lightning flashed quickly between them. A panel opened much like a garage door being lifted to reveal a ramp descending down a lighted tunnel.

Kempler shouted orders to his men. "Get the sweeper and erase the tracks. Then retrieve the airplane and take it to the base. Make sure there is not a trace of anything. I want the airplane gone over with a fine tooth comb. If there is anything at all that is questionable let me know immediately."

Kempler descended into the tunnel and motioned for us to follow as we drove behind him in the Kettenkrad. A few soldiers stayed with us and followed us in. Off in a side tunnel was something that resembled a dog sled made of metal, there was a circular broom bristled sweeper mounted on the front and the back and it was driven by an airplane engine with a back mounted propeller. There was seating for four people and it was armed with a mounted machine gun and an antiaircraft rocket launcher. Not a very visitor friendly vehicle to say the least. This is what they would use to eradicate our tracks.

We were directed to a large indentation on the tunnel wall and ordered to park our Kettenkrad there. Then we were led on foot down the tunnel. I noticed the walls were of wood but traces of white frost could be seen between the section joints where the wood was butted together. An under the ice German controlled base was now a certainty.

After walking past many offshoots of corridors we were finally led to one that contained barred cells much like a prison. How deep under the surface we were it was hard to say. It was now pleasantly warm and I could see beads of sweat on the foreheads of my human companions.

Kempler directed Asil into one cell and she asked if it was all right if Einer could accompany her. Permission was granted.

Parky, Ole and I were put in adjoining cell. It had solid walls inside so we could not see or communicate with Asil, especially since a guard was posted outside of each cell. The clunk of the lock closing as the key was pulled from the door made us feel as if we just might have bit off more than we could chew. For the next few minutes Parky cleaned the blood off Ole's cheek with some cloth he tore from his undershirt. "Just a little flesh wound is all. You'll be fine." Was all he said.

Parky spoke loud enough so the guards or any listening devices in the cell would pick up our conversation. "No need to worry. Our papers are all in order. Once the people in charge realize we are here to help rebuild a greater Germany everything will be fine."

It must have been getting late as the guards brought us supper. We had no idea what time of day it was. Being underground the lighting never changed and besides all of our weapons the soldiers had taken watches and everything from the pockets of my companions. Parky and Ole were served dumpling soup and bread and I was given a bowl of something that resembled whale blubber and unlike the Eskimo's I did not consider it a delicacy. However, I was starving and none of us had eaten since the Carolsea so I ate my food without complaint.

There were two hard wooden cots with one wool blanket for each. When it came time for lights out Ole and I shared one cot. Considering we were inside some sort of ice fortress it was actually fairly warm.

As we lay in the dark I had Ole ask Parky why they were waiting so long to interrogate us.

Parky: "We're prisoners for the time being. When they have thoroughly gone over all our belongings and I'm sure they will also investigate our plane and the Kettenkrad with a fine tooth comb they will hopefully realize we are here as allies to their cause whatever it may be."

Next morning the lights came on and we heard the cell next to us open. Although we could not see what was going on we heard the guards telling Asil that she was to go with them. My canine hearing picked up both Asil's and Einer's footsteps as they walked away. There wasn't anything that any of us dared to say with the guard still at our cell door and the chances were that there were listening devices in our cell. For now it was just best we keep our mouths shut.

For breakfast Parky and Ole had scrambled eggs and bread. I got whale blubber again and Ole once again shared a bit of his bread with me. I couldn't believe they had chickens down here but where else would eggs come from. When I asked Ole about it he laughed and repeated the question as if he was asking it to Parky. Parky gave out one of his big belly laughs and we could hear the guard snickering at the door.

Parky: "Eggs! I've had these before while eating in the army camps. They called them powdered eggs. There's a whole lot more powder than they are eggs. Only a cardboard chicken could lay eggs that taste this bad."

For another hour we sat twiddling our paws, ok, I was twiddling my paws and Parky and Ole might have been twiddling their thumbs I wasn't really paying that much attention, all I know is that I was bored. There really isn't much to do in a jail cell.

Ole: "Guard, could you tell us what time it is? Also, do you have any idea how long they are going to keep us here?

Guard: "It's half past noon. I don't have any idea, wait a minute. Looks like someone is coming to get you."

The guard unlocked our cell and Colonel Kempler stood in the doorway dressed in the black uniform of an SS officer with the skull and crossbones insignia glimmering just below the winged eagle under the peak of his cap as he looked us over,

Kempler: "Well, you three don't look any the worse for the wear. However, your uniforms are wrinkled and you look like you could use a shave and some cleaning up before we go to see the General.

Follow me to the latrine. There are fresh uniforms and a shower there for you. Once you are presentable as German soldiers we will go to see the General. By the way, that scrubby looking dog should be washed and brushed if he is to accompany you."

Of course I was to accompany them. What did Kempler think, that I was just some mutt that you toss in the corner and forget about? You might do that to a cat but never to man's best friend.

We were led to the latrine and Colonel Kempler said he would wait outside for us. We walked in and Parky made a quick check over of our surroundings.

Ole: "Parky what are you looking for? There are fresh uniforms on the shelf over there. Shaving equipment is by the sinks and towels are by the door of the showers. It's actually pretty amazing for a military base to have individual showers with doors on them. Looks like a nice clean comfortable place to me."

Parky motioned for Ole to come near him by the sinks. He hung a hand towel over the mirror in front of his sink and pulled Ole close to him while he whispered in his ear. "First of all I was looking for any small metal pipes or release jets just in case they planned on gassing us. You know they used it on the Jews in the concentration camps. Secondly, there could be hidden cameras, possibly the mirror I covered up could be a two way mirror and they might be watching us. Now if you want to talk just ramble on about anything useless. That shouldn't be too hard for you."

Ole gave Parky a playful sock in the arm and a wry smile like humans give when they are being teased. I of course gave a good tail wag at Parky's comments.

Parky and Ole shaved and Ole set me up on the counter and grasped my head in his hands as he held me still so Parky could use a scissors to trim up my face. I will admit I am not the best customer when it comes to someone waving a sharp scissors around my eyes and nose but Parky was gentle and careful so I can't really complain too much.

Parky grabbed two towels and tossed them over the shower door, it would take two towels to dry off his bulk. Ole did the same except one towel was for him and the other for me. Only one thing comes as close to my list of dislikes as having my face trimmed with a scissors and that's getting a bath. I knew I had no choice in the matter if I was to accompany Parky and Ole to see the man in charge so I accepted my fate. The only thing worse I could think of was if I had to lick a cat.

Ole showered first and then he lathered me up with shampoo and gave me a good rub down with a towel. Once he dried himself off he put me back up on the counter by the sink and combed out my fur as best he could with a people comb. I looked myself over in the mirror and I had to admit I was one handsome canine. Now don't you think I was just bragging and showing off like Parky does. It's not arrogant or egotistical if it's true. Although Ole's next comment was a bit cruel if you ask me as he whispered in my ear. "You look just like a mini-Parkurkakus."

Parky and Ole got dressed in their clean uniforms sans any holsters or dagger scabbards. Once we were finished and looked like professional military men we went back to the awaiting Colonel Kempler.

Kempler: "Well I must say you two look the part of German officers. Now we'll see what the General has to say about your being here. You best hope it's in your favor. If not I can assure you I will enjoy it immensely if he turns you over to me for the final decision on your fate."

Parky, Ole and I all looked apprehensively at each other. Was it possible Kempler knew something and was giving us a hint as to our fate?

Ole: Colonel Kempler. We came as friends to the German cause. We've done nothing more than be model prisoners and to do as we have been instructed. Parky is a professional pilot and Officer with many talents that will be useful in the making of a new Germany. I have combat and military experience and a vast knowledge of history to share with the people stationed here. Asil is a loyal and devoted German who has proven by her being here with us that she wishes to offer her services to a new a better Germany. By the way, can you tell us where she is?"

Kempler: "Genug, halt die klappe!"

Opps, sorry I'll translate for you. Kempler said: "Enough, shut your mouth."

After traversing what seemed to be endless corridors of tunnels we came to a wooden door with a small window cut into it. The window was glass with a German Eagle emblem done in silver in its center. A brass plaque right below the window read General Von Weber.

Considering how military things seemed to have been so far it surprised us that no guards were posted outside the door. Colonel Kempler knocked and a voice from inside said 'enter.'

Colonel Kempler opened the door and entered ahead of us. He undid the snap on his holster and placed his hand on the handle of a Luger pistol. We stood slightly off to the side wondering what was to happen next.

General: "Colonel you are dismissed."

Kempler: "Begging your pardon Sir. You don't know these men or what they may be capable of. They could be spies sent here by the Allies. I would strongly suggest I stay here to keep an eye on them."

General: "Corporal Kempler. I am a General, I did not come by this rank without having military experience and that includes my judgement on which men I can trust and not trust. If you insist on arguing the point you may find that your rank may be quickly demoted to that of a foot soldier, if we were not already in a frozen wasteland I would send you to Siberia in Russia. I'm sure the Russians would welcome a man with your past experience in killing their fellow countrymen during the war. I bet they would enjoy putting you up in a cozy little gulag."

Kempler: "I am sorry Herr General I meant no disrespect. I shall be waiting outside if you need anything."

We looked around the office and we were impressed how warm and homey it felt for a place located under an icecap. Honey colored wood paneling, deep red colored carpeting that felt thick and warm beneath my paws. Brown soft leather chairs and a couch, a hand carved walnut desk. Paintings by a young artist Adolph Hitler of town scenes and architectural buildings that were located throughout Germany, albeit, many of which had been destroyed during the war. A holdover from the past still adorned the wall behind the General's chair. A large portrait of none other than Adolf Hitler. The General was dressed in a German Officers field uniform. He was from all appearances a soldiers solider.

General: "Please forgive Colonel Kempler gentlemen. He is dedicated SS, brain washed into ideologies that I am glad to say are not shared by the majority of the people here. However he does have a loyal band of men that he brought with him and if I were you two I would give them a wide berth.

Now let's get down to the business at hand. Please have a seat. Would either of you like some tea or coffee?"

Parky and Ole both took the offer of tea and took their seats in the two large wing backed leather upholstered seats in front of the Generals desk. The General pushed a button on the top of the desk and male voice answered. He asked the man that answered to please bring in three cups of tea and a bowl of milk. I don't know about my partners but the General just made his second brownie point with me, the first being that he didn't care much for Colonel Kempler.

General: "I'm General Von Weber, I am in charge of this installation. I have looked over your identification papers and the belongings that my men confiscated from you when they picked you up. Your plane has been retrieved and is now in a safe place in our compound hidden from the prying eyes of anyone who may wish to locate it. Your presence here is a bit of a surprise but hopefully not an unpleasant one. You are not the first ones to arrive here unannounced. We have scouts still in the homeland looking for likely candidates to help with our project. Unfortunately for us most of the scouts work undercover and we do not know who they are or who they may send us. It is best it remain that way for the well-being of all of us. Anyone who ventures here will have to know our approximate whereabouts or they would not be here. Even though we assume you are friends you must understand we need to be careful. Our work here is of the utmost secrecy and it may very possibly be the basis for a greater Germany in the future. A Fourth Reich if you will. Only this time we will have a better plan than to trust our military actions to just one man. The Fuhrer had the right idea to conquer

Europe, his mistake was to open a two front war. Our plan will be different."

Ole: "General, do you think it is wise to start another war so soon after we have just lost the last war?"

General: "When the time is right we shall make our move. You may be surprised how far we have advanced in the time we have been here."

Parky: "If you don't mind me asking, just how long has this base been in operation?"

General: "By early 1943 many of the higher ranking military officers could see the tide of the war was shifting. Stalin was building relations with the allies and with their assistance and with the manpower he was able to harness it was just a matter of time before the allies would trap Germany in the center of the two front war Hitler was fighting. It was simple logistics that we did not have the manpower or the resources to fight enemies from both sides. So it was that I and others like me started building this base."

Parky: "That sounds like an excellent plan Sir. We came here to help. What would you like us do?"

General: "I had a long discussion with Corporal Asil and she convinced me that the 3 of you and your two canine companions are indeed genuine patriots. Captain Parkurkarkus you will be assigned to the aerial wing of our operation along with your assistant Corporal Asil. Sergeant Ole, You will be assigned to help oversee our assembly operations. Captain, because of your rank, you will be assigned to your own private quarters. Ole will be assigned a bunk with the other lower ranking officers. Asil will be assigned her own quarters. We have very few women officers here and we do our best to accommodate them."

Ole: "General, can we ask just what is going on here?"

General: "You may not, you will find out in good time as your work moves you into more secure areas. For the time being you will need to build up our trust in you and show us that you are capable of being part of our team. If that is all you are dismissed. Corporal Kempler will show you to your quarters."

The General got up from his desk and led us to the door where he gave orders to Colonel Kempler to take us to our quarters and make sure we were settled in. Kempler did as he was told although he did not seem too pleased about it. He led us to Parky's quarters first and then to Asil's. Then we were led to our barracks and shown our foot locker and bunk.

Kempler: "Sergeant Ole, I do hope you enjoy your stay. My bunk is the next one over. It's certainly not military protocol in my book that I should be in the same room as enlisted men and having a Sergeant with a dog just across from me might prove interesting for us both. Just remember as an officer in the SS I am better trained than any of you regular army fellows. If I were you I'd watch my step. My men and I will be keeping a close eye on you and your companions. If you breathe a word of what I just said to General Von Weber, well, I would hate to see some unfortunate accident befall you or your dog, or maybe the lovely Asil."

What we did not know at the time was that Kempler had his own private quarters but he kept an open bunk in the barracks to keep an eye on the men billeted there.

Ole looked at Kempler with fire in his eyes. I quickly intervened. "Ole, blow it off. He's trying to get you upset so you will do something stupid. He's just looking for a reason to cause a fight."

Ole: "Thanks for all your help Colonel. You know we're here to help the cause. Believe it or not we are on your side. I apologize if I did or said anything to make you feel otherwise. I hope we can forgot our differences and be friends. Just so you know I have fought alongside some of the SS units in the past. Those units are well trained and have no fear. I have only the deepest respect for their abilities."

Of course that took Kempler totally off guard. Ole literally turned that SS wolf into a friendly lap dog.

Kempler: "Maybe I got you wrong Ole. Chow will be served in the mess hall at five. You can wander around until then. Just stay clear of the restricted areas. I have work to do. We'll see you later."

We had had more than enough rest in the cell we had been confined to so we took up Kempler's offer to explore as many areas as we could. The tunnel system was well marked with large arrows pointing to the different areas.   We were able to explore the assembly shops, prefabrication, the kitchen, the recreational area and something that was quite interesting the botanical gardens. How they had managed to grow everything from the common to the exotic species of plants and trees was amazing beyond belief. This large circular area had insulated wooden sides with a system of pipes that sprayed a fine mist on the hour. The roof was some type of crystal clear Plexiglas similar to what was used in the domes on airplane bombers. One thing was this roof was immense in size, about the size of a football field. Its purpose was to let the sun's rays shine into the gardens during the daylight hours.   It could be easily hidden from view by pulling a large lever that would retract a two piece sheet of white Plexiglas that would form a seal in the center and matched the surrounding snow and ice field above us. There were heat vents on the side spaced six-feet apart that generated enough warmth that the whole place had sort of a steaming jungle type of feel to it. A few birds flew around without a care in the world. Parakeets, parrots, cockatoos, robins, sparrows, blue jays and even nuthatches. Not to mention assorted lizards and a few snakes. It was as if paradise had been relocated under the ice. One had to wonder what type of minds had conceived and built such a thing. If they were capable of creating such a beautiful place then what else were they capable of?

CHAPTER 6

A month went by. We had not seen or heard from Asil or Parkurkakus. We had been assigned to a fabrication and minor assembly section. There was a foundry section that we had been able to visit so that we could absorb the processes that were involved and that would in turn give Ole a better understanding as to coming up with new ideas to speed up the process and make it more efficient. He was also instructed to try and come up with ways to add strength to the items they were making. The metal was a composition of aluminum with some flexibility but it needed to be the strength of case hardened steel.

Ole did his best to convey that it would be prudent if his superiors told him just what the items we were overseeing were to be used for. If he knew that he explained he might better be able to come up with something flexible, lighter and more durable if he understood the dynamic of its use.

Was it to resist shell fire from weapons, or was it to build bomb proof buildings or possibly it was to be used to sheath submarines so they could go faster and reach greater depths. Thus far all of his questions went unanswered and he was told to just do his job. Eventually a time might come that he would be privy to more information but not now.

It was a frustrating situation for both of us. Ole was busy supervising as usual. I was on the assembly room floor laying off to the side and out of the way of the workers. My head was on my paws and I was peacefully dozing as I had become oblivious to the constant noise that accompanies the work of an assembly area.

I felt a slight nudge of a wet nose on my cheek. Of course I figured maybe I was slipping into a dream with some pretty little bitch. The nudge soon became a push on my stomach from something that might have been a human foot, but it was a dog's forehead. I lifted my head and looked toward my back, sort of miffed that I was being disturbed.

My supposed anger turned to joy as I stood up with my tail at full wag. "Einer, my friend, my buddy, it's so good to see you. Where

have you been? Are Asil and Parky all right? Have the three of
you found out what is going on around here? Well, what's wrong?
Cat got your tongue? Ha-ha, that was a good one, huh?"

Einer: "Hold on there partner. That's a lot of questions to answer
all at once. First off and most important, Asil and Parky are just
find. Second, we are finding out a lot and it is sort of a mixed
situation. Parky has been his normal I can do anything self. He's
been promoted by General Von Weber to Cornel Parkurkarkus.
After his promotion he was given clearance to the top secret
operations that are going on here and you won't believe your eyes
until you see it."

My tail was going at full wag in anticipation. "So, what is it, this
top secret operation? Is there any chance Ole and I can see it?"

Einer: "Parky is doing his best to figure out a way to get Ole and
you transferred to his command. It may take a little more time.
He's gaining their trust but it's only been a few weeks. As for you, I
think if you come with me no one is going to figure that a dog is a
spy and I have access to everything that Parky has access to. Come
on let's go take a look."

I ran over to Ole and told him Einer and I were going exploring.
He looked down at Einer and was excited to see him as I was. He
gave Einer a good friendly scratching behind his ears as he asked.
'Einer, is Asil all right?"

Einer: "She's fine and so is Parky. I need to get back before they
miss me. Is it ok if Sven comes with? I'll only keep him for a while.
I promise he'll be safe,"

Ole: "No problem. As long as he is with you I know you'll watch
after him. Say hello to Asil and Parky for me."

Einer: "I will. See you soon."

Einer took off at trot as I followed along. He seemed to know his
way around the place much better than I did. He ran by the guards
at the entrance to tunnels that had large signs that read security
clearance required to enter this area. They seemed to know him
and as long as I was with him they let me pass without checking me
over. Then again, we were dogs, little did they know that we could
communicate with our humans or our entrance into these

forbidding places would most likely have been justification for the guards to shoot us dead on the spot.

The first room we entered was filled with technicians dressed in white lab outfits with surgical masks covering their mouth and nose and there were white gloves on their hands. The instruments and equipment they were handling looked as if it was designed for a very modern up to date mad scientist lab like one would see in a monster movie. Sort of a Frankenstein lab as I remembered from the Universal picture of the same name that was produced in 1931. The only thing missing was the monster and the stone walls. Instead of dead body parts the room was neatly arranged with tables filled with strange metal items that resembled propellers, machine body parts and exotic shapes of bolts and screws some so light that the slightest vibration of the tables made them seem to float in the air.

It didn't take long before one of the technicians noticed us. "Out of here! This is a sterile area you know better than to come in here. Plus, I see you brought one of your mangy friends along with you. If Colonel Kempler knew you were here he would shoot you both in the head and take you to kitchen so they could serve you as dog meat stew. Get along, now! Scat! If you know what's good for you don't come back."

I trotted off alongside Einer as the electric door of the facility opened to let us out and then automatically closed behind us just as it did when we came here. I looked at Einer and asked. "I thought I noticed that the humans needed a pass card that they have to put into a slot to get in and out of there. How come the doors open for you?"

Einer: "Parky has moved up the hierarchy with his knowledge about so many things that he has a pass card that allows him access to almost everywhere in the complex. He got one of the technicians to fix him the parts he needed to make a collar for me that has some type of sensor in it that lets all the security doors to allow me access. He figures it will come in handy when the time comes for us to make our move."

"So, what's going on in here?"

Einer: "This is research and development. Of course it's supposed to be a sterile environment so no one is allowed without germ free clothing, masks and gloves. I'm sure Parky will have all kinds of hell to pay if word gets out that you and I were in here. As far as I know they don't make germ free outfits for canines."

Maybe I should suggest the idea to him. If he could you make you a collar to override the safety protocols a couple of sterile suits for dogs should be a cinch."

Einer: "Don't you dare say anything. If Parky doesn't find out all the better for us. If he does there will hell to pay for me. Parky doesn't often lose his temper, in fact I have never seen him do so. Most we might get is a good verbal scolding. However, If Asil finds out she may let you off easy as you were just following my lead. As for me I'd get hell in a handcart and then some. Trust me, she has a temper and I prefer not to be on the receiving end of it."

I had to think that Asil had been changing a lot lately. Einer mentioned her temper and I had noticed that her heart was cooling off toward Ole like the heart of the Princess of ice that she was. It was adding up to a sad state of affairs for my partner's future love life. For now I decided I should keep my thoughts to myself.

The next section Einer led us to was even more heavily guarded than the last.

Einer: "If you thought what you just saw was interesting, just wait. You haven't seen anything yet."

The guards once again ignored us as we trotted by them.

I thought I better ask a question before we went into the next section. "You sure this is going to be all right if we go in? They didn't seem too happy about us being in the last place. I don't want to see Asil or Parky get into any more trouble. Or yourself or me for that matter."

Einer: It will be fine. This is the development and experimental applications section. I looked around and as far as I could see there was no end to the length of the room and it was at least three football fields wide. Looking, up there was an opaque slightly curved dome the color of ice crystals so that if anything passed over it the top would blend in perfectly with the surrounding ice fields.

There was a gap extending from each corner and intersecting in the center. Einer explained to me that the dome was too large to slide away and out of sight. So in this case it was hinged in four sections and it would open outwards from the facility to allow for testing the items that were all around us.

As for those items there was more than I could ever hope to explain or comprehend. It was a literal cornucopia of aviation machines. Flying marvels that only a fertile unbridled imagination could have conceived. Planes that looked like nothing more than flying wings. From the little I knew about Germany's v-bombs, rockets and there jet planes it was obvious that the designers of those airborne marvels had leant their magical genius of destruction to a whole new era of aircraft. However, very few seemed to carry or be built to carry armaments. I took this as a good sign, at least for the time being.

One item in particular caught my attention more than the others. It was a rather ungainly looking thing. I had seen some photos of something similar that was being developed in some countries other than but including Germany. The generic term seemed to be helicopter. Only this one had some very unique additions. The one's I remember had three rotors mounted to the top that spun for lift and could be cantered for forward or backward or side movement. The smaller propeller in the tail section was there to counteract the torque of the larger propellers.

One of the technicians walked over by Einer and I. He talked to us like he knew we understood him. Of course that was pure nonsense in the back of his mind. But I believe he enjoyed showing off one of the many 'toys' that were scattered around us.

Technician: "Well hello there my furry friends. I bet you've come to see some of our many creations. You seem to be particularly interested in this little gem. Right you should be. It is one of my favorites. We have taken what was at one time considered a unique design for an air machine and turned it into something that is an absolutely mind-boggling amazing piece of machinery. Something far beyond what the original designers could have even dreamt of. Of course they were restricted in their visions by the old regimes restraints on time and money. Churning out super weapons to save Germany in its final days of the war was just not feasible considering the time frame those poor designers and engineers had to work with.

But here we are under no such restraints. We are encouraged to let our imaginations run wild. Budget restraints and cash flow are not an issue. I personally don't know where the materials or funding comes from and I don't really care. As long as my associates and I have free reign to do as we please we are as happy as children in a free amusement park.

For you two this is your lucky day. This machine which we have dubbed the jetcopter is due for a test flight. It would be quite interesting to see the affect it has on canines."

All of a sudden I lost interest in this flying jet thingee and its overly friendly technician soon to become pilot. Things started to get rally hairy when I felt myself being scooped up and tossed into the seat of the jetcopter. Einer was either used to flying or much more adventurous than I was as he voluntarily hopped in beside me. The technician got in and strapped Einer and I into our seats by wrapping the seatbelts around our bellies. I had a very bad feeling about this. Einer looked at me and wagged his tail.

Einer: "No need to worry Sven. I've been up in a lot of these experiential aircraft. They have been pretty thoroughly tested and most of the time everything turns out just fine.

"And if it doesn't" I asked.

Einer: "Well, I've seen a few of them crash. Usually if something goes wrong the pilot and any crew have time to bail out and parachute safely to the ground."

"I have two questions. What happens when they don't get out and the aircraft crashes and just in case you didn't notice we don't have parachutes only the pilot does? In your case that's probably just fine seeing you can fly on your own. As for me I'm afraid I'll fall like a rock straight to the ground and go splat like a bug on a windshield of a moving vehicle, make that a huge splat and a very high speed moving vehicle."

Einer: "Don't be such a scaredy cat."

There he goes making cat jokes while I'm worried about my current life expectancy.

Einer: "I'll get us a parachute." He pawed the pilots arm and then pawed the parachute that was on the floor by us.

Technician/pilot: "Oh no. I almost forgot to attach your parachute. One chute should be adequate for the both of you. I'll strap it to you Einer seeing you're the bigger of you two and we'll run an attached strap around your buddies waist so he can float down with you if the need should arise, which I am sure it won't."

Just to get the answer from my two part question and I asked again. "What happened to those that crashed and didn't bail out."

Einer: "They didn't exactly splat like a bug on a windshield. It was more like being attached to an exploding bomb. You can't image how volatile and explosive the fuel is that they power these babies with."

"Thanks a lot for those comforting thoughts. Here I thought we might be in danger." One thing about Einer he had a philosophy about life just like his Mistress Asil. Sort of maritime like with the damn the torpedoes and full speed ahead thinking.

From this point on I'm just going to refer to our technician-pilot as TP at least that was what Einer called him.

TP checked over all the controls and put on a headset that let him communicate with the main operations area.

TP: "Everything here has been checked and double checked. I am ready for takeoff. Two canine passengers on board. I'll attach their oxygen masks once we are in flight. Please inform when roof panels are open and we are clear for take-off."

We could hear the loudspeakers make the announcement. "Now hear this. Now hear this. Jetcopter has been cleared for take-off. All ground personnel report immediately to your safety areas. This is not a drill, this is not a drill."

Sirens began to sound as everyone within our sight scrambled to safety like so many ants heading back to their anthill in a rainstorm.

TP: "Ready boys. Hang on to your ears and your tails, this is going to be a fun trip heading out of here. The turbulence of the wind from the rotors is going to be bouncing off the walls in here like the outside edge of a tornado and we are going to be right on the middle of it. Don't worry though, I've done this before. Once we clear the dome it will be smooth as silk."

TP pressed a starter button and we could hear the rotor blades above us start to turn. As they picked up speed we began to rise off the ground. The faster the rotor spun the blades the higher we rose and just like TP predicted our craft began to bounce around from the surrounding turbulence. TP had both his hands wrapped around the control stick and it was easy to see he was using all his strength to keep the jetcopter under control.

Once we had cleared the dome and were out in the open we shot straight up in the air. The force of our ascent literally pushed me into the seat cushion. We leveled and started to move forward at a brisk clip. I watched TP push a button called auto pilot.

TP: "All right. We're out in the open and you two shall soon see what a jetcopter is made of. But first I better put these oxygen masks over your snouts or you'll lose consciousness once we start putting this thing through its tests."

I looked back and saw the dome closing behind us and had to wonder how we would ever find our way back. Luckily, TP must have read my mind.

TP: "There we go, the homing device is set so we can find our way back. We're going to need it because once this baby gets moving there will be no stopping it. I hope you two don't have weak stomachs, if you do bark or nudge me or something to let me know that you are about to hurl your guts out. If you don't you'll most likely drown in your own vomit as it fills up your oxygen mask. So either paw it off your face or let me know so I can remove the mask for you. You two got that? If you do give me a slight bark so I know."

Either TP was really trusting that we understood him or he was intelligent enough to know that dogs understood a lot of what humans say. Einer and I both gave out a muffled bark through our oxygen masks.

TP pushed the control stick forward and we could feel the rotor above us cantor as we darted ahead picking up speed. Then we shot upward at an angle. I glanced at the altimeter as it showed us climbing from five-hundred feet to eight-hundred feet in what seemed a wag of the tail.

TP: "We are almost there, at twelve-hundred feet I'll show you why they call this the jetcopter. You two might want to lean back in your seats now. Here we go!"

We were sitting in a machine that had a clear dome around us. As TP fiddled with some controls we could hear the roar of a jet engine building up. Just before the jets kicked in the rotor blades of the propellers above us retracted from their normal position to a bundle of the three of them now pressed together in a straight line pointing to the back of the jetcopter. As they locked themselves in that position the jetcopter made a slight dip as we lost momentum and then the jets engines at the mid rear of the jetcopter kicked in. We lurched forward like a rock flying out of a slingshot.

TP: "I hope you two are ready for this. You are about to go to where no dog has gone before. A Hungarian-American physicist Theodore von Karman calculated that at 62 miles above the earth we leave our atmosphere and move into space. You two are about to experience that privilege. With the lack of the earth's gravitational pull you may feel yourselves floating off your seats but not to worry your seat belts will keep you from floating away. Are you ready? No matter, here we go."

TP pulled back the control stick and we shot higher into the air like a, well, like a rocket.

TP: "We'll soon be hitting 1,225 kilometers per hour, or 761.2 miles per hour, when we do you will hear a large explosion, like a bomb going off. No need to worry, it's what we refer to as a sonic boom. It is the point where we will be traveling over the speed of sound. We'll shoot up out of our atmosphere for just a minute or two as the jetcopter doesn't have enough fuel for us to stay up much longer."

Next thing I knew we were barreling through space and I was feeling lighter than air. It seemed like only a split second of flying time when we began a slow turn and then started our descent. I was feeling light headed and not exactly sure what was going on around me. I looked over at Einer and he had a drunken dog look on his face so I'm sure he felt the same as I did, disoriented and confused. I vaguely heard TP talking as if he was far away even though I could have reached out my paw and touched him.

TP: "Control, this is TP we will soon be making our approach for landing. Confirm."

Control: "We have you on radar and all looks to be normal for approach and landing."

As if in a shadowy dream I could see TP working the controls in front of him. I heard the jet engines roar fade away as the blades of the propellers above us moved back to their normal three point position. As the jet engines stopped we seemed to be in a freefall until the blades above us started to spin and took over our flight like a normal helicopter.

TP: "Dome is in sight and it looks to be open. Please confirm."

Control: "Confirm. Dome is open and your landing pad is at the ready. Emergency ground crew is on alert. Start you descent to land whenever you are ready."

My light headiness was clearing enough so that I now understand what was going on around me. I had heard the Control room say emergency crews were on the alert which sort of gave me the willies as to way they were standing by. I suppose it was just a safety precaution that is used whenever an aircraft lands.

As we came in for a landing I regained complete control of my senses. TP lined the jetcopter up over the open dome and slowly eased it down. As in our initial takeoff the turbulence from the wind of the propellers against the walls inside the facility once again bounced us around like a cork bobber on a rough sea. I was greatly relieved as I felt the skid gear touch solid ground.

TP looked at Einer and me as he reached over to undo our harnesses. "Now you two will have something to tell your puppies and grand-puppies about. You have to admit that was an adrenaline rush that few if any canines will ever experience.

Personally I had to admit it was exciting looking death in the eye. However, and quite honestly I think I could do without reliving that experience again. Of course I couldn't wait to tell Ole all about it.

Looking around, I couldn't imagine that if this jetcopter which looked mild in comparison to some of the other craft I could see was capable of doing what it just did the rest of the aircraft here would more than fulfill Hitler's dreams and visions of world domination   secret   weapons.
TP opened the door on the passenger side of the jetcopter and Einer and I hopped put. We were both a bit wobbly legged for a few minutes as we regained our balance.

A crew had rushed over to check out the jetcopter and TP kept an eye on us. Once he was satisfied we were all right he turned us over to a doctor who had two of his assistants carry us to his lab.

TP: "Noting to worry about boys. I'm coming with you. It's routine for us to be checked over after every flight, especially when we enter space. A couple pokes of the needle for blood tests, checking your pulse and heartbeat and it will be all over and you can trot off to wherever you were headed in the first place."

TP was right. The doctors and nurses prodded us, poked us, took our temperatures and seeing we were dogs you don't want to know where they stuck the thermometers, but I will tell you that when someone lifts your tail up and they have a glass tube in their hand filled with mercury you will let out a yelp.

When they had finished they helped us get down off the examination tables and after making us sit and wait for a while they finally seemed satisfied that we were fit to be on our way. TP thanked us for volunteering to see how canines would be affected by space travel and waved goodbye as we left as quickly as our four legs would carry us.

I looked at Einer as we took off for what would hopefully be safer pastures. "I don't remember volunteering do you?"

Einer: "Nope, and after that I'm not going to volunteer for anything around here."

"All in all I had to admit that was absolutely amazing. Just think about it Einer we are the first two dogs to break the sound barrier and go into outer space."

Einer: "You're right it was amazing. Except I think we were more in inner space as the next step up would have sent us into outer space where there is no gravity at all, also no air and probably death for anyone dumb enough to try to go there."

"Well, if anyone is that stupid it just might be these guys. The weird thing is that to be that stupid they would have to be geniuses' and from what we just saw they just might be that smart."

Einer: "If they actually are that smart and I think they are, they might have it figured out as to how to survive in outer space. The only thing is I can't imagine what good it would do them. No one else is there and there is no one to conquer so what's the point?"

Yeah, what would be the point? By the way, am I going to get to see Asil and Parky?"

Einer: "They should be at our next stop. I'll give you a bit of a warning before we get there. This next area is top, top, top secret. No one is allowed in there without the highest clearance from General Von Weber."

"Just how are we going to get in there?"

Einer: "My collar will give us clearance. You just stay right by my side. The guards know me and I don't think they will consider you a threat seeing you're just a 'dog' to them and being with me I figure they will just ignore your presence."

We approached a hallway that was marked with a sign that was in German, just to make it easier I'll tell you what it said in English. 'Stop, no admittance beyond this point without proper clearance. Violators will be shot.' After reading the sign I fell behind Einer as I slowed down.

Einer: "Hurry up, if you want to see Asil and Parky you better keep up with me."

With some trepidation I moved back up to Eisner's side. Better we should die as partners then alone.

We slowed down at the first check point. Two guards stood before a locked set of doors. One had a Steyr machine gun held in his hand at chest height, ready to level it and blast away at any unauthorized intruder. The other guard who seemed to be in charge carried a still holstered Luger at his side.

We stopped at the doors and Einer moved his head a bit to activate the sensor in his collar. The doors opened as the guard in charge looked us over. "Einer, looks like you have a friend. How can we be sure your little buddy is authorized to go beyond this point?"

Einer looked at the guard and barked once and wagged his tail. The guard smiled. "Well, if you vouch for him I guess he must be ok. Parky and Asil are inside someplace. You two have a nice day."

I looked over at Einer with my tail wagging. "Well, that was easy enough."

Einer: "It gets tougher. Just wait and see. I hope you're not ticklish."

I rolled my eyes and down went my tail. The tunnel we were in was lined with white twelve-inch square tiles on its curved walls. The floor was done in large sections of white marble. The lights were recessed into the walls and covered what a thick looking glass, probably bullet proof. At the very far end of the tunnel I could see another guard station. As we approached one of the three guards stationed there stepped in front of us. He raised his hand in the air palm forward to emphasize the command. "Halt. Stop where you are." The other two guards stood with Steyr machine guns held across their chest ready to use them. The guard that stopped us started talking. "Einer. I see you have been out exploring again. You have a friend with you. You know the drill. I hope your companion is friendly. If not and he snaps or growls we may have to shoot him."

Einer looked over at me, "Sven, you heard him. Be extra friendly, wag your tail. Lick his hand if you think it will help."

The guard got down on one knee at my side. It was a bit of a shock to my system as he ran his hand up and down the length of my body, slipping his fingers through my fur like I was some kind of fuzzy kid's toy to be played with. I didn't manage to wag my tail but I did as Einer suggested and turned my head to give him a quick lick of friendliness.

Guard: "This one is ok, Einer you know the drill, your next."

I watched as they did a fur search on Einer and the guard ran his fingers under Einer's collar.

Guard: "Looking good boy. No contraband that I can find. You two are free to proceed. Say hi to Asil for me."

That got a chuckle from the other two guards that made me a bit uneasy. "Einer, what was with the snide comment about the guard made about Asil?"

Einer: "Just guy talk. Half the men around here have a crush on her. She seems even more alluring to them for she won't give any of them the time of day. She's the forbidden fruit they can't have. None of them would dare to say anything to her face. With Parky being promoted to Colonel and the impression that Asil and Parky have given to these grunts she belongs to Parky and no one would dare to cross a German Colonel. Even Kempler gives Parky a wide birth and those two hold the same rank."

We had left the last checkpoint and we now entered a section that made the last area we came from look tiny in comparison. The objects I now beheld varied in size from maybe five-feet in diameter to some as large as baseball field. I had a lump in my throat the size of a fur ball in a thirty-pound cat. This place took my breath away and my vocal cords refused to make a sound. I was awestruck and scared at the same time. Luckily, I was too ignorant to know what I was afraid of. Except, my mind told me whatever I was seeing could not be a good thing for the future of mankind.

CHAPTER 7

I was standing in awe at what my eyes beheld when Einer nudged me with his hip and cocked his head in the direction he wanted me to go. I followed him through a maze of machines that I had never before seen the likes of. We finally came to an office that was free standing in the midst of this madness. There was a swinging doggie door cut into the main door and Einer went through it with me close at his heels. There were filing cabinets along one wall, drawing tables scattered throughout and something that looked like the prototype television sets I had seen in Popular Science magazine. The screens were about twelve inches square and gave off an eerie green glow. Below each screen was a keyboard like one would find on a typewriter.

Asil was the first to see us and she rushed over to pick me up and give me a hug. Parky was busy looking over blueprints at one of the drafting tables. There was a General in his mid-forties standing by Parky and discussing whatever it was they were so engrossed in.

Asil walked over by Parky and said, "Parky, it's time for you to take a break. Look who has come to see us. Parky gave me a big smile and took me from Asil as he hugged me so hard my eyes almost popped out of my head.

Parky: "Hans, pardon us for the intrusion. This is Sven, he came in on the plane with us. He and I will both feel really bad if we didn't spend a little time together."

Hans: "I understand completely. I used to have a dog myself. However, it seems like so long ago. So many things I loved were lost when we went to war. You three go and relax for a while. I'll keep working on these equations."

Parky carried me as Asil and Einer led the way from the office to a break room that was down a small passage way. There were cooks behind the counter and tables just like any ordinary cafeteria. Parky ordered sauerkraut and dumplings for all four of us. He also added cold milk to the menu of course specifying that Einer's and mine be served in bowls. I forgot my manners and dug right into my food.

Asil: "Sven you act like your starving. Don't they feed you where you are bivouacked?"

I looked up as I chomped down a mouthful of sauerkraut. Asil and Parky both laughed at me and Einer did his big smiley tall wag thing.

"What's so funny?" I asked.

Asil reached over and dabbed around my mouth with a napkin. "You're so funny. You have sauerkraut hanging from your chin."

I licked my lips and tried to act nonchalant as I answered. "Well, I guess I can't help myself. Didn't mean to act like a pig. They don't feed us like this where we are. We have to get in line along the cafeteria style counter and we get whatever they happen to be serving. It's like being in the regular army. They really like to serve us beans and bread and some type of meat which we can't always identify. Only good thing is that the cooks must be Catholic because we always get fish of Fridays and it can be delicious at times. We've had whale, sailfish, cod, shark, dolphin and on occasion we get cold water lobster. It sort of makes up for the slop we get on the weekdays."

Parky: "How's Ole doing?"

He's doing all right. We've made sort of an uneasy truce with Kempler. Ole told him how he admired the SS units that we had seen in action and that stroked Kempler's ego. We sure do miss you guys though. How are things going?"

Parky: "Well, as you can see I got a promotion. I've got them convinced I know all about some of their top secret projects and what I don't know I make up along the way."

Asil: "He's every bit the con artist he always has been. He's got them thinking he is a rocket scientist that was under deep cover for Henrich Himmler. Anyone that knows Himmler was not surprised that he would be hiding someone like Parky away from the rest of the scientific community."

"I noticed that you don't seem too concerned about hidden microphones picking up our conversation. Are you sure this place is safe from listening ears."

Parky: "It's not. I doubt anyplace other than General Von Weber's office is safe. I developed a tiny transmitter that Asil and I have sewn into our collars as does Einer that jams anything we say from being picked up by outside sources. I found the design tucked away in some stolen British intelligence files that these guys have. Fact is they have files and information on every country in the world, all most all are marked top secret. Lucky for me they let me wander around and do research in everything they have. What they are doing is truly amazing."

Asil: "Now Parky don't get carried away with what they are doing. Some of it may sound good but I have a feeling that their ultimate goals are anything but helpful to mankind. You don't hide what you are doing under the North Pole for the well-being of civilization. Half the scientists here are former Nazi's and SS. Not the kind you want to put a lot of trust in"

Parky: "Don't get me wrong, I know they may not all be looking out for the good of mankind, however a few of them are sincere in their efforts that this may benefit the world of the future."

My head was swimming with an overload of information. Everything I had seen, the flight to outer space and the discussion that was taking place right in front of me.

Asil: "Parky, forgot all the talk about good and evil. Tell Sven the good news."

Parky: "You think I should? I was hoping it would be a surprise."

Asil: "You're right. It should be a surprise."

"Ah, come on now. You two can't toss a morsel in my lap like that and expect me not to beg for it."

Einer: "Let's not tell him. It will be like tempting a cat with a canary in a cage. He knows it's there, he can see it but he can't get it. Let's make Sven suffer for just a little while."

"That's not fair. I thought you three were my friends. At least give me a hint."

Asil: 'Ok, one hint and that's it. You have to promise if I give you one hint, you will not ask for anymore."

"Ok."

Asil: "Say I promise."

"All right all ready. I promise."

Einer: Say I hope to sniff a cat's butt if I break my promise."

Now this was going to be one serious promise, no dog in his right mind would sniff a cat's butt. So I made a solemn promise and I sure as heck wasn't going to break it.

Parky: "Are you ready for your one hint."

"Of course I'm ready. Let's have it."

Asil "It will happen tomorrow before noon."

"That's it that's the one hint."

Einer: "That's it. We best be getting you back to Ole and your section. Let's go."

CHAPTER 8

Of course it was much easier for us to return to my home base as the farther we got from Asil and Parky the less security we encountered. When we were at the entrance to Ole's and my barracks Einer and I said goodbye and I went in search of my partner. I had been gone for quite some time and I finally located Ole in the fabricating plant.

Ole: "Where have you been buddy? I was getting worried about you."

"I went with Einer and he showed me some absolutely amazing things. Aircraft that looked like flying wings and I went on a ride in a machine called a jetcopter."

Ole: "Hold on their buddy. You're telling me you actually went on a ride in one of those infernal machines. From the scuttlebutt I hear around here most of the machines that we are making parts for in my division are untested and experimental only. The few that get test flights often end in disaster for not only the machine but for the pilot and any passenger that may be with them. I can't believe you were dumb enough to go for a ride in one."

"I didn't really have a choice. Einer and I were standing there admiring this strange looking helicopter when a technician came along and started talking to us just like he would talk to a human. It was sort of weird him acting like he knew we understood what he was saying. Then again he was kind of a geek and probably didn't have any friends to converse with so this was akin to him talking over things with himself is what I figured. The next thing you know he scooped us up off the floor and tossed us into the jetcopter. He strapped us in and put helmets and oxygen masks on us. He said he had flown this before and it was due for another test flight.

You should have seen the place we were in. It was huge and filled with all types of experimental vehicles. The technician we called him TP used a radio system to contact the control room asking permission for takeoff. As soon as permission was granted the area was cleared of human personnel. There was a large frosted dome above that looked like ice and it opened to let us out.

We took off straight up into the air just like the Popular Mechanics magazine said a helicopter should. Except this jectcopter had a hidden feature that the author of the Popular Mechanics helicopter article probably never even dreamed of. The blades attached to the rotor above us moved straight back to produce just one single blade pointing behind us as TP hit a button to activate a pair of jet engines like the Germans were using on their jet airplanes and v-rockets. We were moving at hundreds of miles per hour. TP then used the controls to shoot us up at an angle and a sonic boom was heard behind us as we broke the speed of sound. Now we had entered what they call the Karman line. It's that area where you first encounter the fringes of outer space. Our bodies became lighter almost as if we were going to float away. We were only there for a few moments but it was amazing and really, really scary. If I was ever going to admit feeling like a scaredy cat, and you know I don't take cat references lightly, this was the time I was definitely a scaredy cat.

Once we reentered the earth's atmosphere TP shut down the jet engines as we were running out of jet fuel and he reverted the craft back to propeller drive and regular aviation fuel. He radioed the control room and they opened the ice colored dome to let us back in. I can tell you I was never so happy in my whole life to be back on the ground safe and sound."

Ole: "Sven, are you telling the truth? This whole thing sounds pretty far-fetched to me. A Jetcopter? Really? Traveling above the speed of sound and a journey into space. Talk about cat references sounds to me like you were drinking cat-nip."

"Cat-nip? Now that was just cruel. Have I ever lied to you? It's the honest truth. You can ask Einer when we see him."

Ole: "By the way how is Einer?"

"He's just fine. So are Asil and Parky. If you think my last story was something out of some science fiction story you should see the place where Parky and Asil are working. If I told you about it you would probably accuse me of mixing catnip with schnapps and guzzling it down like there was no tomorrow."

Ole: "Now I suppose you are going to be stubborn as a mule and not tell me anymore?"

"You bet I am. First you accuse me of being a scaredy cat and now you accuse me of being a stubborn mule. I can hardly wait to see what other animal you want to compare me with. I was going to tell you something else but I don't think I will."

Ole: "Tell me anyway."

"No."

Ole: "What do you mean no? I was only teasing you for telling tall tales. Or in your case would that be tall tails?"

"Ha-ha. Very funny. You know you're not making any brownie points."

Ole: "Come on tell me. After all we are partners and partners don't keep secrets from each other. Anyways, look where we are in the middle of a secret German base putting our lives on the line for all of mankind, oh and yes for all of canine kind and the rest of the world's animals, plant life and every other thing. We could be dead tomorrow. The least you can do is tell me the rest of your story."

"Seeing you put it that way I'll tell you what I know. However, it's pretty vague and you have to promise me you won't bug me for more information because I don't know anything else."

Ole: "All right tell me."

"Not until you promise, no more questions. You take my answer for what it's worth and that's the end of the discussion. Promise?"

Ole: "I promise."

"Ok. Are you ready?"

Ole: "Yeah, yeah, I'm ready. You're just like a little puppy teasing me all the time."

I did a fast smiling tail wag. "Ok, here it comes. Are you sure you're ready?"

Ole: "If you don't tell me now I'm going to take that tail of yours and stick it up your bung-hole and pull it out your throat!"

Oh boy, I've got him worked up now. I'm afraid I built this up a little too much. He's going to be really disappointed but here goes. "Parky, Asil and Einer have a big surprise for us tomorrow, but they wouldn't tell me what it was."

I sort of curled my lip up on my teeth and cringed my eyes waiting for the blow-back I was sure to come.

Ole: "That's it? You got me all excited for there's going to be a big surprise and you don't know what it is?

Then he laughed and so did I. I sure hope tomorrow's surprise wouldn't be a letdown after all the fun I had building up to the crescendo.

CHAPTER 9

We got up in the morning and Ole took his time getting groomed and dressed. Guess he figured and so did I that maybe our surprise would be waiting for us. Of course neither one of us could imagine what it might be.

As slowly as Ole hadn't gotten ready for the day we made our way to the commissary for breakfast. Mushy powdered eggs, over-cooked bacon and something resembling mush was slopped onto our trays.

I sat next to Ole at one of the tables like I usually did and of course by this time everyone was used to me so no one ever said anything. It wasn't like that in the beginning but once we had sort of befriended Kempler things had gone from bad to all right.

"Might have been nice if our surprise had been better food." Was the only thing I could think of saying.

Ole: "Friday's food is always good. I've never had such a variety of fish in my life. I suppose that somewhere they have a submarine base around here and most likely trawlers are out in the surrounding open water that they use for everything from catching food to suppling the base to keeping a lookout for any suspicious ships or air traffic that might be looking for this place."

Kempler came to our table and sat down with his tray of food. At first he ignored us as if we weren't even there. Finally he spoke to us.

Kempler: "You two seem to be fitting in all right. You have any complaints or problems? If so you just let me know. There's nothing the SS can't take care of."

Ole: "Nothing I can think of. Thanks for the offer though."

Kempler: "I heard that dog of yours was doing some unauthorized exploring yesterday. Seems he took a ride on one of the experimental aircraft. In case you are not aware of it there are Gestapo agents stationed everywhere to watch for activity like that. I'm the one they come to for enforcing any breaches of conduct. So far your dog is in the clear as it seems the technician was an authorized pilot and he wanted to see what the effects of flight would have on canines. He also took Parkurkakus' dog up with him. Just so you know that could have had serious consequences for your dog Sven if that technician hadn't had clearance to do what he did.

One more thing. Sven also managed to breach security and enter a top secret installation. Colonel Parkurkarkus said he gave permission for Sven to enter the complex. It's a good thing for you two that he did. I'll tell you right now if that dog could talk or communicate anything that he saw or did I'd have to shoot him right here on the spot. I suggest you keep him on a short leash from now on. Understood?"

Ole had turned white in the face and if I could have so would I. Gestapo agents, hidden microphones. This place was going to be harder than we thought when it came to taking it down.

Ole: "Understood. I'll do as you suggest and keep Sven in my sight at all times. Thanks for the warning, I had no idea he could get himself into so much trouble."

Kempler started back on his food wolfing it down as if he were starving. My only thought was that being a combat SS officer he had learned to eat fast before a bullet could find him. For him food was not to be enjoyed it was just sustain life.

 We were just finishing our meal when music came wafting over the loud speakers. It was not very loud but at a volume so the workers could hear it and continue with their duties. However, this was not your normal German music of Bach or Mozart it was modern jazz and it was the Glen Miller band playing it. Ole and I looked at each other and smiled. We figured this had to be Parky's surprise. Music to work by.

Kempler's ears picked up the sound of the music and it took a second for it to register. He spit out a mouthful of food and a string of German cuss words came flying out of his mouth with bits of leftover food. He stood up knocking his tray of food to the floor.

Kempler: "What kind of music is this playing here! American jazz. Satan's music! Who authorized this! Where's General Von Weber!"

He stormed off in the direction of the General's office still ranting and raving. "I'll put a stop to this! Whoever put that record on over the broadcast system will be publically executed by firing squad or my name is not Colonel Kempler!"

I looked over at Ole with worry crossing my brow. "If it is who we think it is he might be in big trouble."

Ole: "You might be right. Except, remember that Parky was promoted to Colonel. Those two are the same rank so it might be a stalemate."

"But, do you think Parky got permission from General Von Weber to do it?"

Ole: "Knowing Parky that's a good question. Maybe we best get back to work and enjoy the music while we can."

The morning in the assembly shop went along just great. Music went from Glen Miller to Tommy Dorsey, the Andrew Sisters, Bing Crosby, Frank Sinatra and many others including some popular German tunes such as Lili Marlene. The workers seemed to enjoy it and productivity was at an all-time high.

We broke for lunch and Kempler was nowhere to be seen. Then we heard a dreaded announcement over the loud speakers. "Ole and Sven please report to General Von Weber's office at once."

We didn't have anything to do with the music so we were not sure what this was all about. Although, Ole had smiled and I gave a tail wag when the music started playing and Colonel Kempler was sitting right across from us. Knowing Kempler and the fact that there were Gestapo agents lurking about that might just be enough to get us in trouble. It might even get Ole demoted.

We got up from our table, our tray half full and slowly walked over to the garbage to dump the remaining contents out and place our tray in the stack of empties. We were in no hurry to get to the General's office but lingering to long would probably get us into even more hot water then we already figured we were in.

The two guards outside the Generals door saw us approaching and one of them knocked on the door and waited for the General to acknowledge.

General: "Yes, what is it?"

Guard: "Ole and Sven are here General."

General: "Well, what are you waiting for? Show them in."

The guard opened the door as he said. "The General is expecting you. Please enter." As soon as we were inside the door closed behind us and we stood there waiting for the worse to happen.

General: "Ole, Sven. Please have a seat. Can I offer you some wine. It's the best there is. It came from France when the German Army was still formidable and a force to be reckoned with,"

Ole glanced at me not sure just what to do. My advice. "Take the wine. Act cordial just like this is an everyday occurrence. The General seems mighty friendly maybe something good instead of bad is going to happen. Let's play along and see where this leads. By the way, don't forget me, I'd like a bowl of wine myself."

Ole: "I'd love some wine. If it would not be too much trouble would it be possible for Sven to have a bowl of wine. Of course if it is too expensive for a dog I would completely understand."

Too expensive for a dog. What kind of crack is that? Human's always acting like their better than us canines. When they want somebody to sniff out bombs or find people lost in the rubble of bombed out buildings or mine cave-ins or avalanches who do they call to do their dirty work. Dogs. That's who they call.

General: "No trouble at all. After all I have heard that you and Colonel Parkurkakus treat your canine companions as equals. I find it a bit strange myself. However Parkurkarkus is a genius even if he is a bit of an eccentric. It is a good thing he has Asil as his assistant, she brings a bit of sanity to his madness."

As the General poured our wine Ole commented. "Yes, Asil is a blessing for Colonel Parkurkarkus. She tends to keep him focused on the things that are really important. I have known both of them since the beginning of the war and if you leave Parkurkakus run loose there is no telling what direction he may take."

I lapped up my wine and the General was right, it was top quality. I really wanted to ask for a second bowl but figured it would be impolite.

General: "I know what you mean. He came to me with two wild ideas this morning. I'm not so sure that the first one is such a great idea but I agreed to give it a try. In fact you have maybe noticed what it was. Would you care to venture a guess?"

Ole: "I did notice something very unusual during breakfast. The loud speakers started playing music and not just German music but Glen Miller and his orchestra. I remember hearing him play while I was still in Norway before the occupation and before I joined the German army to fight the soviets."

General: "What did you think of the music? Now don't hold back, be truthful with me. It's between us and I won't hold whatever you say against you."

Ole: "Herr General, I must admit I rather enjoyed it and the other music that was playing while I was in the fabricating room."

General: "I also enjoyed it. Of course I would never have admitted to such a thing if Der Further was still alive. Tell me, what do you think the workers reactions were."

Ole: "I would say the majority of those I saw were favorable to it. In fact it seemed to increase productivity. Some of the overseer's seemed a bit upset by it. Colonel Kemper was furious. He was bound and determined to find the source and have them shot."

The General laughed. "Ah yes. Colonel Kempler. He was in here ranting and raving as only an SS officer could do. Stomping around, cussing a blue streak of profanities, his face red as a ripe tomato. I thought the man was going to explode right in front of me. It took a good 10 minutes before he finally settled down and sat down in front of me demanding to know what I was going to do about it and that I was to find the perpetrator and turn him over to the SS. It was really hard for me to keep a straight face as I explained the situation to him. Of course you may not be aware of it but most the men you know as overseers are ex-Gestapo who think they are still Gestapo and they report to Colonel Kempler who of course comes running to me with every little infraction expecting severe punishments to be doled out. Being SS, he still think we are a new Nazi Germany. I like to think of ourselves as more progressive than that. Possibly a new hope for Germany with less rules and restrictions and no death camps."

Ole: "Not to be rude Herr General, but just how did the music come about?"

General: "Oh yes. Well, it seem our illustrious somewhat eccentric Colonel Parkurkakus had been rummaging around some of the items that had been captured from the allies over the years. He stumbled upon a box of American and some British musical records. He said he had a theory that playing upbeat music over the loudspeakers would increase the workers productivity and make for a happier work force. I figured it was worth a try. However, I insisted that I be able to preview the records before they were played. One particular record I felt was totally inappropriate, although just between you and I it was a rather catchy tune, but in Hitler's Germany it would have been an immediate death sentence if you were heard listening to it."

Ole: "Would it be to bold of me to ask what the song was?"

The General gave a small smirk and took another sip of wine before he answered. "It was a British tune called 'In der Furhrer's Face.' Even now if it was played here I bet Adolph would be rolling over in his grave."

Ole: "What about Colonel Kempler and his minions? Is he going to cause you trouble?"

General "I'm still in command here. Of course if Kempler had his way he would be in command and the SS would rule this camp with an iron fist. All the good we are trying to accomplish here they would turn into evil to bring the world to its knees. But, that's not for discussion at this time. You will learn a lot more in the very near future. Just remember, what you learn is to be used for the good of Germany. Now, I suppose you are wondering just why I called you here?"

Ole: "The thought had crossed our minds."

The General laughed again. "Ole. Sometimes times I think you are as eccentric as your friend Colonel Parkurkakus. I have to laugh at how you just answered me. It was not an answer most people would expect. Most people would have answered that they were wondering. But not you. You answered for you and Sven with the thought had crossed our minds, not your mind but our minds as if Sven knew what we were talking about. It's rather strange you must admit."

Ole: "I guess it is rather strange to you. However, Sven and I have been together for so long that I consider him my partner. I guess dog people are just a special breed."

The General laughed again. "Special breed. I get it, as in dog breed. Ole you are defiantly a special breed. Now to get down to why I called you here. You are going to be transferred to a different unit effective immediately. In fact your belongings are being move to the unit as we speak. Now there is a special condition that you must swear to before I bestow this privilege on you. You must swear allegiance that nothing, and I mean absolutely nothing about your new position is to be mentioned or discussed with anyone outside of those that are assigned to the same unit as you. In fact with your new position there may be things that will have to be kept between you and your immediate superiors. Are you will to take an oath to me that you will obey my orders?"

Ole: "I am flattered that you would put such trust in me Herr General. You have my oath."

The General smiled as he asked the next question. "Fine. Knowing that you speak for Sven do I have his Oath also?"

The General and Ole looked at me. I wagged my tail and gave out one single solitary bark.

Once again the General laughed. "I took it that was an affirmative from Sven?"

Ole: "It was Herr General."

General: "Now to the second reason you have been called here. Colonel Kempler and his SS men and the mini-Gestapo he controls will not be too pleased with either of the things I am doing but let them be damned. However, to ease the transition I have decided to promote you to Lieutenant and while I'm at it I figure I might as well do a bit more to upset our dear Colonel Kempler so I have had a special collar made for Sven with the rank of Sargent attached to it. Do either of you have any questions?"

Ole: "I have two questions sir? Can I ask what unit we are being assigned to and what did we do to earn your trust in giving us this new assignment and the promotions?"

General: "I cannot answer the first question. You will find that out soon enough. As for the promotions you need to be at least the rank of lieutenant to be assigned to the area you will be working in. In Sven's case, I think an exception might be made seeing he is not human even though the two of you may think otherwise. Being a canine I think the rank of sergeant will do for the time being. If that is all, you are dismissed."

Ole: "Thank you Herr General."

General: "Don't thank me. This might be more than you bargained for. Anyways I was cajoled into doing this. By the way enjoy the music on the way to your new assignment."

We left the office and an armed escort was waiting outside the door for us.

Escort: "If you two will please follow me I will take you to your new assignment. Don't bother to ask me any questions as I am under strict orders not to answer them."

We walked along with Ole in silence but not me as the guard wouldn't know I was talking and I had lots of questions. "Ole, what do you suppose this is all about? You don't suppose it's a trick and Kempler might be in on it. If he is we might be heading off to a firing squad. Boy, I hope they aren't planning on executing us. We don't have a weapon between us. I have a bad feeling about this. What do you think?'

Ole: "Shh. Be quiet."

Guard: "I didn't say anything."

Ole: "Sorry, I was just mumbling to myself."

Guard: "I heard you were a bit of a strange one Sergeant."

I guess word wasn't out about our promotions yet. Unless the guard was talking to me. Wait, he wouldn't know about my promotion either.

We were led through the same corridors that Einer and I had been through the day before. The guards remembered me so they were pretty friendly when looking me over.   In Ole's case it took a bit longer even though our guard produced papers from General Von Weber to give us clearance. Ole was still searched before we were allowed to proceed into each section.

Once we had cleared all the checkpoints we were led down a brightly lit corridor with doors off to each side. Sort of like you might see in the hallway of a fancy hotel. We came to a door made of thick grey wood that I did not recognize. It had a brass plaque attached to it that read Ole & Sven.

Guard: Looks like this is your room Sergeant." He turned the door knob and opened the door for us. "Make yourselves comfortable. I believe there should be food stocked on the shelves and in the refrigerator for you.   I've been told your services will not be required until morning. At that time someone will be here to escort you to your new work station. Have a nice rest of your day and evening."

The guard stepped out of our room and closed the door behind him.

Ole and I looked around the room and both of us were too shocked to say anything. It was at least as big as any luxurious suite in the finest of hotels. A huge bed fit for a king with silk sheets and a fur covered blanket was ready for us to curl into. Of course I find fur covered blankets a bit disconcerting as being a mammal myself it doesn't seem quite right to enjoy the comforts of fur when you know a living creature had given its life to supply it.

Ole opened the refrigerator and it was stocked with wine, beer, soda, milk and assorted snacks including things that looked like vegetables but were different than any vegetable we had ever seem. I believe these were actually vegetables of the sea, some might actually be sea cucumbers.

The cupboards in the kitchenette were filled with canned goods and boxes of assorted staples. There was even sugar and flour in case we decided to do some baking.

The sitting room had a radio and phonograph with assorted records from America, Britain, France and of course Germany. Ole looked at one of the records and asked if I was ready to listen to Speeches by Der Fuhrer. I declined.

"I wonder what the bathroom looks like" said Ole as he made his way there. "Whoa! "Sven you have to come see this."

I trotted over and let out a yelp of surprise. I was almost tongue tied. There on the floor was a two inch high wall of ivory with a drain in the center and a small sign mounted on the wall behind it that said Canine Latrine. I could hardly believe it, my very own potty. This was like doggie heaven. It even had a four rows of metal jets along the edges that when one would exit you would step on a pressurized pad that activates streams of water from the jets to wash the area clean. I stood staring at my potty as I wagged my tail. "Ole, this is amazing. I could get used to this real quick."

Ole: "Sven look around this place. It's all amazing the sink is made from a huge mollusk shell and the bathtub is made from the largest clam shell that anyone has ever seen. The faucets are made of coral and the side lights are made from conch shells. Look at the floor, its mother of pearl. If this is what being a Lieutenant gets you I wonder what a Colonel's room looks like."

"Colonel's room, who cares. I wonder what the General's room looks like." Of course we both laughed at that one.

Ole and I did a thorough search of the room for hidden microphones but didn't turn any up. It didn't meant there weren't any, if there was we didn't find them. Maybe if they figured it was just Ole and I that the room wasn't worth bugging. Then again if we ever had visitors there would certainly be a reason for Kempler and his Gestapo to keep tabs on us.

I asked Ole about that. "You think Kempler and his minions have any authority in this section?"

Ole sat down in a big overstuffed chair that I believe was made from sealskin, and that made me sad. He motioned for me to jump up on his lap and lay my head on his shoulder. This way he could softly whisper in my ear without anyone hearing him.

Ole: "The General acts as if he is not a fan of Kempler's, but that might be all it is. An act. Even though it might be that Kempler is not welcome in this section. But who know who might be working with Kempler. If it's like it was in Nazi Germany there could be spies or Gestapo agents lurking all about. We best keep to ourselves and trust no one until we get the lay of the land. It should be interesting to see what tomorrow brings."

"Do you suppose the music wasn't actually the surprise we thought it was that Parky was giving us? Because that was a gift for everyone here. Maybe he had something to do with our promotions and transfer to this section. If this private room is part of the surprise I'm going to give Parky enough doggie kisses to drown him. If the room was bugged they would certainly wonder why anyone would be sitting in a chair laughing out loud to themselves. As for me I just gave a hardy tail wagging laugh that was quiet as the little noise my swishing tail made in the air.

CHAPTER 10

We shared the bed and because of its size neither one of us knew the other was there except when Ole rolled over. It seems that whatever kind of mattress they were using it was unusual as it was filled with water. So when Ole rolled over it made a small wave that would toss me into the air. Luckily for me Ole didn't roll over very often. We christened our new bed the water bed. Sort of like have our own little ocean to sleep on top of. If one of us had been a female we could pretended we were the good ship Carolsea.

It was a restless night for both of us not knowing what the morning would bring. We got up early and did our morning chores as we were not sure when our day was planned to start in our new section.   Ole paced the room while stopping occasionally at the small table in the kitchenette to take a bite of a cookie and a sip of milk.

I had finished with my cookie and bowl of milk so I jumped back up on the bed and took a quick cat---oops, make that a dog nap. I was awakened from my slumber by a knock on the door. I jumped off the bed and hurried to Ole's side as he answered the door.

The same guard from the day before was there to greet us.

Guard: "Good morning you two. I hope you had a restful evening. I know it can be hard to sleep when you have no idea what is going to take place in the morning."

Ole: "You're right about that. I'm always a bit nervous when I'm to start a new job or project. It's as if sleep doesn't really come. Your mind just flirts with all kinds of scenarios and never seems to stop until you actually wake up."

Guard: "I can assure you that you will be very pleased with your new assignment and your boss isn't such a bad person. The guard looked down at me as I trotted along beside Ole. "His name is Sven isn't it?"

I barked once to acknowledge my name and the guard looked at me and laughed.

Guard: "I'll take that as an affirmative. As I was saying I think you and your dog will be very happy with the new assignment."

Ole: "He couldn't possibly be any happier with the new assignment as he was with his own doggie potty in our room."

The guard laughed again. "Yes, I oversaw the workers when they installed it. I've only seen one other like it. I used to have a dog before coming here so I can understand a man spoiling his dog. But, to be honest I think that might be carrying it a bit too far. I do miss my dog though. They sort of frown on pet's around here. They seem to feel it might be too much of a distraction from our work. Then again this place is not exactly what you call pet friendly. It would pretty hard to take your dog out for a stroll when everything around us is ice, snow and cold."

Ole: "Really, you've seen another one like that. Where was that?"

Guard: "I probably shouldn't tell you. But, with where you're going and who you know I have a feeling I can trust you. The other one was also installed here in this facility."

Ole: "If we're going to be friends can I ask your name. You already seem to know quite a bit about Sven and me."

Guard: "My names Anthony. Everyone calls me Tony."

Ole shook Tony's hand as he said. "Nice to meet you Tony."

It seems our room was already in a secure area as we passed no check points as we entered one of the rooms I had vaguely mentioned to Ole. This was the place I didn't elaborate on as I figured if Ole doubted my story about the jetcopter and the ride into space he would have never believed what was in this room.

The varying size of discs with clear domes on the top of some and some with no domes which had a series of windows around the circumference. Men in white coats were scrambling about like ants swarming around a pile of sugar.

Ole suddenly stopped and stared at the sight before him. "Wee doggies, what in the world is this place and what the heck are those things?"

Tony: "This place is just an extension of the work you were doing at your old job. As to what these things are I'll let your new boss tell you that. Come along now, we're almost there."

We headed towards some doors along the outer edges of the room. As we walked along it became apparent that the room was not square or rectangular but circular in shape. Looking straight up it was like so many other rooms in the complex. A large dome looking like ice was above us. There was no doubt it would open like the one where I rode the jetcopter. Of course if it opened as I thought, then that begged for an answer as to whether these disc shaped things we were seeing could fly.

We finally got to a door with no markings. Tony lifted his hand to knock but Ole gripped his wrist before he could complete the movement.

Ole: "Tony, just a quick question before you knock. How come none of the doors have names or descriptions of what might be there uses on them?"

Tony: "That's a good question. I asked it myself when I was first assigned here. Being a top secret area it was felt best that nothing be marked in case of a breach. If that happened it would be very hard for the enemy to locate any particular area or item they may be looking for. Of course the fun part is to remember who or what is behind each door. I'll tell you it took me some time as we are not allowed to make notes for security reasons.

Ole: "Got it, Ok, go ahead and knock."

Tony rapped lightly on the door, then he tried again harder. He looked at Ole. Some of these rooms are sound proofed, this is one of them. I know who is in there and most likely he has music playing and he can get so engrossed in his work he tends to space out all other sounds. However, if his assistant is in there they'll hear this. Then with the toe of his boot he kicked the door twice, loud enough to get the attention of those workers that were scuttling about. They looked at us and most just smiled or shook their head. It seemed to be not such an unusual course of events.

I heard the faint sound of a dog barking as it was muffled by the sound proofing. Tony and Ole didn't hear it, humans just don't have the ears we dogs do.

The door opened and Einer came flying out to greet me. Asil was standing at the door and held it open for us.

Asil: "Ole, come on in. Tony, thanks for bringing them here. Einer, let Sven catch his breath and then you two get your butts in here and quite making a scene."

Tony: "My pleasure Asil. Take good care of them, they seem like nice fellows."

We entered the room as Asil shut the door behind us. Einer and I went back to greeting each other with a playful wrestling match. Ole made a motion to give Asil a hug but she backed away and offered her hand instead. Ole clumsily shook hands with her.

Ole: "It's really nice to see you and Einer. We missed you."

Asil smiled. "It is nice. We missed the both of you too."

There was a big heavy set man in a white lab coat standing in front of some type of beeping monitor with his back towards us. There was little doubt in my mind who it was. He turned and his eyes lit up and he smiled.

Parky: "Asil, why didn't you let me know they were here?"

Asil: "If you weren't so engrossed in your work you would have heard Einer barking."

Parky: "Einer was barking. I didn't hear him. No matter." He stepped forward and grabbed Ole in his to be expected bear hug of a greeting, lifting my partner right off the floor and squeezing the breath out of him. Ole put his arms around Parky's bulk more out of self-defense to keep himself from being dropped then out of brotherly love, although there was a bit of that too.

"Ole, it's great to see you. Just a minute and I'll turn down the music. I just love the Andrew Sisters, especially this song, Boogie, woogie, bugle boy. Just makes you want to dance doesn't it." Parky grabbed Asil and lifting her off her feet he swung her around in a circle while Einer and I pranced around with them barking along with the music.

Asil pounded on his chest with her fists until he set her down. As she straightened her lab coat and white knee length white skirt she said. "Parky you big lug. How many times have I told you not to do that?"

Parky laughed. "Not enough times or I still wouldn't being doing it would I?"

Parky then grabbed me off the floor and gave me a gentler hug and a really soothing ear scratching. "Sven you little mongrel I sure missed you. Even though I just saw you the other day. Did you two like my little surprise?"

Ole: "Which one? The music over the loud speakers, or this one?"

Parky: "Wait, you thought the music was the surprise. No, that wasn't for you two, although I'm glad to hear you noticed it. Of course having you here is part of the surprise. How about the promotions. Did you like them?"

Ole: "Of course I did."

I chimed in. "Me too, I love being a sergeant in the German Army, or any army for that matter. Thanks Parky."

Einer: "Parky, don't you be taking credit for Sven's promotion that was my idea."

Parky: "Yeah, well, it was Einer's idea. But it was me that got you promoted Lieutenant Ole. What about your room? Did you like it?"

"I love it, especially my doggie potty."

Einer: "Before Parky tries to take credit for that, it was also my idea."

Parky: "Your idea, but my genius made it work. So there!"

Asil: "That's enough you two. This isn't a bragging contest. Parky tell Ole the rest."

Parky: "You my friend, my buddy, my pal are now part of my staff. Top secret clearance throughout the complete facility. You can go wherever, whenever you want at any time. However you need to be a bit carful where you go and what you look at. Midnight sojourns while looking over top secrets files might get noticed, especially by Colonel Kempler's minions. You do remember the Colonel don't you?"

Ole: "Only too well. We've had sort of an uneasy alliance since you left. We were assigned to the same barracks. I'm not sure why he didn't have his own quarters being Colonel and all."

Parky: "Oh, he does. He just prefers not to use them. He like to lurk around the other officers and men looking for ways to make their lives miserable."

Ole: "I noticed that. He wanted to find the idiot as he put it who put American and British music over the loud speakers. If he had his way you would be up before a firing squad. However, General Von Weber seems to have calmed him down. Or so he said when he told me about my transfer and promotion. I was wondering what he meant when I pressed him for why I was getting these things. He said I'd find out soon enough. I guess I did. By the way, I also love our new quarters."

Parky: "It's identical to Asil's. But you haven't seen anything yet. You should see mine. Even the General is jealous but he doesn't dare say anything as he seems very concerned that I am kept happy. I've really got these Kruats wrapped around my little finger. It's not that I really know what I'm doing but I am really good at taking the ideas of those that do and making them think their my ideas. I love it. They are so easy to manipulate."

Ole got close to Parky and leaned his head close to Parky's ear as he whispered. "Is it safe to talk in here?"

Parky: "Perfectly safe my friend. In fact in just a minute I'll make it safe for you and Sven to talk anywhere you want without worrying about being overheard. Originally I had developed pins for us to wear that blocked out all signals from any hidden microphones. Einer has a device in his collar that does the same thing and I have a collar for Sven with Sergeants stripes that will protect him and the rest of us from any unwanted eavesdroppers. I have just perfected the use of my device into these wrist watches. It's a surprise for both you and Asil as she didn't know I was working on these. Here you are you two put them on. Remember do not take them off for any reason. One slip could mean the end of our operation here."

Ole: "What have you found out so far?"

Asil: "Be careful what you ask for Ole. Parky has me a bit worried. He sometimes gets so caught up in the inventions around him that I think he loses the real reason we are here."

Parky: "I'm afraid she's right. The people they have gathered here to work on their projects are absolutely amazing. To say many of them are geniuses would be an understatement. Seeing you are to be my assistant let me show you around."

Ole: "About that, as your assistant just what are my duties?"

Parky: "Well, I told General Von Weber that I would feel safer with a bodyguard and a gopher that I could trust. Seeing we had a history the General let me have you for that position."

Ole: "Gopher, as in go-for whatever you ask me to do or get for you."

Parky: "You hit the nail right on the head. However, more importantly you and Sven will add a much needed extra set of ears around here. I know most of what is going on but it never hurts to have someone as non-descript as you and Sven around."

Ole: "Gee, thanks, I think."

Parky: "No offense meant my friends. You know what I mean. We're a team, no rank can separate us."

CHAPTER 11

Parky: "Asil would you mind showing Ole and Sven around the complex. I have some more things I would like to work on."

Asil didn't seem real anxious to take us out on her own but she agreed. Einer on the other hand was very excited to show us around.

We left the office and worked our way around the outside circumference of the facility.

Asil: "We'll start our tour on the far end. That is where the older inventions and early prototypes are kept."

Einer seemed to sense the hesitation in Asil's voice and manner at being our tour guide. I didn't want to ask but I knew from my doggie instinct that she was cutting Ole loose and didn't want to lead him on. Most likely Odin had told her it was time. This being our last mission together meant it had to be done soon. I'd been warning Ole it was going to happen but I know that this was going to be a bitter pill for him to swallow. He had avoided opening his heart to anyone of the opposite sex since the last time he was burned. That was many years ago. I was afraid after this time it would be the last time he would ever love a human female again. Yet, he had me, sometimes best friends are the most loyal and loving ones that one can ever have in their lives. I certainly fit that bill and so did Ole. We'd get by.

Once we reached the far end of the complex Einer took over as our guide.

Einer: "These are the early stages of the developments in jet flight. V-rockets that terrorized England. Jet airplanes that became the terror of the skies over Germany towards the end of the war. Unfortunately for Hitler and his promises of secret weapons to rule the skies they came a little too late. Not enough material or manpower to build them, not enough fuel to power them and few pilots trained to fly them.

Now we move on to the flying discs. These have been designed and a few were even made with the ability to fly, albeit in a very limited capacity as the war was ending. This was a pet project of Himmler's and of course he saw these as the next great super weapon. Just how he envisioned it is hard to say. Bombers, gunships, long range aircraft that could enter outer space and attack from the unseen depths of outer space. Who knows, it's a secret he took to the grave with him."

I spoke up for Ole and I as it was best Ole didn't say anything in case he might be overheard asking the wrong questions with so many workers and scientist's about. The nice thing is that Asil and Ole would understand any conversation Einer and I were having and hopefully it would benefit us all.

"Einer, did Hitler know about these round things/"

Einer: "The flying discs. From what we have been able to learn he was kept in the dark about them. We think if Himmler had mentioned their development that Hitler would have pressured him to take shortcuts that would have harmed the project, or Hitler may have shut down the whole project as a waste of manpower, time and money. It's also very possible that Himmler seeing the end of the war was coming and the situation for Germany was lost that he might have hoped to become the new head of the German government and then he could continue the research and development for a new rise of power for Germany. Or, maybe he hoped to trade the technology for his life and concessions that would be more favorable to Germany after the war. He was a shrewd man, very manipulative. This knowledge might have been a valuable asset to the United States or England. Himmler probably figured those two countries would do almost anything to keep this technology from the Soviets. If he was right then Himmler might just have been holding the trump card."

"Are the ones in here armed with guns and bombs?"

Einer: "Not yet. Most of the scientists that are working on the project don't want it to be used as weapons, at least not at this time. They have other things in mind for them. It's complicated, best let Parky tell you about it."

As we made our way around the room I was amazed at the different sizes and subtle differences in the many flying discs. Most were painted black or grey and a few were done in white or military green-black-brown camouflage. One thing they all had in common was the German cross that was painted somewhere on them. Amazedly none of them had a swastika anywhere on them.

"Do these things actually fly?"

Einer: "Some of them have been on very short test flights, a few have been on longer flights, one or two of them have actually been on extended flights. We best get back to Parky's office. There will be plenty of time to discuss the machines later."

Ole's eyes were wide as the saucers we had been looking at. His mouth was slightly open as if he was having trouble breathing.

"You all right partner" I asked.

He looked down and mouthed the words to me. "I'm fine. Just amazed."

Once we were back in the office Asil took a seat at a table and started going through paper work. Parky told us to have a seat at another table and handed us a pile of files.

Parky: "You two can browse through these files. There is all kinds of information on the machines you just saw with specifications and their history. You will also find drawings of failed experiments, pictures of crashes and successful flights and even some prototypes that never made it past the drawing board. Do your best to familiarize yourselves with the working units. They are the ones that will most concern us. Take special note of the fuels that are being used or in development. This is well beyond anything I have ever seen of or heard of before. The United States had something called the Manhattan project that has been working on nuclear fusion by their military. It was that research that led to the two nuclear bombs that brought Japan to its knees. Something the Germans have also been toying with. Remember when the allies blew up the heavy water plant in Norway. That was one of Germany's projects although it had not reached near the seriousness that they have done here. All this nuclear fusion and exotic fuel development is going to change the world we live in. If it is used for evil it could destroy the world as we know it. Let's pray the Allies keep control over this doomsday weapon and that they never use it again. As for the people here, there are too many different mindsets. From peaceful to vengeful. I think we will have no choice but to stop them. But first I want to see just how far some of their developments have gone. Maybe we can take some of this knowledge back with us to share with the Allies and hopefully it will put a stop to the Soviet juggernaut that is swallowing up Europe."

Ole: "I'm not sure what to say Parky. You just rattled off enough information to scare the bejeebers out of me. Sven and I will look this stuff over and we can talk about it later. I don't suppose we can take some of it with us to our room and look it over there."

Asil: "No! None of it can leave this office. It would be a breach of military secrets and we don't need to draw any undue attention to ourselves. Be careful as to agreeing to anything Parky tells you. He's so caught up in this technology that he thinks it might be good to share with the world and he has lost sight to our purpose here. If the rest of world had access to what they are doing here it would destroy the planet. The one true God had Odin send us here for a reason. He seems to figure with the current balance of power the world will survive. Satan will still be amongst us but at least there will be enough believers in God and his son Christ Jesus that things should balance out until God decides to the rid the earth of evil and sin. As far as I can tell this technology should never go any farther then it is right now. You give these people free reign and it will only be a matter of time before Kempler and his minions take control and either take over the world for their own evil desires or destroy it trying."

Parky: "Asil. You are such a doomsayer. There is some good technology here, some of the people have good hearts and care about the welfare of the human race. What about them? Are we going to destroy them to?"

Asil: "If we have to. Kempler and his people will enslave them to do their will just like the Nazi's did to the people in the lands they conquered. If you don't do as they say they will not threaten them, they will threaten to harm their families, relatives and friends. A man may give up his life for what he believes in, but very few men will give up their loved ones. These Nazi's are a clever people, and they are ruthless."

Parky got rather quiet after Asil's little outburst. We had all seen what evil men were capable of, Asil, Parky, Einer, Ole and I first hand as we made our way through war torn Europe on our previous assignments and then again when we were sent to the future to save The United States from a corrupt and ruthless President who was bent on turning a 200 year old republic of free trade into a police controlled country run by one man and his followers.

Of the five of us Asil was by far the most passionate to stop evil-doers. She was alive when the Viking raiders pillaged, killed and raped their way across the British Isles and much of Europe. She had heard about the many wars that followed and she had no desire to see another one. This was to be her last quest at saving mankind from possible total destruction and she meant to do her job to the best of her abilities. She also was of a mind that the other four of us would do our duties that the one true God assigned us to do. Hopefully she remembered we were to do it with the least amount of bloodshed as possible. After all, Parky was probably right that many of the people here had good hearts and the best of intentions for their inventions. How or if we could separate them when the time came for a final showdown was yet to be seen.

Parky had the Victrola wound up and he was swaying to the music of Tommy Dorsey and his band. Asil had stuffed cotton in her ears and was working on her own projects. Ole and I both liked the music but we found it hard to concentrate on the journals in front of us. Sure it was easy to look at the pictures but it was hard to make sense of all the written technical information with the music breaking our thought patterns. I suggested turning the music off or at least turning the volume down but Ole said that it would just disrupt Parky's concentration on his project and that was surely more important then what we were doing.

Even with the music playing we managed to hear the door of the office open. We both turned to witness a man probably in his mid to late 40's walk in. He must be important to have a key and access to this office. He had on a German Generals uniform and his bearing told us he was not a man to be trifled with. Ole quickly stood at attention and saluted the General. The General looked at us and gave a Nazi Palm up salute with a quiet Heil Hitler.

General: "I'm not sure what army you are from Captain, but by the looks of your uniform you are from the German Army. It's proper when addressing a German officer of a higher rank to give the Nazi salute in respect for our late Fuhrer."

Ole: "Please accept my apology Herr General. I am new to this complex and have not been brought up to date on protocol. I meant no disrespect for the late Fuhrer or our Fatherland."

General: "I accept your apology Captain. I suggest you brush up on protocol. I see Colonel Parkurkakus is still playing that foul American music and he of course is too engrossed in his work to take notice when a General comes to see him."

The General took a few steps towards Asil and cocked his head so he could see her ears.

General: "Ah, yes. The beautiful Asil has cotton stuffed in her ears. She's is a good soldier to block out the American trash playing on the Victrola."

The General walked over to the Victrola and drug the needle across the record in a deliberate effort to scratch it as the music stopped.

Parky stopped what he was doing and angrily turned around to see who had caused such damage to one of his records.

Parky: "Who the hell…Oh it's you General. I must ask that you refrain from ruining my records when you come to see me."

General: "How else am I supposed to get your attention? You may be a brilliant engineer but you do try my patience. I'd order you to get rid of the music but I just came from General Von Weber's office and he says that since playing the music over the loudspeakers even for such a short time that the worker's seem to be happier and it looks as though it will show in an increase in productivity. If that proves to be the case I guess I will have to accept it. Your biggest problem and mine by the way, will be keeping Colonel Kempler from going on a rampage to stop it. That man is stubborn as that Winston Churchill fellow when he gets an idea in his head. He'll never give up come hell or high water. If that damn Churchill hadn't been that way we could have conquered that spit of an island empire and moved our forces back to one front against the Russians and we would have won the war. In a few years after winning the war we would have finished what we are working on here and then we would have been able to conquer the whole world."

Parky held his composure and decided to change the subject.

Parky: "General have you met my new aide. This is Captain Ole and his canine companion Sven.   Captain, this is General Hans Kammler he is the head of this whole project. The General oversees every engineer, scientist and theoretician in the complex."

Ole: "I had no idea that you were in charge here Herr General. You must be a brilliant man. From what I have seen of the equipment in the complex your accomplishments must be equal to or greater than the concepts that Albert Einstein put forth."

The glare Ole got from the General could have melted the wall of ice that encompassed the whole complex. I knew right away what Ole had said was going to get us in big trouble. Unfortunately my partner sometimes speaks before he thinks. This was one of those times. A worse choice of comparisons would be hard to imagine."

General: "Parky!   What kind of idiot did you pick for your assistant?   Einstein was a Jew, intellectually inferior to even a peasant German laborer. The man had no idea what he was talking about. He's an idiot. If you were not working for Parky I would have you taken out and shot. Take this as a one and last warning. If you ever dare to speak of a Jew as an intellect or a superior being to the master race it will be the last word you ever speak. Is that understood?"

Ole: "Understood Herr General. Pardon me, I was a fool. Of course you are right about the Jews. I just forgot that he was Jewish. It will never happen again."

General: "Colonel Parkurkakus. Your man has me so angry I forgot what I came here for. If you'll excuse me I'll take my leave now. You best get Captain Ole under control. Another meeting like this and it will be his last."

The General turned and stormed out the door. Parky raised an eyebrow as he looked at Ole.

Parky: "Well, that went better than could be expected."

Ole: "Better. How can you say that?

Parky: "You have to admit things could have been worse if he had ordered you shot. Trying to pull your ass from the fire this late in the game would certainly have put our schedule here at a disadvantage. Asil, don't you agree?"

We all looked at Asil whose back was still towards us. She was busy doing her work with no indication as to what had just transpired."

Parky: "Einer. Get her attention and tell her to take the cotton out of her ears and don't mention to her what just happened here. Ole, if she would have heard what just happened she would have made the General's anger look mild in comparison."

Einer pawed Asil's leg to get her attention. He communicated to her about the cotton and she removed it. She turned around and looked at us.

Asil: "You two look sheepish. What have you been up to? No good would be my guess."

Parky: "Nothing much. I was just thinking it might be a good time to call it a day. Why don't we all meet at my room and I'll make us a good home cooked meal."

Ole: "That sounds like a great idea to me. Only thing is I don't know where your room is?"

Parky: "No problem. You two go rested up for a bit. I'll send Tony to get you in about an hour."

Ole was a bit confused as we left Parky's office as to where our room was. Luckily for him he had me. I put my nose to the ground and followed our scent right back to our new cozy little home base. I jumped up on the bed for a quick nap. Ole grabbed a beer and sat in our little sitting room as he fretted over the mistakes he had made today. I knew it would do no good to tell him to forget about it. Humans, unlike dogs seem to worry much more about the little things. Dogs, we prefer to forgive and forget and start over. I'm really glad I'm a dog and not a human. All that worry has to be hard on a person.

I heard a knock on our door and before I could react Ole was on his way to open it. The word's hello Ton…and he stopped as the word was out of his mouth before he realized the person at the door was not who we had expected.

Ole stood back holding the door open as he spoke. "Captain Kempler. What a surprise. I didn't expect to see you here. Did you miss me?"

Kempler: "Miss you? Why would you think that? I don't miss anybody."

Kempler walked around our apartment like a drill sergeant inspecting a barracks.

Kempler: "Nice place you have here, I think it's even nicer than mine. You going to offer me a drink or not?"

Ole: "Of course. Pardon me. I just wasn't expecting company. Please have a seat. What would you like to drink?"

Kempler: "Bring me a beer. No glass I prefer it in the bottle. Make sure it's room temperature. None of that sissy cold beer like the Americans drink. By the way you don't chill your beer do you?"

Ole glanced at the refrigerator and prayed Kemper didn't get to nosey. There was a case of beer under the counter by the sink and Ole pulled out three warm ones. He handed one to Kempler, poured half a beer in a bowl for me and then he sat down across from Kempler with his own beer in his hand.

Ole: "What do I owe for the pleasure of your visit?"

Kempler: "I hear you have been a naughty boy my friend. Disrespecting a superior officer when he came into the room. Speaking kindly about the Jews. Not acceptable behavior. What have you got to say for yourself?"

Ole: "Grave mistakes on my part. I apologized to General Kammler. I give you my word it will never happen again."

Kempler: "Only thing that saved you for now is that Parkurkakus likes you and you are working for him. However, he won't always be there to pull your ass out of the fire. Just you know this. I'll be watching you. You'll never know when or where but I'll be there."

Kempler finished off his beer and set it down with a thud on the end table. He got up and walked to the door. Ole got up to see him out."

Kempler: "No need to see me out Ole. I'll let myself out. You have nice day." With that said Kempler shut the door behind him.

I looked at Ole who was still standing by the door looking rather worried. "Well, we have had nicer visitors over the years."

Ole: "You can say that again. It's probably a good thing we don't have any Nazi friends. Not the friendliest folks are they?"

"I should say not. I think I'd rather befriend a cat than a Nazi."

There was another knock on our door. Ole looked at me and I looked at him. "I'm sort of afraid to answer it this time. How about I open the door and you stand there and greet whoever comes in?" said Ole.

"Unless it's Einer I don't think that will work."

Ole opened the door with much less enthusiasm this time. Standing there looking at us was Tony.

Ole: "Boy are we glad to see you."

Tony: "I bet you are. I must apologize I'm a bit late. I arrived just in time to see Colonel Kempler knocking on your door. I do my best to avoid him. So I ducked down the corridor and around the bend to stay out of his sight. When I heard him leave I figured it was time to get you two. The last thing we need is for Kempler to know you are paying a social call on Parkurkakus. He and Parky are the same rank and Parky seems to hold a bit more sway around here being the rocket scientist that he is. Kempler on the other hand has seniority but it doesn't hold much sway with Parky. Parky loves to spar with Kempler and he usually wins. Kempler would like nothing more than to catch Parky with his pants down and get him demoted or shot before a firing squad. Enough small talk. If you two are ready we best be on our way."

Our trip to Parky's wasn't very far. The corridors looked about the same but the distance between the rooms was much greater.

Arriving at Parky's door Tony knocked and the three of us waited for an answer.

Asil answered the door and invited us in as she thanked Tony for escorting us.

Asil: "Have a seat you two. Parky's in the kitchen busy playing chef. I'll get you a drink. What would you like?"

I saw Einer sitting on the couch and jumped up next to him. He had a bowl on the arm of the chair. "What you drinking buddy?"

Einer: "They call it whale's milk. I sure would like to see how they milk a whale."

"I'll have the same. Ole, you want to try some?"

Ole: "Asil may I ask what you're drinking?"

Asil: "I'm afraid nothing quite as exotic as whale's milk. Parky has a still set up in one of the labs he uses. He's been fomenting seaweed with yeast and sugar to make some sort of grog. It's not bad if you can get by the green color."

Ole: "I can't say it sounds good but I'll try some."

Ole took a chair near Asil and the four of us sipped on our drinks as Asil passed a tray of appetizers around. They were round and crunchy, had sort of a nutty flavor.

Ole: "These are different. I don't believe I've ever tried them before. Do I dare ask?"

Asil popped a few in her mouth before she answered. "You dare. But first do you like them?"

Ole: "Actually I do. How about you Sven what do you think?"

"I do. I detect a bit of oil in them. Almost a bit on the fishy side. I believe they are some kind of nut, I just can't place them."

Einer: "Welcome to the world below the ice where not everything is as it seems. You boys have just had a delicacy known as smoked fish eyes."

Well, our eyes got a bit big and we had a slight gag reflex that we withheld. However, they were good and one just had to get by the prejudice that new things weren't necessarily bad things.

Parky came from the kitchen and sat down by us. A big tankard of his home brew in his hand ready to quench his thirst.

Parky: "It will be a few minutes before supper is ready. Have you two had a chance to explore my little domain? I designed most of it myself."

Ole: "Actually we just got here. Asil was kind enough to get us Hors d'oeuvres and drinks."

Parky: "Follow me." He led us across the room to what looked to be a blank wall. He pushed a button and the wall split in the middle as it retracted into the ceiling and the floor. What was once a wall was now a solid sheet of thick glass holding back the ocean. Stalactites of ice hung down and a few arctic species of fish swam about. A blueish hue of light came from the sun trying to penetrate this frigid world of water we now beheld. "One hell of an aquarium isn't it boys?"

Both Ole and I could only come up with one word between us. "Wow!"

The rest of Parky's place was no less impressive. His bathroom was twice the size of ours. He had a separate bedroom and kitchen all Parky sized. The Kitchen had a huge stove which Parky explained to us had come from the sunken ship Lusitania. With our food cooking I took in the aroma and couldn't wait to eat.

Parky ushered us out of the Kitchen and we all sat at a table in his dining room that just so happened to command a view of the glassed wall aquarium that was of course made up of the ocean that surrounded us.

Parky: "Please everyone be seated. Lunch is about to be served."

Asil: "Parky I have been here often enough that you need not consider me a guest. How about if I help you serve our meal?"

Parky: "Offer accepted. Come with me."

Einer, Ole and I sat in our chairs and watched the ocean view through the glass walls of the room. A giant squid scuttled by and by giant I man this thing could have been the squid that drug the Nautilus beneath the sea in Jules Verne's 20,000 Leagues Under the Sea novel.

Asil came in with salads for all of us and Parky followed with a wheeled butlers tray made from coral. A large silver cover engraved with the logo for the White Star Lines covered the main meal from our sight.

I looked at the salad and it was a mixture of greens, browns and a bit of red types of vegetables none of which looked familiar. Remembering our snack of fish eyes I figured if it tastes good it must be good for me so I tried it. Not bad at all.

Ole: "I probably shouldn't ask. But what is in the salad?"

Asil: "The people here have learned to improvise. Of course they could have developed greenhouses to grow the food we are used to but they decided that that would be a waste of their time and valuable space they needed for their other projects. So they cultivate most of their food from the ocean. The salads are made up of assorted types of seaweed and kelp. The dressing is made from mollusk oil and flavored with the juices from lobster meat. Do you two approve?"

"I do. Being a canine I'm not a big fan of salads but this is good."

Ole: "I have to agree with Sven. Very tasty indeed."

We finished our salad and Parky stood up next to the butler's tray. Ever the showman he removed the silver cover with a flourish of his hand. Sitting on a bed of seaweed and surrounded by huge shrimp that looked to be holding it up was the biggest lobster I had ever seen.

Parky: "I figured the best surprise I could make you two for our first meal together in the complex would be something you actually recognized. I know both of you love lobster so here it is. Of course the shrimp is just an added extra. As for the warm butter it was made from walrus milk. Quite tasty if I say so myself. You must remember that they call a female walrus a cow so how much different can it be from cows on dry land." With that Parky gave one of his trademark belly laughs.

Parky pulled an oven mitt from the butlers cart and then grabbed hold of the dinner plates that had been kept between hot towels. He set them down at each of our places and then proceeded to cut the lobster and dole it out to us.

Ole: "Parky, these plates look to have a German style eagle on them but not one that I readily recognize. Is there a history behind them or were they produced for use here at the complex?"

Parky: "Ah, yes the plates. The folks here have been scavenging things from ship wrecks all over the world to use here. It saves them from having to produce what they consider the more mundane items of daily use. These plates were in use from 1898-1918 by the German cruise lines and the military for higher ranking officers. I confiscated them from one of the storage units that is in the complex. Much of the items they are scavenging from the sunken vessels they use to raise cash for the things they cannot produce or acquire from their land contacts. They have developed a rather lucrative trade throughout the world for antiquities from the bottom of the sea. Pretty much every nation worth it sea-salt, get it not worth its salt but sea-salt."

Asil: "They get it Parky, It wasn't that funny."

We of course laughed anyway. It was the polite thing to do.

Parky: "Yes, getting back to what I was saying. Almost every nation has historical relics that were lost at sea and they are willing to pay good money for them or barter things of value. Rare metals, fuel, iron, ore, steal you name it. If this system had fell into Hitler's or even Himmler's hands Germany would have conquered Europe and eventually the world."

Ole: "About that conquering the world. Just what have you found out about what they are doing here?"

Parky: "Yes, that's an excellent question. Asil and I have figured out some of it but there are a few things that are still a mystery."

I quickly asked the question. "What do you mean a mystery?"

Asil: "What Parky means is if even with all his bullshit and clout he has not yet been given the keys to the kingdom. Have you my rotund friend?"

Parky: "Asil, that's what I like about you. No beating around the bush. Yes, she is correct. There is one section that is off limits even to me. However, I am close, very close to being allowed access. All I need to do is to get the project I am currently working on to work. If I can do that they will have no choice other than to let me help with whatever it is that they are so secretly guarding.'

Ole: "What makes you so sure they will let you see what's going on? If it's so top secret that you haven't seen it. They surely aren't going to just let you waltz in a take a look see."

Parky: "General Kammler told me that if I can bring my current project to fruitarian that I will have proven myself as a loyal follower of his and the German Homeland. Once that happens he said he would be putting me in charge of the most important project in the complex. One he claims will be the game changer in how the world perceives a new and greater Germany."

Ole: "Tell us just what you need to accomplish to see this great secret that General Kammler has promised to show you?"

Parky: "It's nothing really. I just have to figure out how to get the large flying disc outside my office to fly."

Asil: "Parky. There's a bit more to it than that, isn't there?"

Parky: "Maybe just a little bit."

Ole: "How little bit might that be?"

Parky: "It has to leave the earth's atmosphere and enter the first layer of space. "

Asil: "It has to enter the Karman line which is considered the area where outer space begins."

Ole: "Is that all. Sounds like a walk in the park to me."

Of course my partner was being sarcastic and sending a projectile like a rocket or even the jetcopter into outer space is one thing. Sending a huge round flying disc seemed a bit more difficult."

Asil: "Tell them the rest Parky."

I raised my ears a bit to show I was paying rapt attention. "Yeah, Parky, tell us the rest of the story about your flying saucer."

Parky: "Flying saucer. You know what Sven, I like that name a whole lot better than flying disc. I think that officially I will change the project name to flying saucers. Thanks for the suggestion."

Asil: "Parky! You're avoiding the subject. Now, tell them the rest."

Parky: "Well, you see it's like this. The flying disc, oops, I mean flying saucer we will use in the test can hold up to fifty people. There are a series of propeller like blades at the bottom of the saucer. These will spin at a high rate of speed to create lift. The glass dome at the top is the control area like the cockpit of an airplane. With the controls up there the blades can be tilted at different angles to control direction, lift or decent. Initial liftoff is created by jet thrusters powered by aviation fuel. As we near the sound barrier the aviation fuel will be switched off and a special mixture of rocket fuel will be turned on. This fuel mixture is highly unstable but creates an immense amount of power to slingshot a craft of this size past the sound barrier and into the Karman line of outer space. At that point the flying saucer will seem to almost float on its own as it leaves most of the earths gravitational pull below it. The next step will be to leave the Karman line and break into actual outer space. Once we are in outer space the flying saucer will be free floating. No gravitational effects from earth will be affecting it. The inside of the saucer is pressurized to equal the gravity and atmosphere we are used to on earth. If this was not the case we would be floating around like helium filled children's balloons. There you go, it's as simple as that."

Einer: "It's not as simple as that. Tell them the rest."

Ole: "There's more?"

Parky: "Just a tiny bit more." His face scrunched up as he looked at us. "I'm supposed to have a power source perfected to take over once we are in outer space that does not require the use of fuel as we know it."

Ole: "What other source would that be? Even electricity requires a fuel source. You can't be talking about batteries as a power source."

I chime in. "Ole, even batteries would be considered a known fuel source. So I guess I'm stumped. What else is there?"

Parky: "Perpetual motion."

Ole: "Wait just a minute. Perpetual motion? Isn't that where power is self-generating and requires nothing other than its own movement to power itself?"

Parky gave a wry smile. "Yup, that's it, easy peasy, huh?"

Asil: "Parky, you may be a con artist and even fairly smart but not even you can pull off a con like that. What were you thinking promising the General something you can't possibly deliver?"

"We're sunk." Was all I could say?

Parky: "Wait just a minute. This isn't as far-fetched as you may think. Asil, you are right about one thing, I'm not smart enough to invent something like perpetual motion and actually have it work. However, there are scientists and engineers in this complex that have proved it is possible on one of the four-foot diameter flying saucers. They actually had it self-power itself for almost twelve minutes."

Asil: "So you stole their ideas?"

Parky: "No I didn't steal them. Remember this is a team effort. This complex was set up to be a huge think tank and everyone here works together to accomplish the main goals that the whole group is hoping for. Preputial power benefits everyone. Some of them such as Kempler and his minions would use it to power military weapons of destruction. Others with families and morals to humanity look at it as a way to supply free power with no pollution or adverse effects on the earth's resources or atmosphere. Just imagine. A source of everlasting clean pollution free power that would not depend on coal or oil to be pulled from the belly of the earth."

Ole: "I have a question. You said this perpetual power lasted twelve minutes on a flying disc that is probably one-hundred times smaller than the one you plan to propel into outer space. If that's the case you might be lucky to power your craft for a minute at most.   Will that be enough to satisfy the requirements of General Kammler?"

Parky: "If it works at all that will be enough to prove that it is possible. For the time being that should be enough to convince even the harshest critics that we have proven that perpetual motion is possible. I believe General Kammler will be more than happy with the results."

Asil: "So, let's assume it does work. Just what do you think General Kammler is planning on using it for?"

Ole: "That's the million dollar question. With technology like that he could equip a fleet of bombers filled with atomic bombs and hold the whole world hostage."

Sven: "With enough inertia almost anything might self-power itself. One minute isn't going to satisfy the German high command. I have a feeling we're about to become dead ducks. I bet Kempler will volunteer to shoot us from the sky just for target practice."

CHAPTER 12

All of us jumped as we heard a loud knock on the door. We sat still as if we were mice hiding from a cat.

Asil whispered to Parky. "You expecting anyone?"

Parky shook his head no as the knock came again, this time much louder and more forceful.

I whispered for all to hear. "Do you suppose it's Kempler and his goon squad of SS men?"

Einer: "It could be, if they know all of us are together it would be just like Kempler to try and catch us doing something wrong."

Ole: "You don't suppose your jamming devices quit working and they know what we are talking about."

Parky: "Even if they quit working this room is built so that no signal could possibly be picked up from outside. There's no way they could have any valid reason for disturbing us."

I said what everyone else was probably thinking. "Kempler doesn't need a valid reason. He's just a Nazi fanatic trying to make everyone else's life as miserable as his own. He's only happy if he can make someone else suffer."

Einer: "Maybe if we sit here real quiet like he'll think no one is home and go away."

Asil: "Or, knowing Kempler he'll try to pick the lock and let himself in."

Parky: "That lock is un-pickable. I designed it myself. Kempler is not going to get in that way."

Ole: "If that fails he might just have his goon's bust the door down and you can bet he'll have some lame excuse for doing it that he'll justify to everyone later.

Asil: "Ole's right. Parky, I think you should answer the door."

The knock came again, louder and more forceful sounding then before.

Parky got up and moved as if in slow motion until he got to the door. He looked back at us with worry on his face as he turned and unlocked the door and slowly turned the handle. We all watched with baited breath as Parky opened the door.

Parky: "Tony. What in the world are you pounding on the door for? We thought you might be Colonel Kempler."

Tony: "No sir Colonel Parkurkarkus. Something happening down in the submarine pens. I'm not sure what it is but it must be important. Generals Kammler and Von Weber are on their way there now. Colonel Kempler and his SS men are also on the way there."

Parky: "What's going on?"

Tony: "I'm not sure but I thought you would like to know. Maybe you should go and see what's got everyone so riled up."

Parky took off his chef's apron and rushed off to his bedroom to get into his Colonel's outfit. He hollered back to us as he ducked out of sight. "Asil, Ole, you two rush back to your apartments and get into uniform. We're going to the submarine pens to see what all the excitement is about. We'll all meet back here in ten minutes so hurry."

Ole was still buttoning his shirt as we rushed back to Parky's place. Asil was tucking her blouse into her skirt and Parky was zipping up his pants as we all hurried of with Tony in the lead. Once we arrived at the submarine pens we were stopped by two of Kempler's SS stooges.

One of the stooges stepped in front of us as the other pointed his Steyr submachine gun at us. "Halt. You've gone far enough. There is no admittance to this area without written permission."

Parky: "Written permission from who?"

SS guard: "General Von Weber, General Kammler or Colonel Kempler."

Parky: "Colonel Kempler does not out rank me and from what I have been told both the Generals are here so it would be extremely hard for me to get written permission from any of them. So let us through."

SS guard: "I've been told by Colonel Kempler that you would say just what you said. He informed me he has seniority of rank over you so yes he does outrank you."

Einer cocked his head to the side to let me know I should follow him. The two guards were so busy watching our humans that they didn't notice as we slipped past them. A submarine was just easing its way alongside one of the docking stations. General Von Weber was dressed in a housecoat with his uniform pants sticking our below it. He must have been in a hurry to get here and hadn't time to get on his complete uniform. Einer pulled the General's pants leg with his teeth. The General looked down. "Einer, what you doing here without Asil?"

Einer ran towards the area where we were waiting. He had to do it three times before the General took the hint.

General Von Weber: "You want me to follow you boy?"

Einer barked twice and ran towards where our humans were waiting for us. The General quickly followed us.

General Von Weber: "This better be good because this submarine affair looks to be very important."

As soon as the General was within ear shot Parky hollered over to him.

Parky: "General, boy am I glad to see you. These two goons of Colonel Kempler's are refusing to let us pass. They say they need a written order from you."

General Von Weber: "I never gave such an order. You two, let these people pass immediately. Just who gave you orders to detain them? Never mind, SS guards, I smell Kempler's orders all over this. Come on you five let's go. Stay close to me and there won't be any other incidents. Something is going on down here and I am here to find out what it is."

I looked back at the two SS guards. They had an angry look of defiance after being chastised by the General. I am pretty sure this will come back to bite us in the butt as us dogs would say.

We followed the General to the submarine pens. This was an area Ole and I never even realized was here. Of course we should have known that the complex must have had some way of getting goods delivered without anyone being any the wiser. I sort of thought things might be coming in by air but that would be too obvious for the allies would be sure to spot that much airplane activity. It was doubtful the allies had set up radar this far north for they would doubt there was much to track, a good reason that the Germans were set up here, it made it easy to test their experimental aircraft away from prying eyes. However, if the Germans had been flying in supplies from other locations it would just be a matter of time before allied aircraft would have spotted them. I had to give these Germans credit, they were a crafty lot.

There were at least a half dozen submarines in this under the ice harbor. The walls and ceiling in this dome were carved from ice so that the lights inside the complex shone off the ice and made the room seem twice as bright as it would have been if it was sheeted in man-made materials. In some places where the ice was a bit jagged or depressed the lights caught it at an angle to cause small colored rainbows or the glitter of what looked like jewels and diamonds. It was a beautiful room filled with underwater crafts from an ugly war.

A crowd had gathered around a submarine that had just arrived. Being a dog and not very tall I could not see over all the humans that were blocking my way. Luckily we were with General Von Weber and he had the clout that when he said move, people moved. The last thing anyone wanted to do was to disobey a direct order from a General and especially a German General in a German run complex.

We finally made our way to a section that was being cordoned off by Kempler's SS men. They had locked arms and the only ones now in the open area near the submarine were General Kammler, Colonel Kempler and ourselves. Kempler of course gave us a dirty look but seeing we were accompanied by General Von Weber he didn't dare say anything.

The submarine that was at the dockside was huge. For a moment I thought it had to be the biggest submarine in the world. The conning towers number and the depiction of a Viking long ship painted below the number U630 brought instant recognition to my eyes. Was it possible that this was our old friend that was captaining this vessel? On its deck stood it's Captain. He had a full beard and his Captains outfit was a bit bedraggled and had seen better days. His first mate was busy giving orders to a motley looking bunch of deck hands of all shapes and sizes. All of them seemed to be bundled up in clothes that hid all their features except for their eyes. As soon as the ship was tied to the dock stanchions the crew quickly disappeared below deck. Only the Captain and the first mate remained on deck. The first mate was a huge man, close to seven feet tall with a long beard and muscular build, almost like a demi-god.

Some of the bases workers slid a gangplank out to the submarines deck. General Von Weber being the senior officer in the complex stepped forward. He stood by the deck as the Caption of the ship gave a traditional navy salute to the brim of his cap and not the Nazi raised hand. There was also no Heil Hitler verbiage to accompany the salute. General Von Weber returned the salute but he did add in Heil Hitler which the subs Captain chose to ignore. Much to the disgust of Colonel Kempler.

Sub Captain: "Permission to come ashore Herr General?"

General Von Weber: "Permission granted."

The Captain crossed the gangway and stood before General Von Weber. The two of them shook hands as the Captain introduced himself.

Sub Captain: "General, I am Captain Kavan Hammerbeck of the German Navy. I am here to offer the services of my ship the U630 and its crew to your cause of rebuilding a greater Germany."

General Von Weber introduced himself and the rest of our immediate party. Parky, Asil, Ole, Einer and I had not recognized our old friend with his shaggy beard and bedraggled appearance. Once we heard his name and the fact he was Caption of the U630 we all had to do our best to pretend we were not glad to see him or the ship. The human's shook hands all around and Einer and I got a pat on the head, Kavan gave my human companions a wink as he was introduced and we all took the hint to pretend not to know each other.

Von Weber: "Captain. May I ask how you heard about us and how on earth did you find your way here under the polar ice cap?"

Kavan: "The scuttlebutt of your existence is a well-guarded secret. The allies figure it is just a rumor spread by Germans who are grasping for one last hope to return their country to its former glory. We happened to put ashore a small crew in our dingy at Svalbard to get some much needed fresh fruit and vegetables. I knew a loyal German officer was stationed at the airport and I went to his house to ask for assistance. After much discussion and learning we were both of the same mind he told me he had recently sent an airplane your way. He then gave me the coordinates on how to find you"

Von Weber: "On behalf of myself and the rest of us at the complex we wish to welcome you and your crew. I'm sure you have had a long voyage and from the looks of you I might assume you could use a good bath and fresh clothes. As for your crew they are welcome to come ashore and I am sure we can find room for them to clean themselves up and I will have the commissary open to serve them a good hot meal."

Kavan: "I appreciate the offer but my crew wishes to stay on board. However I would be grateful to accept your offer for myself."

General Kammler: "If you wouldn't mind Captain I would like to take a closer look at your submarine. I have never seen any submarine the size of yours. I would love to see what powers such a massive submersible as this."

Kavan: "I beg the Generals pardon but I allow no one on board other than my first mate and my crew."

Colonel Kempler: "I think you misunderstood the General Captain. He wishes to board your submarine and take a look around. He is a General and you are a Captain, he outranks you. I strongly suggest you take him up on his offer to look your craft over. If you refuse, well, I think you get the point."

Von Weber: "No need for any of us to get defensive gentlemen. We are all here to unite under a common cause. I'm sure that at a later date the Captain would be more than happy to give us a guided tour of his vessel. For now I suggest we let him get cleaned up and rested and then we can all share a meal together tomorrow evening. Of course if that fits in the Captains schedule."

Kavan: "Thank you for your understanding gentleman. Being land based officers I release that you may not understand a Navy man's attachment to his vessel. We sort of feel like our ships are like our women and we tend to be very protective of them. Just so there is no misunderstanding from any of us my first mate will be standing guard to make sure the U630 is not violated in any way. Oh, I almost forgot to mention this in response to Colonel Kempler's comment about rank. I belong to the German Navy and according to protocol an Army or Air Force General does not have the authority to override my decision. If any of you were German Admirals I would be more than happy to bow to your wishes. "

The looks Kavan got from General Kammler and Colonel Kempler were of course none to friendly. General Von Weber was still the ranking officer so what he said was law. I looked at General Von Weber and he had a slight smile on his face. I think he really enjoyed seeing his two cronies being put in their place.

As we left the U630 behind us we headed along the corridor to where Kavan would be led to an empty apartment. Kavan made a comment that must surely have ripped at the very soul of Colonel Kempler.

Kavan: "General's if I am not being to bold could I make a small request as to tomorrows dinner arrangements."

Von Weber: "If it is within reason I see no problem at all with your asking for anything we can offer. Maybe Lobster or champagne or maybe a few of our female associates to lighten the conversations from men talk."

The woman comment defiantly drew fire in Asil's eyes. Especially when there seemed to be very few women at the complex.

Kavan: "Oh no, nothing as exotic as that. I was just wondering if Colonel Parkurkakus, Captain Ole and Corporal Asil might be willing to attend. It would make for a much more pleasant evening for this old Captain to have a few new faces to talk to. Being aboard ship with a bunch of grimy sweaty men for months at a time can leave one starving for fresh conversation."

General Kammler: "I don't think that would be possible. I'm sure Parkurkakus and his assistants have other plans."

Colonel Kempler: "Yes, I'm sure they do. Might I suggest you accept the offer of General Von Weber for some female companionship? We have some rather lovely wenches that we keep for laborers in another part of the complex. I could have a few of them made presentable and you could do with them as you wish. I'm sure being at sea with as you say a bunch of grimy, sweaty sailors that your manly urges must just be begging for a release. When you are through with them we could give them over to your crew to do with as they wish. Then maybe we can take that little tour of your ship that General Kammler and I were hoping for."

Asil: "Colonel Kempler. I find your comments totally disgusting and unbecoming of an officer or even a solider of the German Army. Just where are these women laborers and where did they come from?"

I got the distinct feeling that we had just stumbled upon a secret that Colonel Kempler was not supposed to reveal. It seems that not only had the SS migrated to this complex but it was also leading to the fact that the complex was most likely built with slave labor and those laborers were somewhere in this complex. If that is the case than destroying the complex might endanger a large population of innocents.

Kavan: "I must agree with Asil on your comments and your assumption that I am a man who would be tempted by sins of the flesh. I also must strongly lodge a complaint with General Von Weber as to your conduct of attempting to bribe me with women to get yourself or anyone else a tour of my vessel."

Von Weber: "Your protest is duly noted Captain Kavan. I will deal with Colonel Kempler on this matter as soon as time permits. I am very sorry if you were offended. This complex is under my command and I must admit that if Colonel Kempler has been using these laborers for any purpose other than to do their jobs here it will be dealt with as to the severity of his actions."

Of course that comment had all of us smiling except for General Kammler. Whether he was party to any of Kempler's actions or not was hard to say. Personally I think he is to straight-laced to be a wine and womanizer type of guy but sometimes the quite studious ones are the ones you need to keep an eye on. Take Himmler for example. He was just a wisp of a man, with a bum leg and bad eyesight and he rose to a positon that entailed the killing of tens of thousands of innocents in mass murder and concentration camps.

Parky: "General if you don't mind I'd like to change the subject to something a bit more cheerful before each of us goes our own way."

Von Weber: "I think that is a splendid idea. Just what did you have in mind?"

Parky: "Some of you may not be aware of it but it just so happens that in my repertoire of accomplishments I happen to be an accomplished chef. I would be honored if all of you would be my guests at my apartment and let me make you a meal fit for the German officers that we are."

Kempler: "Colonel Parkurkakus. I assume you mean only the senior officers and not the likes of your staff people?"

Parky smiled at Kempler as he answered. "Colonel Kempler sometimes your rudeness even surprises me, although I have long become too accustomed to the uncouth words that flow from your mouth so the shock value has long since subsided. To answer your question everyone here with us right now is invited and I expect them all to be treated with dignity and respect. After all that is what the esprit of German military etiquette requires. Don't you agree my dear Colonel Kempler?"

Kempler: "If you say so Colonel Parkurkarkus. I only hope some emergency does not arise that would prevent me from attending."

I for one was hoping for just such an emergency. Although I knew I would not be disappointed. Kempler had pre-made his excuse and it was pretty obvious he would be elsewhere. Now only if General Kammler would come up with an excuse not to attend my day would be made.

General Kammler: "I for one shall be glad to attend. I am curious to see if our dear Colonel Parkurkakus is as accomplished at the culinary arts as he is at science and aviation."

I glanced at Kavan as he raised an eyebrow to the General's comment about Parky's expertise at science and aviation. Kavan was proving to be a good actor but I think that one took him for a bit of loop.

We soon separated as each of us went our own way. General Von Weber took Captain Kavan under his wing and I was sure he was in safe hands, at least for the time being.

General Kammler and Colonel Kempler left together as I watched Kempler rambling on in an animated fashion to General Kammler on how Captain Kavan and his crew were probably spies sent to infiltrate the complex. Of course I hoped that he was right. Until one of us could be alone with Kavan we couldn't be one-hundred percent sure which side he was on. After all he had switched from the side of the Germans to the allies in the past. Had he become disillusioned after the war and might be looking for a new cause. I prayed not.

CHAPTER 13

Ole and I returned to our apartment. Once we settled in for the night and both of us were all comfy cozy in our bed I asked. "Ole, it was sure a surprise seeing Kavan and the U630 show up here. What do you make of it?'

Ole: "Surprise is an understatement. You suppose he was recruited like we were to find out what is going on here? Maybe Odin and the one true God figured we were taking too long and sent him to help us out. And what about that big fellow that Kavan says is his first mate. I don't remember him from any of the missions we made with Kavan do you?"

"I don't. Except he wasn't the only strange looking one on the U630. What about the deck Hands? We might not have been able to see their faces but the way they were covering themselves to disguise recognition I'd bet a cat's paw that they were trolls. If they are, and you can kiss a cats butt if I'm wrong, I bet Krympe is somewhere inside the U630."

Ole: "You might just be right about the trolls. If you are I would have to agree that Krympe is involved. No matter what Odin told her to do her first loyalty is to Asil. The first mate, I don't think he is a troll. I caught a glimpse of his long beard and his eyes and nose. He wasn't very good looking but he wasn't ugly enough to be a troll."

"Ole, I'm surprised at you. Trolls are not ugly to other trolls and they probably think humans are ugly. Especially you."

Ole: "All right, that's enough from you. Good night and God bless."

We reported to work in the morning and once again our day's assignment was to pour over the specifications and drawings of various projects from the past to the present. Parky told us that by doing so we might just learn enough to be helpful on our upcoming mission into space. As he was quick to point out, you can never have enough knowledge. Looking at Parky who was very knowledgeable about many things I had to wonder if that was why he way such a big man, bulk wise that is. Maybe he had to be that big to store all that knowledge inside of himself. Certainly one brain was not big enough for all the things he seemed to know.

We ate a light lunch in the commissary as Parky had told us to save room for the feast he would be preparing for our dinner party to welcome Kavan on board. I could not image how he was going to top last night's dinner of Lobster with all the trimmings. Yet, knowing Parky he would do it.

After our shift at work was completed we went to our room to rest a bit and get refreshed before going to Parky's. There was a set time we were to arrive there and Ole was instructed to wear a dress uniform that was waiting in our room for him. I was told it was to be a formal affair so of course there was a black tie collar on the bed waiting for me. I'll be the first to admit in case no one else does that Ole and I made a pretty spiffy pair of gentleman when we were all dolled up for high society. If you can call a bunch of German officers high society.

This time there was no Tony to escort us. I guess we were expected to know our way around well enough to find Parky's apartment on our own, which we did. We were hoping to arrive first and to get the lowdown from Parky on how we were to handle the Captain Kavan situation. Unfortunately General's Kammler and Von Weber along with Captain Kavan had arrived early and we ended up being the latecomers.

Asil greeted us at the door and she was dressed in a floor length bright red gown. The v-neckline of her drees ended at a point that drew Ole's eyes to her supple, well you get the picture. A white pearl necklace was draped in a double strand around her neck and on her wrist was a black pearl bracelet. Red high heels accented the slit on one side of her dress that went half way up her thigh. Real silk nylons finished things off.

Ole gasped for his breath as he first beheld her. He stuttered out as any typical awe-struck human male would do. "Asil, you, you, ah, you look. Well, you, um, ah, look…'

Asil looked at him and smiled. "I look?"

Ole: "Ravishing."

Asil: "Thank you. Parky picked it out.   It seems a bit ostentatious to me. Parky figures it will draw the attention of the General's away from Kavan so we might get a chance to get him alone. Please come in and join us in the sitting room."

If Asil's beauty and that outfit didn't get the General's attention than those boys would have to be dead.

We were served drinks and Parky was of course absent for the time being as he was busy in the kitchen.

Kavan: "It looks like we are all here except for Colonel Kempler. I certainly hope that the emergency he was hoping to avoid did not crop up and that he won't be attending our little get together."

Kammler: "I had a short conversation with the Colonel just before I came here. It seems an emergency did arise. He sends his deepest regrets at not being able to attend."

Asil gave a wry smile towards Ole and me. "Oh my, that is such a shame. He tends to be such interesting company. Such a soldier, a real man's man as he so aptly puts it. From what he says he has been in almost every theater of the war. I am sure if Germany had an army of Kempler's we would surely have won the war."

Von Weber: "Yes, from the way he talks he would have won the war single handedly if our Fuher would have just held out for a bit longer."

Whether or not Kammler was serious I'm not sure but he raised his glass to make a toast. "To the Fuhrer." All the humans raised their glasses and in a rather subdued tone said "to the Fuher."

Kammler immediately made another toast. "To Colonel Kempler, if only Germany would have had more men like him." Once again and in an even more subdued tone, in fact it was so subdued my dog hearing had trouble picking it up. 'To Colonel Kempler."

At this time Parky came from the kitchen to join us.

Parky: "I have a few minutes to visit while some of my items are simmering. Did I miss anything important?"

Kemmler: "I was just…"

Before he could finish Asil cut him off.

Asil: "Nothing important. Just the men folk wishing for the good old days and reminiscing on how a few good men might have turned the tide of the war."

Kavan: "Not to put a damper on your memories of the past gentlemen. I personally feel that the biggest mistake the Fuher made was to open a two front war. If he would have concentrated all his efforts on defeating Britain then Stalin would have sat tight thinking the treaty we had with Russia was keeping him safe from German aggression."

Von Weber: "Possibly you may be right. I know a lot of the officers I knew would have agreed with you. However, in the beginning we drove the Russians all the way to Stalingrad. It wasn't the Russians that defeated us there. It was the winter."

Kavan: "Stalingrad. Yes the weather was what killed our advance. It also gave them the propaganda they needed to say look we stopped the Germans. They aren't invincible. If Britain and the United States supplies us with equipment and weapons we can push the Germans back to Germany and if the allies will land in France and move inland we can destroy Germany in a huge pincer movement. Which is just what they did. The biggest error was when the little lance Corporal decided he could take over as supreme commander of the German forces. We might have had a chance if he had left the decision making to the more experienced officers."

Kammler: "If this was the old Germany you would be shot for such treasonous talk. If Colonel Kemper were here you would probably be dead by now."

Von Weber: "Gentleman. This is just a little social get together. I think for the time being we should avoid talk of politics. The time we all remember is done and over. The Germany of old was defeated and we have moved on to where we are now. This is a new beginning for all of us. We can build a Germany that will be a better place and one that shall not be marred by the mistakes of the past."

Kavan: "Just what do you gentlemen have planned for this new Germany you speak of? I came here to find out for myself and my crew. If you are actually planning a place for the betterment of the German people and not world domination we might just be interested in joining forces with you."

Kammler: "Captain Kavan. I think you misunderstand your position here. It is not you who will make the decision of joining us it is us who will decide if we wish to bring you into our confidence. After all, you have a submarine to offer us. We already have lots of submarines. If one wished only to hide from his enemies under the sea or to sneak up on them and sink their ships like a thief in the night then you might have something to bargain with. As it is, you have nothing to offer us that we do not already possess."

Kavan: "You may be right as to the fact that you have many submarines. However, I saw the excitement in your eyes and in the eyes of everyone else when they saw the U630. It is the largest, most advanced submarine the world has ever seen. You've read or at least heard of the Jules Verne book 20,000 Leagues under the sea and Captain Nemo's submarine the Nautilus. Compared to the U630 the Nautilus was a mere child's toy in a bathtub. My U630 is the thing that dreams and science fiction can only image."

Kammler: "Typical boasting of a seafaring man. As far as we are concerned here the ocean has already been conquered. It is the skies that beckon man now. I'm not talking just the sky above that you can see but the universe of the stars and other planets. You bring up your Jules Verne, we would prefer to look at the H.G. Wells 1901 book First Man on the Moon. Mankind has visited the seas and the oceans but as of yet no man has stepped foot on the moon or any other planet in our vast solar system."

Von Weber: "Gentleman we seem to be jumping from one controversial subject to another. Undersea exploration, exploration of the heavens. As both of you have quoted books written by writers of science fiction why don't we all just agree that mankind has many dreams he would like to see fulfilled. This is just a nice little sociable get together let's keep it at that."

Parky: "I agree with General Von Weber. We are here to enjoy ourselves and we should make our newest member feel welcome. Now, if you gentlemen don't mind I think it is time for everyone to make their way to the table for supper. If you will please excuse me I will go to the kitchen and bring out your meal. Captain Kavan, I realize you are the guest of honor and I really hate to impose upon you, but being a seafaring man I think you might just enjoy seeing how I have prepared my specialties. They come from the same oceans that you have plied with your ship the U630. Maybe you might have a few suggestions on my preparation. If you do I am always anxious to learn from others."

Kavan: "I would be honored to accompany you. It is not often that the Caption of a ship is allowed to observe a master chef in action. Although you may have flattered me by thinking I have any knowledge on the preparation of undersea delicacies. The cooks on board most submarines are not what you would call experts at making fancy meals. Although the U630 being the size it is does have an actual chef on board and with so many men needed to crew a vessel of her size we eat in shifts and the chef takes great pride in the meals he serves. If circumstances permit I hope the two of you can get together and maybe share a few culinary secrets with each other."

Parky: "Asil, if you would be so kind, would you mind seating our guests and keeping their conversations along a pleasant note until we return?"

Asil: "It would be my pleasure. It's not often that one woman can have the company and attention of such a distinguished group of gentleman."

I had to admit I had never imagined that Asil could be as charming as she was being tonight. If she was not the Princess of the Drogon she could have had a very lucrative career as an actress.

As for Parky he had just pulled off the coup we were all hoping for. He was about to get Kavan alone and away from the prying eyes and ears of the Generals.

Once Parky and Kavan were alone in the kitchen there was a rather tense moment as they kept their distance and had a stare down like a cat and dog might have to see which of them would back down first. Parky as always was the first one to strike. He smiled a big old Parky smile which of course gave Kavan the opportunity to smile back. As soon as Kavan smiled Parky rushed him and embraced him in a typical Parky bear hug which lifted Kavan right off the ground.

Kavan: "OK. I get it. You're happy to see me. Now would you put down?"

Parky: "I'm just glad to see you. What are you doing here? Did you know we were here? Who sent you? You are on our side and not theirs. Aren't you?"

Kavan: "Slow down Parky. This place might be wired for sound. If it is you just blew my cover and yours."

Parky: "No need to worry. I've done some fancy field work on my apartment and the whole place is safe as a mother's womb. Every room is sound proofed so need to worry that those in the other room can hear us. Even if they could with the way Asil is dressed and her playing hostess those Generals are way too occupied with her to worry about us."

Kavan: "All right. To answer your questions. If you remember right I went to work for the United States Navy. With the end of the war I was thinking about retiring and moving to England. Thought maybe I would get me one of those seaside cottages overlooking the English Channel. You know a place just big enough to let my parents move in with me. As you know we had already smuggled them over to England to get them out of Germany to a safer place. Well, I was on my way there courtesy of a British troop ship that had been requisitioned to bring United States troops back to their homes. Seeing it was a return trip to England the ship had very few passengers. Being a Naval officer I was assigned one of the few state rooms on board. My commission was still good for another month until my retirement became official so I could be called back to duty if the need arose, but that was rather doubtful so I arranged for a place on the coast and settled into my stateroom with dreams of a nice idyllic life with my family in jolly old England. I could live off my pension and not have a care in the world. I finally had time to leave the war and the world's problems behind me. Oh, if only I wasn't such a soft hearted fool."

Parky: "And?"

Kavan: "And what?"

Parky: "If only you weren't such a soft hearted fool. What happened next?"

Kavan: "What happened next? I'll tell you just what happened. There I was lounging in a nice comfy deck chair watching the ocean go by. The sun was shining and only one small white cloud dotted the sky. I was the only one in sight. All alone I closed my eyes and with my dreams and thoughts of the peace and tranquility that would soon envelope my life. Suddenly the warmth of the sun left my face and I opened my eyes. The single little white cloud had blocked the sun and seemed to be moving towards me at a rapid pace. I thought I must have fallen asleep and was dreaming. It was not possible for a cloud to move from the sky like that and target a person. I shook my head trying to wake myself as the cloud came closer and closer. Then there it was, twice the size of three men right in front of me. I reached out to try and touch it, even though I knew clouds were just made of moisture and it was not a tangible thing."

"Before I could reach out it changed into the shape of a man, at first hazy and surreal. Then the shape took solid form. It was a man. A big man with a long hair and a long beard. He looked vaguely familiar but I couldn't quite place him. My hand involuntarily kept reaching out to touch him to see if he was real. Then he bellowed out at me"

Man: "Don't you even think of touching me mortal. I am Aegir King of the deep. I have an assignment for you."

"Sure enough, I seemed to have either seen him or heard of him as being involved with Asil and the rest of you. Of course I figured this really was a dream. No way would some Norse god be coming to me for help. However, he seemed to read my thoughts or at least he guessed what I was thinking."

Aegir: "I believe they call you Kavan do they not?"

I stammered out with a feeble "yes."

Aegir: "In case you're wondering this is not a dream. I am as real as you are. Asil, Einer and her human companions are on an assignment of the utmost importance to stop a surviving faction of the Nazi's from once again trying to rule or destroy this world as mankind knows it. Your assignment will be to join them and assist in saving the innocents that may be involved. Are you ready?"

"First off Aegir. I'm not ready. I'm retired from fighting. Al I want to do is spend the rest of my days in peace and quiet with my family. I'm not your boy. I suggest you find someone else."

Aegir: "You do not understand. This is not a request it is an order from Odin the King of the Norse. The greatest Viking of all time."

"Aegir then calmly sat down in the deck chair next to mine."

Aegir: "Here is how it will be. I have your submarine staffed with trolls and waiting to sail as soon as we arrive. I will play the part of your first mate to keep the secrets of the U630 from falling into enemy hands. I will also guide you to our destination. I have been retired by the one true god so I cannot use my powers of old to assist you. However, I can assist you as a mortal. So that is how it will be."

Kavan: "The next thing I knew we were on the U630 with a crew of trolls. We docked here and Aegir stayed on board the U630 to keep any Germans from trying to board. I was sent ashore to assist all of you in whatever way I can. So, what's going on here?"

Parky: "There's no doubt in my mind that they are developing aerial technology that rivals anything you have ever seen or read about. In fact from just the examples I have been working with they are making the dreams of a science fiction writer into realities. Flying discs or as Sven calls them flying saucers. I'm about to test one tomorrow. They want me to prove the existence of perpetual motion."

Kavan: "That's somewhat reasonable if you have the means to do it. After all the U630 runs on the flames of hell and they never burn out, I guess that would be considered perpetual motion. Although I can't image an aircraft running on an engine driven by the flames of hell. However, giving it a second thought I suppose it could be possible."

Parky: "Interesting analogy. The scientists here have actually developed an engine with propellers, hoping that if they spin fast enough and at the right angles their draft will energize the propellers behind them to keep them moving on their own accord.

If it works they will keep generating their own power. Free energy that will cost nothing and could power almost anything. Just think a complete city run by perpetual motion. If it can be made to work the possibilities are endless. No more power shortages. No digging coal or pumping oil for power, no pollution. It would revolutionize the world as we know it."

Kavan: "Or if it is used by the wrong hands and the minds of evil men take control of it. Well, you know what will happen then. They will use it in weapons of destruction, taking the whole world hostage, or destroying the world as we know it."

Asil popped her head into the kitchen door. "Parky, our guests are waiting. Remember I can only act charming for a short while. If you don't hurry and serve the food you might just find I turned them into icicles."

Parky: "Sorry, we're on the way."

The food arrived and Parky ever the showmen explained each dish as he served it. The courses ran from seaweed salad to smoked sailfish with Parky's very own homemade rolls and butter churned from walrus cow's milk.

CHAPTER 14

Meanwhile and unbeknown to us Colonel Kempler had an agenda of his own. The emergency he had told General Kammler he needed to take care of while the General made his apologies for Kempler's absence at the dinner meeting.

Kempler had gathered four of his SS men who were highly trained in the act of camouflage and infiltration. Three of the soldiers were dressed in black wet-suits and they smeared black greasepaint on their face and hands to better hide themselves. Each man carried a dual edged knife in a scabbard attached to their leg. Luger pistols were loaded and slipped into water proof bags then holstered around each man's waist. Waterproof explosives were slipped into pouches that were attached to their gun belts. They gathered for a final briefing in a dark corner of the submarine pens. It was getting late and seeing the area was considered a secure space there were no guards on duty and the workmen had long since went back to their barracks. Only a few lights had been left on for the night for with no workers it was not necessary to waste the power on excess lighting.

All the submarines that were at the docks were devoid of people. No crewmen were posted on watch and any crew that was not necessary for around the clock duties had joined the outside workers and gone to the recreation area or back to their barracks. The only exception was the U630. It still had a full crew on board and one lone watchman was posted by the gangplank. This watchmen was not the first mate as he had went below deck to join the crew for supper and then relaxation.

Kempler gave a last minute briefing to his men. Three of them were dressed in black cold water wet suits and were told to slip into the icy waters from the docks opposite the U630. Kempler and his sergeant were dressed in black SS uniforms and were not in blackface.

His plan was to try and gain access to the U630 through typical Nazi cunning and subterfuge. The signal for his three men on the far side was that once Kempler and his aide approached the guard on board the U630 the other three would slip into the water and swim across to the U630. Kempler would distract the guard so that his men could approach unseen. They were to use the ropes and grappling hooks they carried around their shoulder to hook onto the decking or stanchions of the U630 and pull themselves aboard. They would thus provide backup if needed for Kempler and his aide. If anything went wrong they were to drop back into the water and place their explosive charges below the waterline of the U630. Each charge would be set for five minutes to give them time to escape to the far side of the docks. Kempler figured if he couldn't gain access by invitation or trickery to look over the interior of the submarine he would either try to enter it by force and kill or capture anyone who got in his way or if that failed he would destroy the U630 and all those aboard.

Out of the shadows stepped Kempler and his aide. The night watch on the U630 was leaning against the conning tower with his head dropping down as if he was asleep or if not he certainly didn't seem to be very alert. Kempler figured this was going to be much easier he then he had thought. He and his aide stealthily made their way to the gang plank. There was a rope hooked across it and Kempler quietly undid it and let it hang loose just in case they had to make a quick getaway.

The two of them worked their way slowly up the gangplank which made a slight creaking sound but Kempler was sure it was not loud enough to wake the sentry. The submarine was shrouded in darkness and other then the shadow of the sentry it was hard to make out much more. Unbeknownst to Kempler the Sentry was resting but he had a sharp sense of hearing and an even sharper sense of smell. He heard the two intruders from the time they had slipped out of the shadows. His nose had picked up what his senses told him were Nazi's. His vision matched his other senses and he could see as well as cat in the dark. 'Boy, I do hate cat references but in this case it is appropriate.' The sentry slipped from his position at the conning tower and in the shadows repositioned himself. He watched as Kempler and his aide made their way to the top of the gangplank and started to unhook another rope that had been fastened there. Kempler finished letting the rope quietly down so as to make no sound. He stood up and bumped into the sentry who happened to be about the same height as he was.

As Kempler stepped back in surprise he bumped into the sergeant and the two of them stumbled. If not for the side ropes on the gangplank they would have both fallen overboard. They grabbed the ropes and managed to regain their footing.

They now stood a few feet from the sentry and Kempler could be heard cussing out the sentry and his bad luck. Finally Kempler quit his tirade of under the breath swearing and stood straight and tall trying to show his dignity as an SS officer.

Sentry: "May I help you two?"

Kempler: "I am Colonel Kempler and as a German Officer and the Officer in charge of security at this base I am here to inspect your ship."

The sentry was dressed in German naval gear, except he had on a hooded sweatshirt, the hood was pulled up and was a bit oversized for his head so that it hid his facial features.

Sentry: "I am sorry sir. No one is allowed to board the ship without the permission of Captain Kavan Hammerbeck."

Kempler: "I have his permission. You see we were at a dinner party with General's Kammler and Von Weber and I asked your Captain if he would like to give me a tour of his ship. He was having such a good time he told me that if I wanted to see it I was welcome to do so. I was bored with the attitudes of the top brass bragging of all their war time exploits. I'm sure you know how they can carry on so and take all the credit for what the men on the front lines have accomplished. They are just a bunch of blowhards who don't understand what a real fighting man like you and I have to go through. So, I excused myself telling them I had to get up early to work on security measures and make sure everything was up to par. I really wanted to come see this marvel of the oceans that your Captain has so much pride in. Now if you will let us pass we will take a quick tour and then be on our way. We don't even need a guide. I'm sure we can find our way around."

Sentry: "Did the Captain give you written permission?"

Kempler: "No he did not. I know I should have requested it but I really didn't want to bother him with such a trivial thing. Finding paper and a pen at a party would have put such a damper on things for the others that were there. I'm sure you understand. No need to bother the brass with unnecessary things. His verbal permission should be more than enough. After all, if you can't trust an officer in the SS who can you trust?"

Sentry: "I am sorry Colonel. Verbal permission is not acceptable. I'll have to ask the two of you to leave."

The sentry turned as he heard a sound behind him. Kempler's three men were just crawling up onto the deck. The sentry did not have time to run for the button on the conning tower to sound the alarm so he pulled a bosons whistle from his pocket and raised it to his lips. His back was turned towards Kempler when he felt Kempler's hand clamp over his mouth and the blade of Kempler's dagger slip between his ribs and thrust upward in a twisting motion to puncture his lungs.

Once Kempler felt the sentry's body go limp he quietly lowered him to the deck.

Sergeant: "Colonel, there's something very strange about that man," He leaned over and pulled the hood back from the man's face. Kempler and his aide looked down at the sentry's face.

Kempler: "He's hideous. Look at the size of the nose, and his eyes, they bulge like they should pop out of his head."

Sergeant: "Look at those ears, there huge, no wonder he heard us coming. The man looks like some kind of monster. I sure hope the rest of the crew looks better then him."

Kempler: "Maybe that's what Kavan is trying to hide from us. This ship might just be racked with some horrible disease and he is hoping to spread it throughout the complex and kill us all. Do you have that machine gun under your jacket that I told you to bring with."

Sergeant: "I do"

Kempler: "Give it to me. We'll go below deck and check it out. Hopefully the rest of the crew is sleeping. If they look like this man we'll blow this ship to kingdom come and stop any infection it might have on board."

Sergeant: "Colonel. I'm not so sure that's such a good idea. Us going below decks. I sure would hate to catch what that fellow has"

Kempler: "If we see the infection has affected the rest of the crew we'll high tail it out of there."

Kempler looked around trying to make out his other three men on deck. Finally he whispered just loud enough to be heard. "Men if you are on board. Count off so I know where you are."

Each man counted off one-two-three followed by their names.

Kempler: "Have you set the explosive chargers?"

An affirmative was acknowledged by each man.

Kempler: "We're going below deck. If you hear me tell you to set the charges or if we get killed or captured, set those charges and get away as fast as you can."

One of the men in the darkness was heard to say. "Colonel, we can't leave you behind, if you need help we are all in this together."

Kempler: "That's enough. You heard me. Now that's an order. Do you all understand?"

A quietly mumbled "affirmative" was heard from the three men.

Kempler motioned for the Sergeant to follow him. The two men climbed the conning tower figuring it unlikely any of the crew would be on watch there since the ship was docked. They made their way down the ladder and slowly touched down on the deck inside the ship. So far so good for them. Not a soul was in sight. Kempler held the machine gun in one hand as he moved along the deck inspecting the control panels. His sergeant held his luger pistol at the ready in case anyone might unexpectedly show up.

Kempler quietly whispered to the sergeant. "Look at these controls and panels I've never seen anything like this on any ship or submarine that I have visited in the past. The safety depth indicator does not red-line until twelve-thousand feet. That's not even possible. The average depth of the ocean is about twelve-thousand one-hundred feet. If this sub can actually withstand depths that deep it could literally be out of range of any other vessel in existence. About the only place it could not go would be the Challenger Deep which is approximately thirty-six thousand two-hundred feet.

The average submarine is only able to stand depths of six-hundred to maybe a maximum of nine-hundred and twenty-feet before the pressure from the water outside the hull will crush it."

Sergeant: "Colonel. Look at the metal of this hull. It shines like its nickel plated. Have you ever seen metal like this on a submarine or any other ship for that matter? The same metal is used on the decking. The instrument panel seem to be made of titanium. Is any of this technically possible for a submarine? I mean, I know we are working with some pretty exotic metals in the complex but I've never seen anything like this. Do you suppose this thing can really reach a depth of twelve-thousand feet without being crushed?"

Kempler: "I don't know. I told you that Captain Kavan was hiding something from us. Come on we need to make our way to the engine room. If this thing is capable of reaching the depths of the ocean it must have an engine and drive system to match the rest of its capabilities. I can only imagine what we'll find down below.

The two of them quietly made their way into a few other compartments and still had not encountered any of the crew. With their weapons at the ready they both started to get an uneasy feeling that something was drastically wrong with this scenario.

Sergeant: "Colonel, do you think maybe the crew snuck ashore for R & R?

Kempler: "If they had come ashore for rest or relaxation my Gestapo would have alerted us. Nothing goes on in this complex least of all any stranger roaming about that I don't know about. They are here somewhere. Most likely in a vessel of this size they have a huge crews quarters."

The two of them soon came to an actual stairway leading to the next level. They crept down and found themselves in a good sized library with red carpet floor, wood paneled book shelves that were filled with thousands of books."

They quickly passed through this room and entered into a room that was dimly lit by four large tortoise shaped crystal chandeliers that illumined rows and rows of green velvet seats arranged in rows that went in single steps down from each row and ended about twenty feet from a large movie screen.

Sergeant: "Colonel. I think I'm dreaming, this looks like a movie theater. No submarine in the world is large enough to have its own movie theater."

Kempler: "Be quiet. I bet they have some kind of projector that is making us see images of things that don't really exist. Come on, we'll back track until we find the ladders or stairs or whatever to the next level, Sooner or later we're about to either run across the crews quarters or the engine room. Hopefully it will be the engine room so we can check out what powers this thing."

Sergeant: "I don't know Colonel. This place gives me the creeps. Maybe we should get out while we still can."

Kempler: "That's enough out of you. You're supposed to be my top man, not only are you my aide but you are a Sergeant in the SS. You telling me you're scared like a little lost girl? You going to start crying big old crocodile tears on me?"

Sergeant: "Sorry Colonel. You're right. They have some apparatus that's playing tricks on us. Let's find the engine room."

They stealthily made their way along the corridors that connected the adjoining sections of the ship. Kempler was in the lead and he reached back with hand held to stop the Sergeant.

Kempler: "Did you hear that?"

Sergeant: "I don't hear anything except the pounding of my heart in my chest. There's something drastically wrong here Colonel. We haven't seen a soul since we came below decks. I'm beginning to think this is a ghost ship. Like the tales they tell of the Flying Dutchman. A ship crewed by the dead. You know what they say? The dead are always looking for new recruits. I'll tell you right now, I don't relish the idea of being the newest member of the crew on a ghost ship."

Kempler: "Sergeant, I thought you were a man with common sense. You talk like a kid swapping ghost stories around the campfire. Ghost Ship my eye. You're an idiot. I thought I heard a sound like the squeak of hinges opening a door. I guess that wouldn't be so strange. Let's get moving"

Sergeant: "I may be an idiot but then you tell me, where is the crew?"

Kempler: "It's a huge ship. They are probably all asleep in their quarters somewhere. Just be thankful we haven't seen any of them. If we do they have to die quickly and silently so they don't alert any of the others. You understand?"

Sergeant: "Of course I understand. But, I'm not so sure you can kill a ghost."

Kempler just shook his head in disgust and began moving forward again. They went down two more sets of ladders and figured they were now at the bottom deck.

 Kempler: "I smell something that smells like fire and sulphur. Do you smell it?"

Sergeant: "I do. Reminds me of my church going days."

Kempler: "Now what are you babbling about?"

Sergeant: "It smells like I always imagined fire and brimstone would smell when the preacher would tell us of the perils of sin and going to hell. Colonel, if it's all the same to you I think we should give up this quest and get back to shore."

Kempler: "Sergeant, one more word out of you about fire and brimstone, hell or ghosts and I'll send you there myself."

That kept the Sergeant quiet for the time being. The two of them worked their way along the corridor and finally came to a water tight door. The plaque on the door read 'engine room.'

Kempler: "It's about time. Sergeant, be prepared, there's sure to be least one or two crewmen keeping eyes on the engine."

Kempler turned the wheel of the engine room door as quietly as he could. It made a small grinding sound that one would expect from the gears meshing into each other to release the bolts that held the door in place. He slowly opened the door and it creaked just enough to make him nervous.

They stepped into the engine room and beheld two men sitting at a work table playing cards. Both of the men had hoods pulled over their heads that hid their features. Neither of them seemed to have heard Kempler and the Sergeant as they entered the room. A fact that both the SS men pondered as being rather strange. Kempler motioned for the Sergeant to keep his gun aimed at the two crewmen as he stared at the massive boiler with what looked like super thick isinglass windows cut into the boiler doors. There was no coal or a smell of diesel or even gasoline to fuel the boilers and the room seemed warm but not hot as it should have been with such flames going in the fire grates.

Kempler put the palm of his hand near the glass, then he got braver and pushed his palm onto the glass. It was warm but not hot. In reality he should have been burned. He looked back at the two men who seemed oblivious to the fact that anyone else was in the room with them, then he looked at the Sergeant who just shrugged his shoulders.

Kempler quietly said to the two men. "You two. Hands up."

The two men just kept playing cards as if they hadn't heard a word.

Kempler cleared his throat and much louder he said. "Are you to deaf and dumb? I said hands up!"

Without looking at them one of the men answered. "We heard you. Can't you see we are busy playing cards? Why don't you two go away and leave us alone?" Kempler had a look of total surprise on his face. He looked back at the Sergeant who once again just shrugged his shoulders.

Kempler: "This is the last time I'm going to ask. Put your hands in the air and stand up. If you don't I'll shoot the both of you."

The two crewmen put their hands in the air and they stood up facing Kempler and the Sergeant. Their loose fitting hoods covered their faces so that Kempler and the Sergeant could not make out their features.

Kempler: "What powers these engines? There should be heat blasting from the metal the way those fires are burning."

1st Crewman: "Are you sure you want to know?"

Kempler: "Of course I want to know or I wouldn't have asked."

2nd Crewman: "You really want to know? You may regret it."

Kempler" "You'll regret it if you don't tell me."

1st Crewman: "I say we tell him."

2nd Crewman: "All right if he insists. However I doubt he will believe us. Here goes. The ships power comes from Hades himself. He has supplied us with eternal flames from hell to power our ship. The flames have to remain just warm enough to put the fear of god into the wicked but not so hot as to burn them up or they would be of no use to Hades or Satan or Lucifer depending on what teachings you believe. For this ship it is an everlasting source of perpetual power. It never dies and never needs to be replenished.

Sergeant: "See, I told you so. This is a ghost ship from hell. Let's get out of here."

Kempler: "Sergeant! You stay where you are or I'll shoot you on the spot and your boogeymen and goblins."

The Sergeant was looking awful scared. He was white as a ghost if you'll pardon the pun. He started to back away from the two crewmen and made his way to the door behind them. He was ready to make his escape with or without Kempler.

Kempler: "I've had enough of you two and your games of let's scare the Colonel and the Sergeant. Remove those hoods from your heads and let me see your faces so I will remember them when you are court martialed for insubordination to an Officer of the German SS."

The two crewmen slowly pulled their hoods away from their heads and let them dangle behind them.

Sergeant: "God in heaven Colonel. There monsters! I believe this ship is powered by the flames of hell. If those two are the devils minions, well, I don't know what else they could be. Let's get out of here. This is Satan's ship there's no doubt about it."

The Sergeant turned and ran for the door.

Kempler: "Damn you Sergeant. I warned you what would happen if you ran from your duty!"

Kempler turned and a short burst of bullets from his machine gun mowed the Sergeant down as he fell face first to the floor and his blood drained from his body like a leaking water hose.

Kempler: "I hope you two satanic devils are happy now. You just made me shoot my Sergeant. Now you tell me in plain words just what powers this ship and what the hell are you two? You some kind of mutants formed by this radio-active nuclear stuff that they used to bomb Japan. Or are you two just that dammed ugly."

1st Crewman: "You won't believe us if we tell you."

Kempler: "Try   me?"
2nd Crewman: "Ok, here goes. We are trolls, in our case straight form the mountains of Norway."

Kempler: "The hell you say. You could have at least pretended to be from Germany. If you really are trolls and I'm not buying it for a minute, but let's just pretend and say you are what you say you are. What are you doing crewing a German submarine?"

1st Crewman: "Captain Kavan needed a crew and we volunteered."

Kempler: "You mean to say this whole damn submarine is crewed by trolls?"

2nd Crewman: "Not quite. But close. The Captain and First Mate are not trolls"

Kempler: "I've met your Captain. He seems human enough. What about the First Mate. I saw him on deck when you first docked here. He was a very large man. What was he? A giant or maybe an ogre?"

A voice came from behind Kempler. "You should be so lucky if only I were a giant or an ogre. What they would do to you would be mild in comparison to what my plans for you are. By the way, we haven't met. I'm Aegir, retired God of the deep. But, still the King of the oceans. You have killed one my friends,"

Kempler: "Killed who? I don't remember killing any gods or kings?"

Aegir: "The troll you killed topside was one of my crew and he was my friend. I am afraid his death cannot go unpunished."

Kempler: "I am in Officer in the SS. I demand a trial by my peers or an honorable death in battle."

Aegir: "There will be no trial. However, if you want to die in battle I think that can be arranged. My friends here will be glad to escort you to our training area where you can show your prowess as a warrior."

Kempler's mind was working at full speed on ways to avoid having a one on one confrontation with anyone. He was more of a man who felt he was a leader and that others should be ordered by him to do the fighting.

As the two crewmen approached to take him into custody he pulled the trigger of the machine gun and let go a volley of bullets as he swung around to mow down Aegir and to make his escape. Only things did not go as he had planned. Aegir waved his hand into the air and created an invisible force shield that stopped the bullets before they could reach their targets. The leaden projectiles of death flattened against the invisible screen and fell harmlessly to the floor.

Kempler couldn't believe his eyes and tried again. He continued to fire until the gun was empty. Then he threw it at Aegir who caught it with one hand and then taking his other hand he twisted it up like a pretzel and tossed it back to Kempler who caught it in his hands.

Aegir smiled as he said. "Here. I believe you dropped this."

A look of disbelief at what had just happened filled his eyes. The trolls grabbed him by the arms and as he pleaded for mercy they drug him along the corridors and up one flight of steps to a room that had been emptied of its contents and was now filled with the rest of the crew of trolls that were manning the U630.

They tossed Kempler into the middle of the room. A troll much smaller than all the others walked to the center of the room and as Kempler lay in a heap on the floor the little troll squatted down on her haunches and grabbed a handful of Kempler's hair and pulled his head up so that he had to look her right in the face. Her big round eye's sparkled as she said. "I am Krympe the only female troll on board. All of these trolls are my friends and it was I who asked them to crew this submarine to rid the world of scum like you. You have killed one of our own with no provocation. Aegir said you wished to die like a warrior. We will give you that chance which is much more than you gave my friend. Are you prepared to die? No matter, yes or no you will die and not nearly so quickly as my friend died. We want you to enjoy dying. Maybe then your mind will have flashbacks of all the men, women and children you and your men tortured and killed during the war. You best stand up now and meet your end."

Kempler struggled to his feet. He looked around at a crowd of trolls that was surrounding him. One being stood out amongst the rest. It was Aegir. With pleading eyes Kempler looked at Aegir. "Please you must have some human decency in you. Stop this madness and let me be judged by humans."

Aegir: "Decency? Human Decency? You really must be mad. Humans and especially humans like you know no decency. They start wars and kill off hundreds of thousands of their own kind. Have you ever heard of Trolls starting a war? I don't think so. Yet humans tell stories to their children that trolls are evil and live under bridges or in caves just waiting for an unsuspecting child to come along so they can capture them and eat them. Humans who refuse to understand beings that are different from themselves, who only wish to destroy those that don't fit the mold they have made to live in. You and your men Kempler killed one of our crew to try and find out the secrets inside the U630. Before you meet your opponent we have a little surprise for you. Would you like to see it?"

Kempler: "If I die you will receive a surprise from me. How's that for an answer?"

Aegir: "Interesting answer to say the least. However I will bet your life that my surprise will be more interesting than yours."

Kempler: "Will you and all these trolls honor your bet if I tell you what the surprise is?"

Aegir: "If you tell us and deliver your surprise as you promise we will let you go free."

The trolls let out a cheer as Kempler's three men were brought into the room. Each was bloodied and beaten to near death. They were tossed on the floor within sight of their Colonel. Kempler swallowed hard and his fear made him weak-kneed and almost ready to fall down. His throat was dry and words refused to come from his mouth.

Krympe ran towards him and looked up into his face her eyes big and shining as she spoke. "Your surprise would not have been that in case of your death these three were to blow up the U630 and kill all those on board? Would it?"

Kempler slowly nodded his head yes to her question.

Krympe: "One thing you probably did not know is that Trolls have an excellent sense of hearing. We heard your men as they came onto the ship. You were only able to kill our lookout because he was distracted by these three men and he had no idea that you would be so treacherous as to kill him without warning. Now, let the fun begin."

Aegir: "To make things a bit more sporting we have found a troll of about your size Kempler. Of course trolls have the strength of at least two and sometime three normal humans. I would wish you good luck but that would be a lie on my part."

A troll came from the crowd dressed only in a loincloth. He was about the same height as Kempler but he had muscles in his body that rippled with power. His light wood colored skin and straggly green hair streaked with white gave him an evil continuance in Kempler's eyes. The Troll slowly approached Kempler, then he stopped and smiled. With teeth that shone with a rainbow color of green-red –blue and dazzled in the light.

The troll held out his hand to offer a sportsman like handshake. "I am Moss, your opponent human. You killed my friend. I will be the last thing your eyes will ever see."

Kempler bent down and pulled a hidden dagger from his boot. He lunged at Moss who jumped back but still received a slash across his stomach.

Kempler: "Take that you ugly bastard from hell."

Moss stepped back and looked at trickles of blood running down his skin. The crowd booed at Kempler's treachery.

Aegir: "Not very sportsmen like Kempler. Yet, to be expected from a human of your sorts."

Moss crouched down as Kempler made a dash at him with the daggers blade looking for more blood. Moss deflected Kempler with a forearm across his knife arm as the blade slipped mere inches from Moss's chest. A well placed leg thrust from Moss tripped Kempler so that he dropped the dagger and tumbled across the floor into the waiting crowd of trolls. They quickly grabbed him and threw him into the arena and into Moss's waiting arms. Moss grabbed Kempler as he was on the fly and spun him around so that Kempler's back was pressed against Moss's chest and Kempler was facing the crowd of trolls. Cheers from the trolls filled the room as they raised their hands and then gave a thumbs down like the Greeks used in the arenas of yore.

Moss whispered in Kempler's ear. "You will now die for the killing of one of ours."

Moss took one of his massive troll hands and squeezed it around Kempler's neck until the Colonel's eyes bulged and popped from their sockets landing on the floor and rolling towards his men. Next his tongue protruded from his mouth until it fell limp onto his chin. Finally with all the bones of the vertebrae in his neck broken Kempler's head flopped over onto his chest as Moss released his grip. Then he left the lifeless body fall to the floor.

Krympe: "Now that that piece of human scum has been dispatched what should we do with his men?"

The crowd of trolls shouted in unison. "Kill them like their leader!"

Krympe: "I don't think that would be wise of us. These men have killed none of ours. We would not want to bring ourselves down to the level of humans would we?"

A low mummer of agreement went through the crowd. Krympe looked at Aegir and asked. "Aegir, you have observed humans for centuries. Do you have any suggestions?"

Aegir stroked his beard and contemplated for a moment before he spoke. "I think we should set them free so they can tell the others what happens when you try to sneak aboard a ship and kill a crewman without provocation. However, they should be made to leave the way they came on the water side of the ship and not down the gangplank as if they were invited guests. We should supply them with a rubber dinghy from our ship as none of them seems capable of making the swim back to the other side of the docks. Just to show we have compassion we should make sure they leave with all that they brought with them including their weapons and their Colonel's body. Oh yes, and the body of the Sergeant that the Colonel shot and killed"

The trolls took the prisoners to top deck and loaded them into the dinghy along with Colonel Kempler's body and all of the gear they had brought with them.

As the men painfully started to paddle across the water Aegir handed Krympe a small box with a timer and a red button on it.

Krympe: "What is this?"

Aegir: "I guess we forgot to give our friends this box. Maybe if you push the red button it will call them back to get it."

Krympe smiled and told all the trolls to wave goodbye to their unwanted guests. Then she pushed the red button.

A large explosion tore apart the dinghy and the men hat were aboard it. Very small pieces of rubber and blood rained down onto the water where that dingy had been.

Krympe: "Whoops. I'm afraid they meant to use this to blow up the explosives they thought were attached to the boat. We told them we would let them have all their gear back."

Aegir: "Too bad. Now the ship will be short one dinghy. I suggest you and the troll's best go below deck and I will take the watch up here. I'm sure that explosion may bring a few curiosity seekers to the area."

CHAPTER 15

We had finished an excellent dinner compliments of Parky. Retiring to the sitting room we watched the view of the ocean through the window in Parky's apartment. Even though it was night and darkness ranged throughout much of the placid waters below the ice occasional glimpses of luminescent undersea creatures would fascinate us all.

Ole: "Isn't amazing that the wonders of God reach even the depths of the world's coldest ocean?"

Kammler: "If you believe in such things? If your God is so amazing then we shall soon see if his wonders also include the farthest reaches of the heavens."

Asil: "General Kammler. May I be so bold as to ask just what you mean by such a statement?"

Kammler: "If the tests that Parky is to perform in the next few days are successful everyone in this room will become privy to the next step in our plan. Of course that is if General Von Weber is in agreement with me to move the three of you into the final phase of our operation here?"

Von Weber: "I so no reason not to. Of course if Parky can actually prove that perpetual motion is possible."

Parky: "I have heard rumors, mind you that they may be just that. That there is a second complex in South America working along the same lines as we are. What if they should beat us to it? Or, is it possible that we might combine our knowledge with there's and accelerate the development of the final solution to both our efforts?"

Kemmler: "In the beginning there was hope that two bases of operations could be set up. However even the densest of jungles did not offer the security we have here. The second base of operations had to be scrapped and all efforts were put into this base. The only thing South America provided was a secure refuge for the Nazi members who managed to escape Germany at the end of the war. None of them had the knowledge to further our activities here so may they now live in peace and obscurity from the vengeful eyes of those who wish to do them harm."

Asil: "Some of them were found guilty of war crimes in absentia. Don't you feel they should have stayed to defend themselves and then maybe they could have proven their innocence and helped to rebuild Germany?"

Kammler: "Defend themselves? Are you so totally ignorant woman as to believe the Russians, British, French or even the Americans would find them innocent even if they were? Vengeance is the tool the victors use to show their power over the vanquished. They would have all been found guilty and executed as would some of the people in this complex. Now that you have joined us I am quite positive that the three of you would now be considered the same as the rest of us. War criminals who are trying to revive the honor of Germany."

Einer had given out a low growl at Kemmler's comment about Asil being ignorant but luckily it was ignored by the two Generals.

As luck would have it the current discussion was cut short by a muffled roar and then the shaking of the entire apartment. Everyone stopped what they were doing and silence prevailed. A look of worry came to everyone's faces.

Kammler: "What the hell was that? You don't suppose the ice is shifting the entire complex do you?"

Von Weber: "I don't believe that would be possible. Unless of course it was caused by an internal explosion."

Kammler quickly arose from his chair and went to the telephone that connected all areas of the complex. He rang Colonel Kempler's office and there was no answer. He rang the main switchboard and ordered for Colonel Kempler and his men to meet him at the door of Parky's apartment.

Kammler: "All of you come with me. Kempler and his men should be here if a few moments and we will get to the bottom of this."

Asil: "General, you certainly don't expect me to go with you dressed like this do you?"

General Von Weber grabbed his great coat from the chair that he had worn to our gathering and helped Asil to slip it on."

Asil: "Thank you General. You are a gentleman." Of course she was stalling for time just in case the explosion had something to do with the crew of the U630. She glanced at Kavan and raised her eyebrows as she mouthed the words. Your doing?"

Kavan shrugged his shoulders and looked as surprised as the rest of us had been. The Generals were worried that the noise and tremor we felt might have meant we were under attack either from within which would point to sabotage or from without which would mean the complex had been compromised and all that they had worked for would now be worthless to them but a goldmine to the enemy. We figured that if it was sabotage it was certainly in our favor that we were with the Generals when it happened for once Colonel Kempler was located he would surely try to lay the blame on us.

It didn't take long for three of the General's Gestapo agents to show up. They had been under the command of Kempler and he kept a tight rein on them. The lead man was a man called Fritz, he was dressed in a black suit which made him stand out from the more relaxed outfits most of the workers wore. The other two agents were dressed in sweatshirts and slacks and would fit in to most of the workers areas in the complex. A definite advantage I am sure they used to spy on people.

Kammler: "Where's Colonel Kempler?"

Fritz: "I don't know General. I have all our agents searching for him. To the best of our knowledge he and four of his men are missing. There are six of his men still here but they know no more than we do. It seems he seldom confines in his own men as to what his missions are or where he is going."

Von Weber: "Kempler. Always being secretive about what he does. The man never was one to accept the authority of others. I should have demoted him a long time ago."

Kammler: "What about the noise we heard and the tremor that followed it?"

Fritz: "Best as we have been able to ascertain it is possible that there was some type of explosion at the submarine base. I have Kempler's SS men and the Gestapo investigating it as we speak."

Von Weber: "What are we waiting for? Let's get down there and see if they have found out anything."

The Gestapo had cordoned off the area from the large crowd that had gathered there after the sound of the explosion. As we arrived Asil had to endure the wolf whistles of a few of the more uncouth male members of the crowd. Although, she did have a slight smile on her face so maybe endure was not the right way to put it. The trench coat covered three-quarters of her dress but not her high-heeled red shoes and a rather shapely leg that was visible as the slit on the side of her dress moved as she walked. The General's seemed oblivious to the male gawkers as their minds were engrossed in the possible threat to their complex and there future of ruling the world to be bothered by the attention a pretty lady might garner from a base filled with mostly men.

Kavan: "If the General's don't mind I would like to board the U630 and talk with my first mate to make sure my ship is all right. I can also question him as to whether he or any of my crew might have seen what happened"

Von Weber: "That's an excellent idea. Let us know as soon as possible if any of your men witnessed anything. Would you like one of the Gestapo to accompany you so they can take notes?"

Fritz: "That's a splendid idea. You know we are trained to gather information that sometimes people are reluctant to share."

In my mind, trained and torture were synonymous with the Gestapo technique of gathering information.

Kavan: "Thank you for the offer but my crew are very leery of strangers. I think it best if I handle this."

I could see the disappointment on Fritz's face. He might have lodged a protest with the General's but the two of them were much too busy scanning the area and questioning the agents that were investigating the area.

Asil motioned for me to tag along with Kavan which I did. I'm not sure if she totally trusted him yet or not. He didn't seem to mind and I was glad to act as a spy for Asil. However I felt her doubts were totally unfounded.

The first mate was waiting for us as we stepped off the gangplank. I should not have been surprised that he was none other than Aegir.

Aegir: "Hello Captain. Sure is a lot of activity going on around here."

Kavan: "There certainly is. I don't suppose you would know anything about it?"

Aegir: "Possibly. However, I'm not so sure you would want to know."

Kavan: "Possibly, I just might. Did you have something to do with the explosion and the tremor that rocked this place?"

Aegir: "Captain, I'm surprised at you. You know I am only along as an observer. Odin gave me strict orders that I was not to interfere in any way on a personal level. All I can do is observe and give my opinion when asked to do so."

Kavan: "All right. How about you give me your opinion as a neutral observer."

Aegir: "Well, in my opinion there was a large explosion right out there in the middle of the waterway between the two docks."

I could see that Aegir was enjoying himself immensely in stringing Kavan along and making him beg for every detail of what actually happened. This was probably going to take a while. Looking around the docks that were crawling with the Gestapo I figured we had plenty of time. Their thoroughness and the General's watchful eyes meant that if there was any evidence it had better be found and found now.

Kavan: "Just what was it that exploded?"

Aegir: "My educated guess would be a bomb or some other type of explosive."

Kavan sarcastically. "Really, a bomb or some other type of explosive. Of course that makes perfect sense. Was there anything that a bomb or explosive might have been attached to?"

Aegir: "Now that you mention it I believe there was."

Kavan: "And, just what was it?"

Aegir: "I believe it was one of our rubber dinghies from the U630. By the way, I am sorry for the loss of that dinghy."

Kavan: "I think I can forgive you for the loss of the dinghy. Did there happen to be anyone aboard the dinghy? Possibly Colonel Kempler and some of his men?"

Aegir: "Now that you mention it I do believe you may be right."

Kavan: "So, you killed them all. Just how many were there?"

Aegir: "No, I didn't kill any of them. I'm just a neutral observer remember? Anyways the Colonel and the Sergeant were already dead before the explosion. There were three other of the Colonel's men on board the dinghy and they were alive when I last saw them."

Kavan: "Had they been snooping around the U630?"

Aegir: "They most certainly were. The Colonel and his Sergeant had killed the troll who was on lookout duty. Then the two of them snuck down below decks to the engine room where the Colonel shot and killed his Sergeant."

Kavan: "Why would the Colonel kill his own Sergeant?"

Aegir: "That's a good question. You will have to ask the two trolls who were in the engine room."

Kavan: "Who killed Colonel Kempler?"

Aegir: "The trolls held a trial and found him guilty of murdering a troll in cold blood. Kempler tricked the toll into looking the other way and stabbed him to death. Of course in troll law killing a defenseless troll brings the penalty of death as the only logical sentence when one is found guilty. The trolls were not really concerned with the fact that Kempler also killed his Sergeant. After all the Sergeant was just a human. Which would make that a human problem and not a troll problem."

Kavan: "How did they carry out the death sentence?"

Aegir: "It was actually very civilized as far as I was concerned. Something to make a Viking proud. They gave Kempler the chance to save himself in a battle of one to one contact. Human against a troll. Of course Kempler cheated. He pulled a hidden dagger from his boot and lunged at the weaponless troll cutting him. The Troll still prevailed and got Kempler into a headlock and then proceeded to squeeze his head until his eyes pooped from their sockets and his tongue hung loosely onto his chin. Finally Kempler's vertebrae in his neck were crushed and he was dead. It was really quite a sight to behold. In all my years as a god to the humans I must say this was by far the most novel and interesting way to kill a man I have ever seen."

Kavan: "Was Krympe there?"

Aegir: "She was."

Kavan: "She's the leader of the trolls on board ship, why didn't she try to stop it."

Aegir: "It's the law of the trolls. She had no say in trying to stop it."

Kavan: "All right. We've gotten this far. Just how was it that there were three live humans on the dinghy when it exploded?"

Aegir: "The three who had distracted the troll on guard duty were still on the deck when Kempler and the Sergeant snuck below decks. It seems they had orders to blow up the U630 if anything happened to the Colonel and Sergeant or if they did not return topside. The trolls are not barbarians so they let them leave with the bodies of their two comrades. They even gave them the use of the dinghy to get back to shore. Why they even let them keep their weapons and explosives that they were going to use to blow up the U630."

Kavan: "So, the explosives they had just went off all by themselves?"

Aegir: "I guess so. The trolls or myself did not throw them at them. They were just paddling the dinghy across to the side they had come from and boom! Next thing you know there was a shower of rubber, blood and flesh and no more dinghy, no more SS men. You should have seen it. All the deep red blood and the tiny black pieces of rubber almost looked like fireworks in the sky. What a sight it was."

Kavan: "I bet it was. I think we best keep this to ourselves. You let the trolls know that this is a ships secret."

Aegir: "Will do Captain."

The Generals were anxiously awaiting our return. We had barley joined them when Kammler blurted out. "Well Captain. What do you have to report?"

Kavan: "I did learn something from my First Mate. My crew did hear the explosion and they are fairly certain it came from somewhere in the water between the two docks."

Von Weber: "Did any of your crew notice Colonel Kempler or any of his men in the vicinity around the time they heard the explosion?"

Kavan: "I really can't say sir."

I had to give Kavan a lot of credit. He had a way of skirting the subject without actually lying about it.

Fritz had been in a huddle with some of his men and he soon approached the General's.

Kammler: "Fritz, did you or your men find anything?"

Fritz: "I believe we did. We have located some small derbies that seem to be pieces of cloth and rubber. Some of the rubber is the thickness that one might find used in a rubber dinghy like those stored on a submarine or some of the smaller ships. However, some of the rubber is much thinner and more pliable, possible from a wet suit. It's hard to say about the cloth. It is black in color and made of wool. Possibly from a uniform."

Kammler: "Do you suppose Colonel Kempler and his men were performing some sort of exercise in the water and had explosives with them?"

Von Weber: "The Colonel did seem preoccupied with the U630. Maybe he wanted to get a closer look at it without the crew's knowledge. Although, that does not explain why they would have explosives with them."

Parky: "Unless our dear Colonel was upset that Kavan would not let him come aboard and out of revenge he might have planned to blow the U630 up."

One of Fritz's men came running towards us. In his hand was something that was round in shape and dripping wet. The man was out of breath as he stuttered the information about his find. "Sirs, we found this floating under the docks, it was hooked behind a wood piling. You may want to look inside along the sweat band."

General Kammler grabbed it from the man's hand. He flipped it over and then his face went white as the snow expanse that covered the complex.

Kammler: "I'm afraid that it very doubtful we will ever see Colonel Kempler ever again. It's his name inside the band of the hat." He turned it over so all of us could see that it was a German SS officer cap. "I would say it is safe to assume that the Colonel and his men were most likely conducting a training exercise using live explosives. Of course we must assume that something went drastically wrong. We will hold a memorial service for them in the morning. Fritz you are now in charge of Colonel Kempler's operations. Your fist assignment will be to arrange for the memorial service. I suggest you hold it at nine-hundred hours and it should last no longer then one hour for Colonel Parkurkakus, his crew and myself will be departing the complex by twelve-hundred hours. Do I make myself clear?"

Fritz: "Very clear Herr General. Heil Hitler:"

As we returned to our apartments Kavan asked the General's if it would be acceptable for him to spend the night at Parkurkakus' apartment explaining to them that he wanted to help Parky clean up after the dinner party as it was the least he felt he could do as a thank you for such a nice meal.

The Generals were too preoccupied with Colonel Kempler's death to object or for that matter to see anything unusual about the request.

Parky motioned for me to follow them. I had to leave Ole behind but he understood that I was needed elsewhere. As soon as the three of us were alone at Parky's place I was given my instructions. I was to return to the U630 and let Aegir and Krympe know that a small container of the flames from hell was to be installed aboard the flying saucer that would be unobtrusive to anyone on board,

I ran back to the U630 being careful not to be seen. Panting as I ran up the gangplank I told Aegir I needed him to summon Krympe for an important meeting. Once the three of us were together I explained what needed to be done.

Aegir summoned Hades and told him what we needed. Hades appeared in a black suit with red velvet cuffs on the sleeves of the coat and a black cape that had a red velvet lining. Hades at first objected as he didn't know if he had the authority to grant our request. Aegir quickly pointed out to him that to save mankind it was imperative that he help us. As Aegir than put it to Hades. "No mankind no more souls for hell." Hades got the point and conjured up a bell shaped container with flames from hell.

Hades: "Should be more than enough here to supply the power for the flying saucer you have described. Just set it in the center of the blade system and its energy will take over when you flip this switch. Now if that's all I'm out of here."   Ever the showmen he snapped his fingers and disappeared in a puff of red smoke.

Krympe: "Sven and I will take this to the flying saucer. No one can be as stealthy as a troll and I am one of the best. Come Sven we have work to do. Lead me to the saucer."

CHAPTER 16

Krympe and I made our way down the gangplank of the U630 and headed to the flying saucer.   Krympe's sense of hearing combined with my own warned us of anyone that might be lurking nearby.

At each guard station Krympe would use her magical powers of camouflage to blend in with the walls and slide past the guards. Each time she would tip over something on the guards table or tweak there ears or noses so that their attention would be distracted just long enough for me to scurry past. Parky had supplied me with a collar similar to Einer's that would open the security doors to let us pass. The poor guards on duty would look at the door as it opened and shake their heads figuring it was some sort of malfunction.

Luckily when we reached our destination the area was deserted. I guess they figured the security precautions we had to pass through were enough to keep the area secure.

The area was dark and the only semblance of light came from the clear dome above us that was allowing a bit of moon shine to filter in. Looking up I was amazed how the stars seemed twice their size and twinkled more brightly then usual due to the lights refraction of the dome that made them seem twice their normal size.

Canine eyesight is pretty good in the dark but with so many of the various flying saucers painted black it was hard for me to distinguish which one was our destination. I did remember that near the entrance door there were small white letters that read 'Colonel Parkurkarkus, Pilot.' I relayed that information to Krympe.

One thing you should know about trolls, not only do they have huge ears to pick up the most sensitive of sounds but they also have saucer sized eyes that enable them to see extremely well in the dark. Krympe did a quick scan of the myriad of flying saucers before us and quickly picked out the one with Parkurkakus' name on it.

The gangway was down and we entered the saucer with no problems. The main lights were off but the control panels were always powered so that certain functions would not have to be reset before the unit was ready to fly. Small green, red and yellow lights flashed from the various information panels and white strips of light were illuminated along the corridors of walkways. These items were always lit in case of a main power failure and they were powered by an auxiliary battery backup system,

We followed the lighted corridors until we came to a ladder that was marked with an arrow pointing down that said engine room. Krympe carefully made her way down the ladder using one hand as she gripped the ladders side, her other hand was busy keeping hold of the fires from hell canister. Being a dog I was stuck where I was for dogs are not to adept at climbing ladders.

I heard her talking to me as she put the canister into place. "Sven, I am putting the canister on top of the main propulsion unit. I have some wiring that Hades sent with and I will run it along the wires to the control panel that is in the pilot's cockpit. The wires are routed through a round tube that is big enough for me to crawl into. I'll meet you by the exit door as soon as I am finished. You can tell Parky that there will be a new button on the control panel that will be red in color and have a symbol that looks like a flame in its center. When he pushes it the flames from hell will be active, a second push will deactivate them. Once they are active they will act like a silent self-propulsion unit. This should satisfy any of the Nazi scum that are on board that Parky has accomplished what he promised them."

With the flames from hell power source installed we made our way from the flying saucer back to the U630 without incident. Aegir greeted us at the gangplank and congratulated us on a job well done.

I quickly made my way back to Parky's apartment. I was stopped dead in my tracks as there were two guards stationed outside the apartment door. I slowly approached and as I stood in front of the door one of the guards made an effort to kick me as he said. "Get away from here mutt. General Kempler gave us orders no one is to enter this apartment and that includes dogs. Now scat."

I avoided his kick and figured it best I return to my own apartment and let Ole know what was going on. Once I was there I told Ole that Krympe and I had located the flying saucer and the power supply was installed and ready to use during tomorrows test flight. I then proceeded to tell him how I was stopped at Parky's apartment by two armed guards. From what I could ascertain the General had put a watch on Parky's place to make sure no one would interfere with tomorrows test flight. Both of us agreed that there must be a lot riding on this test for the General to go to such lengths at tightening security.

We were sure Parky would be worried about whether we had the new power source installed so Ole decided to take a risk and call him. Maybe he could let Parky know everything was ready for the test without saying so directly.

The telephone switchboard informed Ole that all calls to Colonel Parkurkarkus had been blocked by orders of General Kempler. It was easy to deduce that Kempler did not totally trust Parky and tomorrow would be the ultimate test for both Parky's abilities to produce what he had promised and also his loyalty to the new German Reich.

CHAPTER 17

After a long restless night with very little sleep we heard a knock on our door. It was 0600. Ole drowsily got out of bed to see who it was. I lay on the bed figuring we were about to be informed that Parky was on his way into outer space or at best we were to be invited to watch the takeoff.

Totally unknown to us was that Parky had hand-picked his crew for the test flight of the Parky flying saucer and Asil, Einer, Ole and I were part of it as was the one soldier that Parky had put his trust in. Tony who had kept us informed of many of the goings on around us was also to be on the test flight as our own on board security person.

Tony led us to a 'ready room' as it was known to the flight personnel. Ole was given a grey jumpsuit to wear with his name tag sewn above the top right pocket. I was fitted with a doggie style jumpsuit of my own which covered everything but my head and tail. It even had my name on a tag on my left side shoulder. Once we were dressed we were told to wait in an isolation room all by ourselves. The whole thing was a bit creepy if you ask me. Ever since hearing about gas chambers and torture tactics used by the Gestapo and the SS I have been a bit leery of some of the Germans that were involved in the war.

Half an hour later and we were led by two armed SS guards to Parky's flying saucer. We stood at the bottom of the ramp leading up into the saucer as one of the guards commanded us. "Well, what are you waiting for, you're the last to board so you best hurry along, the others are waiting for you."

We made our way to the main control area, a glass dome was over our heads and there were chairs like you would see bolted into an airplane cockpit, each made of pressed aluminum and unlike an airplanes seats these were well padded and had a recliner mechanism built in for long distance travel. The center decking was built so that it and all the chairs attached to it could be swiveled in any direction. Unlike a conventional airplane the saucer did not require that it be turned to change direction.

Parky was quickly explaining all of this to the crew as he sat at the main control panel and started checking his controls and instruments before take-off. He then excused himself to go to the bathroom.

The crew consisted of Parky, Asil, Einer, Tony, General Kammler, Ole and myself.

Ole: "Where is General Von Weber? I thought he would be joining us on such a historic flight."

Kammler: "Someone had to stay and watch over the complex. I took it upon myself to be here. Von Weber is to easy going and he might overlook some of the more important aspects of this flight. Providing of course that Colonel Parkurkarkus can actually accomplish what he has promised he could do. If not I would not want to be in his shoes when this test flight is over."

Sitting in our assigned seats we all looked around at each other until all eyes were on Parky. He gave a weak smile to Ole hoping for some sign that the perpetual motion system was installed and actually going to work. Ole wasn't taking the hint so Parky moved his gaze over to me. I winked at him and he smiled in response.

Parky: "Everyone buckle in. I expect a smooth take off but as we leave the earth's atmosphere things could get a bit shaky.

Einer and I looked at each other. Being dogs we had no seat buckle, what we did have was a safety harness attached to our chairs and with paws and even teeth there was no way we could put them on and fasten them ourselves.

Asil was the first to notice this and she came to our rescue. As she slipped on our harnesses and attached them to the chairs she said. "From this point on I expect you both to keep your harnesses on at all times. That way if you are up and about and an emergency should arise you can hop onto your chairs and I can snap your safety buckle to your harness. I expect no fooling around about this rule. Do both of your understand?"

We both gave out a quiet bark as an affirmative that yes we did understand and were taking her suggestion seriously.

The clear round dome that surrounded us inside the flying saucer gave us a birds-eye-view of the people scurrying away as we heard the outside speakers inside the saucer make the announcement to clear the area and proceed to safety. Parky asked for final clearance for takeoff. A few moments later we heard the control area say that the area was secure and the roof dome was open. 'Takeoff when the count reaches zero' was the next voice that we heard and the countdown began at the count of sixty. Einer looked over at me sitting in the chair next to him as he spoke to me.

Einer: "Just so you know, there have been test flights of numerous saucers but this particular saucer is the largest one they have made so far and it has yet to be tested in actual flight. According to Parky and the other technicians in theory we should be just fine."

"In theory" I asked?

Einer: "Yes, in theory."

I sure hoped Ole hadn't heard that. Practical flight tests were one thing. In theory was not a very reassuring prospect.

Parky flicked some switches and with just his fingers he controlled the saucer using a control panel mounted into the arms of his chair. From below us we could hear the whir of the propellers as they slowly gained sped. Soon the momentum from the propeller blades began to lift us into the air. Parky kept the saucer level as it slowly rose from the ground and made its way out of the open dome that had been above us. I was thankful that the thrust of the propellers had kept everything smooth as we left the safety of the complex. It was reassuring that we were not buffeted about as we had been when we were in the jet-copter.

Once we were clear of the dome Parky began to put the saucer through some preliminary maneuvers before we ventured into space. We felt no motion whatsoever as Parky sent the saucer skimming along at high speeds just a few feet above the ice. Looking behind us I could see the plum of ice shards filling the air as a furrow of fresh cut ice marked our path.

Kammler: Colonel Parkurkarkus you idiot! Get this thing up in the air! You're leaving a trail a blind polar bear could follow. The last thing we need is for some foreign power to stumble across that furrow in the ice and have them discover our location.

I could see a smirk on Parky's mouth and I knew he had the same idea as the General. Of course, unlike the General, Parky wanted the Nazi's secret base to be discovered. If the Allies found the base it would be less complicated for us and might very well mean extra help in destroying the facility.

We continued to cruise around for a while as Parky explained to the General that he needed to get comfortable with the controls and the saucers handling characteristics before we made our leap into space.

Kammler: "Just don't take too long. It's one thing for some of our more conventional aircraft to be visible doing testing but this saucer is top secret. That's why I ordered this flight to take place before dawn. If you'll take note the saucer was painted black for a reason. It was to camouflage it with the surrounding darkness in case any foreign aircraft or even some Eskimo's might be in the area and see it. It's a shame the test couldn't have waited until the ice cap was in its period of perpetual darkness. For the time being the sooner we enter outer space and away from prying eyes the better."

Parky: "Whatever you say General. You're the boss. Outer Space here we come!"

I watched Parky as he deftly moved his fingers over the control panel. He told us we had just entered the first layer of space above the earth's atmosphere. Unlike my trip in the jetcopter I felt no sudden jerks or pressure on my body and there was no sonic boom. Next we heard Parky mention that we had now left the first layer of space and we were now entering what the scientific field considered outer space. Absolute zero gravity and no breathable atmosphere. It was also pitch black.

I Asked Ole to relay a question to Parky as to why we had felt no motion as we moved along our way and left the earth's atmospheres. Surely we must be traveling faster than the speed of light to leave the gravitational pull of the earth.

Parky: "Good question Ole. The saucer is fitted with gyroscopes which counteract any movement that would cause us any distress or that might cause us to veer off course or lose control of the saucer. In layman's terms it keeps us stable at all times."

We were now in deep space. A frontier no human had ever experienced. The saucer's pressurized interior and the gyroscopes balancing power made our journey seem like nothing more than a walk in the park as Parky so simply put it.

Looking out the dome of the saucer we could see the earth below us looking like some surrealist style painting.

Asil: "Parky, why does the earth seem so blue from up here?"

Parky: "The reflection from the sun makes the earth seem bright from up here. The earth's surface is covered with seventy-percent water, from our vantage point the water seems blue in color. If you look closely you will see brown areas that are land masses and the white areas might be clouds or even polar ice caps. Pretty amazing isn't it?"

Kammler: "Enough of this pretty blue earth and sky talk. I want to see this machine of yours work under perpetual motion. After all that's what we are here for. Or are you procrastinating because you are afraid this invention of yours will be a flop. If it is, you and every one of your crew that is in this saucer will be executed when we land. You will all be finished, kaput, dead. It won't be quick and easy for any of you, I'll make sure it will be a slow and painful death. Something like hanging with a short drop so you will slowly suffocate, or being tied upside-down on a stake and having a fire lit below you so you can keep breathing until the fire consumes you, or better yet, I might have a bowl tied on your stomach with a rat inside and then I will heat the bowl until the rat is forced to escape by eating its way through your insides. Parky, I'll save you until last so you can watch your friends die in agony. Have I made my point clear to you?"

I'm sure all of us were of the same mind set on Kammler. This guy was a major or should that be a General psycho. No wonder he was in the SS.

Parky gulped hard and looked at Asil and Ole with pleading in his eyes that the fires of hell were on board and hooked up correctly to work. They both gave him reassuring smiles but I also noticed both of them had their fingers crossed as both of them were whispering prayers to the one true God that everything would work as it should. I of course joined them with my paws crossed and said a prayer of my own.

Kammler: "Well, Colonel, we are in outer space are we not?"

Parky: "Yes sir General. We are officially in space and I dare say this is the farthest mankind has ever been from the earth's surface. Pretty awesome huh?"

Kammler: "Enough chitter-chatter Colonel. I want to see this perpetual motion machine of yours in action. Remember it better work, or else."

Parky looked around at the rest of us for encouragement. Asil made a click the switch motion with her finger as she gave Parky a weak smile. Parky nodded his head and smiled weakly back at her.

Parky: "Is everyone ready? If all goes as planned which I am sure it will the humming of the engines and the whirring of propellers that we can hear should cease once I flick the switch on for the perpetual motion. Once the system kicks in there should be no sounds other than our breathing. Well, here goes."

We all sat deadly still as we watched Parky's finger flick the switch to the on position. Even over the current hum of the engines and propellers we could hear the click of the switch. The saucer seemed to hesitate a bit as it lost momentum, which we could feel even in the vacuum of space. Then the saucer gave a slight lurch as if someone had pushed it along from outside. The sound of silence was eerily met with the sound of everyone in the cockpit holding their breath. Slowly as each one of us exhaled and relaxed the ship seemed to be sitting still.

Kammler: "What the hell Colonel. We aren't moving. You promised this invention of yours would work. You're a dead man. Turn on the main engines and take us home."

A look of terror came over everyone's face except for Parky's. He was too busy watching the saucers gauges on the control panel in front of him to be worried about any threats that General Kempler had made. Parky finally stood up and looked at the General.

Parky: "General I think you had better see this."

The General rose from his seat and strode over to Parky as if it was a great imposition on his part.

General: "Colonel Parkurkarkus this had better be good. You've already wasted enough of my time. Not to mention the fuel this saucer is eating up because of your so called invention. As you well know fuel is a precious commodity for us."

Parky: "General I suggest you take a close look at that gauge on the control panels."

The General looked down at the gauge. "So what. There's a number that says 1.0. Whatever that means."

Parky: That 1.0 is how fast we are currently traveling. 1.0 means we are traveling at the speed of light. The perpetual motion device is doing everything I said it would and more. At this speed we are circling the earth 7.5 times per second."

Kammler: "If this is true how long would it take to travel from the Earth to the moon at this speed?"

Parky: "If I figure correctly approximately 2.5 seconds. Of course it is doubtful the saucer can sustain such high speed for any length of time without damaging the outer hull from the heat that is built up at such speed. Realistically to safely get to the moon at a reasonable rate of travel for our saucers we should figure two to three days.

Parky throttled back our speed and made a quick observation.

Parky: "General look outside at the saucers outer finish. Notice how the metal is glowing red. A bit longer and the metal would have melted which would mean certain death for all of us. I suggest we head back to the base as quickly as we can, of course slowing down to a safe and reasonable speed so the saucers outer structure can start cooling down."

Kammler: "All right I'm satisfied with the test results. Get us back to earth and our home base as quickly as possible. I can't wait to share this with General Von Weber. This is the break through we've been waiting for."

Parky turned off the switch that controlled the preputial motion as he quickly clicked on the switch to take the saucer back to its normal jet powered engines. We quickly descended through the void we knew as space and back into earth's atmosphere. It was nice to see the blue sky above us and not below us. Even the whiteness of the ice capped North Pole looked inviting after streaking through the bleak darkness of space. Parky pressed the microphone button to alert the main base that we would be arriving in a few minutes.

Main base: "We read your transmission. We are opening the dome now and are anxiously awaiting your arrive. We have been trying to contact you to no avail. Is everything all right?"

Parky: "Everything is fine. I'm sure the loss of contact was due to the fact that we had left earth's atmosphere and the radio signal could not reach us."

Kammler heard Parky's comment and I could see his face turning red as he was building up with another one of his tirades.

Kammler: "Colonel, that simply is unacceptable."

Parky knew what the General meant but he had a way about him that just begged for him to press the General's button and make him even angrier then he usually was.

Parky: "Unacceptable or not General that's the way it is. Space is still an uncharted frontier for mankind and we really don't know what to expect as we explore it."

Kammler: "Just get us back to the base and stop all that philosophical mumbo jumbo that you're always spouting off about."

We landed at the base with no problems. As we walked down the gangway of the saucer a large group of scientists and workers had gathered to cheer our safe return. Many of them were asking if the saucer performed well and what was it like in outer space. None of them were privy that the real test was for the perpetual motion machine. The Nazi's made sure such important information was kept under wraps.

Kammler: "I have arranged for armed guards to take all of you to your rooms. You are to have no contact with anyone until tomorrow morning. At that time we will hold a briefing with General Von Weber to discuss the next step of our project. Tony will serve as our armed guard during the meeting. Any questions?"

There were no questions and everyone was led to their rooms and locked in for the night.

CHAPTER 18

Next morning a knock at our door presented two armed guards to take us to a secure sound proofed briefing room. A long table and chairs was in the center of the room. A film projector was off to the side and a large movie screen was on one wall. The smell of hot coffee filled the room. Luckily for Ole and I there was also orange juice and milk along with assorted pastries for a morning snack.

Tony, Asil, Einer and Parky were already there seated and snacking on goodies. We sat down with our own little breakfast items and waited. A few brief good mornings were shared as the only words that broke the silence of the room. We had no idea as to what to expect next.

General Kammler was the next to arrive. He poured himself some coffee and ignored the pastries as he sat down with a brisk "Good morning" coming from his mouth. "Where the hell is Von Weber? That old bastard is always late. You can tell he is not a real Nazi at heart from his lack of punctuality."

Kammler pulled a pack of cigarettes and sucked the first one down faster than any of us had ever seen before. As quickly as he finished the first cigarette he lit a second. Being the only smoker in the room the rest of us were forced to tolerate the situation as he outranked all of us. Einer and I both laid down on our chairs as the smoke tended to linger higher up in the room and the air was cleaner where we were. Finally the door opened and in walked General Von Weber. He went over to the table and poured himself a cup of coffee and took a seat at the opposite end of the table from General Kammler.

Kammler: "Glad you decided to join us General. I was beginning to think you had forgot about the meeting."

Von Weber: "No such luck for you General, I remembered, it just took me a bit longer to get here than I expected. You seem to have added a few security checkpoints that I was not aware of."

Kammler was now lighting his third cigarette as he sat back in his chair and crossed his legs looking as if he was in complete control of the meeting.

Kammler: "Yes, I did add a few more security check points. What we are here for is of the utmost importance to the future of the Fourth-Reich. From this point on security and secrecy most be at the maximum. I'm sure you will agree with me once you are aware of the importance of Colonel Parkurkarkus' invention."

Von Weber: "I'm all ears General. However, I also have a nose and eyes that find the smoke and stench of your cigarettes quit unbearable. Would you please be so kind as to finish the one you have and not light anymore?"

Everyone in the room sighed a breath of relief at General Von Weber's suggestion.

Kammler: "Anything you wish General. In fact I'll even put this cigarette out right away just to please you."

Von Weber: "Thank you General. Now, can we get down to discussing this invention of Colonel Parkurkarkus'?"

Kammler: "Certainly. As you know we returned to the base late yesterday after doing a trial run of the perpetual motion apparatus that Colonel Parkurkarkus had installed in the test flying saucer as he likes to call it. I have taken the liberty of having the saucer and the engine room photographed so we can see close up views of the apparatus. Tony, if you will please turn off the lights and man the slide projector."

Tony did as he was ordered. The first slide popped up. It was a picture of Parkurkarkus, Asil and Einer in their lab.

Kammler: "As you can see this is our intrepid rocket scientist as he laid claim to when he first arrived here with his assistant and her mutt. 'The mutt comment received a low growl from Einer'. I must admit I had my doubts about the validity of Colonel Parkurkakus when he first arrived but I will be the first to admit that my doubts have proven to be unfounded.

"This next slide is the test saucer that was used in yesterday's trial run of the perpetual motion apparatus that Colonel Parkurkarkus installed. The test was done with his assistant Asil, along with Ole and Tony to act as witnesses. I allowed the Colonel to pick these people of his own accord. I will admit that I was in favor of his selection as I knew he was not about to risk their lives should his apparatus prove to be a failure. Lucky for them the tests were satisfactory.

Next we have a photo of the engine room, followed by close-up photos of the jet engine system. Note these photos were taken a few days before we launched ourselves into space.

Now, note the following photographs taken after we returned from our mission. If you will notice something has been added to the center top of the engine section. This something was not there a few days earlier as our photographs show. So exactly how and when was this new piece of equipment added. Certainly not by the Colonel or any of his hand-picked crew as I had them all in lockdown and heavily guarded the night before our takeoff. I asked some of the Colonel's colleagues to take a look at the item but they are baffled as to how it might work. They tried to remove it but said that whatever was holding it in place was beyond their comprehension as to how to remove it.

I wonder Colonel if you could explain how this addition was made without my or anyone else's knowledge?"

Parky: "It's really very simple Sir. Remember when I excused myself to go to the bathroom. I had hidden the device days earlier in the closet of that very bathroom amongst the cleaning supplies. I did not want to take a chance that any saboteurs or jealous fellow scientists might board the saucer and discover it. Once I retrieved it, it took only a few minutes to install it on the main propulsion system with self-welding bolts of my own invention. Once the bolts were in place they would weld themselves to whatever they were attached to. The more you try to tighten or loosen them the more the welds will bind themselves to the object they are attached to."

That's our Parky, ever the con-artist through and through. I especially liked the story about self-welding bolts.

Kammler: "In that case, just how are we supposed to remove this propulsion unit of yours so we can duplicate it?"

Parky: "That the beauty of it Sir. Only I can remove it and I will only do so if you give me your word as a Nazi officer and gentleman and put it in writing signed by you and General Von

Weber. From this point on the perpetual motion device is to be my baby. Wherever it goes I and my crew go with it. The secrets of how it works are locked in my mind and nowhere else. Let's call it a little insurance just in case anyone decided my crew or myself are disposable."

Kammler: "You can't do that. You are a member of the Nazi Party. You must obey orders without question!"

Parky: "That's where you're wrong General. I never joined the Nazi Party. As a German officer I still have the right to do as I feel is best for the German people. In this case I think it is best that I keep the secret of my invention for the time being."

Von Weber: "I'm afraid he has us there General Kammler. We probably need him more then he needs us at this point in time. I do believe it is time for us to disclose the final part of our plan and to get our operation going as soon as possible. You never know if or when the allies or worse the Russians may discover our hideout."

Kammler: "You know I am not at all in favor of the Colonel's keeping this to himself but I guess I have no choice in the matter. I would like to make the request that the Colonel's associates are not privy to what we are about to discuss and that they leave the room."

Parky: "I beg your pardon General but I will have to respectfully deny your request. They are my team and I trust them with my life. They stay or no deal on whatever the next step of the operation may be."

Kammler: "Very well. However, let me remind you if there is any breach of secrecy the offending party will be executed on the spot. Is that understood by everyone in this room?"

Everyone answered in the affirmative. It was obvious whatever Kammler and Von Weber had been keeping secret was of the utmost importance as to why this base was here. This was finally the opportunity we had been waiting for. So far fancy science fiction type flying machines and flying saucers were very interesting but none of them had been armed with weapons of destruction as of yet. So were they a threat to mankind or just a very novel technological inventions?

Von Weber: "I'll take over for the next phase of our operation. It has been code named Green Cheese. Tony, would you please bring up the next slide. As you can see by this photo we have a picture of a flying saucer similar in design to the one you used for your test of the perpetual motion device. Of course you will notice that the two people standing next to it are non-other than myself and General Kammler."

Asil: "Pardon me General, but the two of you look like ants next to the saucer. The picture seems clear enough, but is it distorted or is it some sort of trick photography?"

Von Weber smiled. "Good observation and a very good question Asil. The answer to both of your questions is 'no'. The picture is very real and very accurate. The flying saucer you see dwarfs the one you used in your test. It was designed on the same principle except using much larger jet engines for lift and thrust. It has made some very limited test flights and everything seems to be working satisfactorily enough that we feel we are ready to proceed to the final stage of our operation. Of course that will depend on if Colonel Parkurkakus' perpetual motion device can be adapted to handle a saucer of this size."

Ole: "Just how big is this saucer?"

Von Weber: "I'm sure this will be hard for all of you to comprehend or to even believe but it has been designed to hold one-hundred people plus a crew of ten to operate it."

A low whistle left Asil's lips as the rest of sat in awe at what had just been said."

Parky: "I'm a scientist and even a bit of a dreamer and I'll be the first to admit that even in my wildest dreams I cannot actually believe that a flying craft of the size you are talking about could ever actually leave the ground. Especially carrying the weight of one-hundred people plus provisions."

Von Weber: "Well, you best believe it. It has made short test flights using jet propulsion and it was loaded with weight to approximate the payload that we need for it to carry to fulfill our plans. Our only obstacle up to this point was that the saucer could not carry enough fuel to reach the destination we have in mind and still return to earth. With your invention and its perfection as a working apparatus we now have not only the vehicles but the propulsion unit needed to accomplish our goals."

Parky: "If I am to be a major contributor to this project with my invention I think it would be prudent for my team and I to take a look at this monster saucer of yours."

Kammler: "Might as well show it to them now as sooner or later they will have to see it. The sooner the Colonel and his team can look it over the sooner they can design the apparatus we will need to complete the next phase of our mission."

Ole: "Just what is the mission?"

Kammler: "That is privileged information known only by a select few. You four are not included in the group."

Einer and I looked at each other as Einer whispered to me. "Don't you like how they always leave us dogs out of their discussions?"

"Yeah, but that's all right, I would just have to growl at them if they treated me like they are treating our humans."

Einer: "I'd like to bite Kempler in the balls if it wouldn't get Asil in trouble."

Asil looked at Einer and mouthed the words. "I heard that. Behave."

Parky: "I hate to be a stick in the mud, but I am not going to design anything for anybody if I don't know what my invention and the thing it is powering is to be used for. If the hierarchy, which is you two cannot trust me after all I and my team have accomplished since coming here then the deal is off. You can find yourself a new mad scientist to carry out your work."

Von Weber: "General Kammler, I don't see any reason why we shouldn't trust them. After all what Colonel Parkurkakus just said is true. They have proven themselves to be loyal to our cause. They came here of their own free will to help us. I think it is time they become privy to our plans. After all, it may just motivate them more when they learn how our mission will benefit the Fourth Reich and restore Germany to the World Power that Hitler had dreamed it would be. Now if you will follow me I will take you to the most top secret place in the complex."

We followed the General to the door and he led us to General Von Weber's office. We went inside as General Von Weber went to the bookcase and reaching for a book called SvenSagas he pulled it back at an angle and then he stood back as the bookcase pivoted in the middle to reveal a passageway.

We followed the General down the passageway which was nothing more than a tunnel bored through the ice. After about 500 feet we came to an elevator. We got in and General Von Weber pushed the down bottom. It took some time for us to reach the bottom level.

Asil: General, just how far under the ice are we going?"

Von Weber: "Three stories."

Once the elevator stopped we exited into a huge cavern carved out of solid rock.

Ole: "This isn't an ice cavern it's rock. How did we end up in a cavern of rock?"

Kammler: "Quite simple really. When we were carving out the main facility above us our engineers stumbled upon a massive mountain located under the ice. We decided to keep the mountain a secret and use it for the most top secrets of our program. Once this carven was completed we made sure that none of the laborers lived to tell anyone of its existence."

Asil: "In other words you killed your own people to build this."

Kammler laughed as he answered. "Our own people, don't be naive Asil. You should know we wouldn't do that, we need our people for the next step of our project. We used slave labor from other countries to build this. There deaths were not of any great loss to anyone."

I looked at my human companions and I could see the look of horror and sadness on their faces that another human could be so flippant about the lives of others. We all knew about the Nazi concentration camps and the gulags and cruelty that Stalin had and still was dishing out to not only his own people but also to the countries that they had occupied and refused to give back to the people that lived in them. So Kemmler's remarks should not have come as a surprise.

We were standing on an elevated level of the cavern that allowed us to see how huge it was and how many workers were scurrying around below us. But the thing that assailed our senses were five humongous saucers. All were painted dull black. The most unusual thing about the saucers was that contrary to Nazi Germany's normal practice of bolding marking everything they made with swastikas or some sort of visible makings to identify the objects as German the saucers had no markings on them other than near the door openings where the numbers 1-5 had been painted to identify each saucer.

Kammler: "Well, what do you think? I bet you never imaged that German engineering and technology could produce such machines as these and that they can actually fly."

It took a few moments for our little group to comprehend what we were seeing and we all stood in silent awe waiting for one of us to say something.

Parky: "I'm the dreamer of this group and have to admit I would never have believed it possible. You have actually tested these saucers and they can really fly?"

Kammler: "Not only have we tested them we have sent them into inner space more than a dozen times to make sure they were capable of handling the stress. They have been loaded with enough weight to compensate for the amount of people we hope to transport and all the necessary items to fulfill the needs of our project."

Asil: "Just what are the needs of the project?"

Ole: "And what exactly is the project?"

Kammler: "General I suppose we have to let them in on it. The Colonel has made it very clear to us that he will not continue without knowing what is going on. Plus, even after his threats I must admit that he and his team could prove to be very useful once we reach our destination. He is also the only one who will be able to repair his perpetual-motion devices should one of them malfunction."

Von Weber. "Let's go to Saucer number one and take a tour. I'll explain our plans as we go along. It will show you just how well prepared we are to take this next step in our journey. If any of you see anything that we might improve upon please do not hesitate to offer your suggestions. Asil, if you don't mind maybe you could take notes."

Asil's first thoughts were of course always the woman to do the secretarial work. Yet she was in no position to object being surrounded by a bunch of male colleagues. Parky and Ole would understand that they all shared responsibilities equally but two German General's would not be so understanding.

We all went into saucer number one as a group. The tour started on the lower level which consisted of the shafts that drove a set of huge propeller blades. 20 per rack slightly offset from each other to form two levels one offset slightly above the other. Kempler explained that by having four sets if one engine should fail the other three or even two would be capable of keeping the craft air borne and still let it be maneuverable.

To move on to the next level up we had to climb a ladder which with the help of Parky and Ole lifting Einer and me up we found ourselves on the second lowest level of the saucer. General Von Weber ordered Tony to close the heavy metal hatch at the top of the ladder and explained that it was air-tight much like a submarine but with even more seals so as to not let any of the controlled atmosphere from the main living area of the saucer to escape or any of the unbreathable atmosphere of space to contaminate the rest of the saucers insides.

This level was filled with tools and building materials. Sections of Plexiglas, rolls of rubber strips, sealants like the ones used to seal aquariums, pumps and filters. On one side were lockers filled with what looked to be deep-sea diving suits complete with air hoses and lead souled boots.

Parky: "This is a very odd collection of building materials and the work clothes look like you have some sort of deep sea exploration planned. In fact come to think of it, those Plexiglas sections and air pumps and purifiers, are you planning to take these saucers to the bottom of the ocean and build a domed city that no one could ever find?

Wait, that makes no sense at all. These saucers aren't designed for deep sea use. You plan to go into space and land on another planet. If it cannot sustain life due to the planet's atmosphere you plan to erect domes and colonize it by creating your own atmosphere. I see you even have crates of tractor parts and farming tools."

Von Weber: "You are correct Colonel. We will be landing on the moon. We do not wish to risk polluting our own atmosphere within the dome so the tractors we are taking with are made to run off batteries. Our scientists have found a way to harness the suns energy to charge the batteries. They call it solar power, although the batteries will only last for about an hour before needing to be recharged we hope to increase this time as our scientist will be devoting all their energies to harnessing the suns power to power a complete city. We are very close and if we conserve our energy usage to daylight hours and shut down all but the necessary power usage at night to sustain life we can live on the moon indefinitely.

Tony: "What about food until you can grow your own, and water, it will take lot of water to sustain life on a planet that might not have anything you need to live."

Von Weber: "We have enough food stores on the saucers to last six-months on regular rations. Each saucer is equipped with deep freeze lockers to prolong the shelf life of any perishables. We have water distillation units that can take moisture from the air which in the domes will be plentiful from the normal breathing of the population and if necessary we can distill human urine to be drinkable. We also have a good supply of vegetables and trees that have been started and can be planted in the dome. I'm sure all of you will see that we are very well prepared for our little adventure to a foreign planet."

Kammler: "Foreign planet? Surely you jest General. The planet will no longer be foreign once we land on it. As soon as we touch down we will claim the planet in the name of the Fourth Reich of the German Empire. That planet will from that time on belong to the new Germany."

Ole: "In other words you plan on leaving earth behind you and settling a new planet?"

Von Weber: "That is correct."

Kammler: "Not just a new settlement but a planet shaped in Nazi ideology. A place where the Aryan race can grow and prosper. Once we have conquered this new world we shall return here and wipe out the lesser spices of mankind to be replaced by our own people."

It was easy to see you can take the Nazi off our planet but he will still be a Nazi no matter where he ends up.

Asil: "Just how do plan on conquering earth when you return. Our Fuher tried and unfortunately failed. Do you feel you have better plans then he had?"

Kammler: "Of course we do. The v-rocket project was just a beginning to test our new development in rocket technology. Our scientist will have an atomic bomb ready within the next year that with one rocket we can wipe out an entire city of 5,000 people. With the technology of perpetual motion there will be little need to waste fuel as we launch one rocket from the moon to each of the major powers on earth and with the might of that one rocket destroying one of their cities they will all quickly capitulate to our demands. If not we will continue to destroy city after city until our demands are met."

Parky: "What's to stop the current powers from killing you or overthrowing your government once you return? Surely you realize they outnumber you in such quantities that they could easily stop you."

Kammler: "We have thought about that and the answer is quite simple. We will leave our base on the moon and in fact we shall expand it to cover enough area that we will control the moon as we will control the earth. If any of the governments on earth resist it will simply be a matter of us launching more rockets to destroy that country. If we must level a country to prove our point then so be it."

Parky: "I've studied the pros and cons of an atomic weapon. Of course its pro is for mass destruction using a fairly small payload to deliver the warhead. The con it is believed that it will leave a nuclear fallout that may be poisonous to not only the people but to all living things within miles of the detonation. This fallout may even be spread farther through the air so that it could affect all living things within hundreds of miles. The long term affects are only to be speculated on at this time but the general thought of the scientific community is that this nuclear fallout could take years or even centuries to completely disappear so that anything living might safely live there again. Have you and your scientist considered this?"

Kammler: "Of course we have. If we need to wipe out the human race in certain areas that is of no real consequence. Or if every living thing is destroyed in some rebel country so be it. As our Fuhrer so aptly stated this will be a thousand year Reich. If it takes a few hundred years to heal the area we can wait. Once the dust settles our people of strong Aryan stock will repopulate the areas and we will have a perfect Utopia for the German people."

Asil: "I'm a bit confused. Am I to understand that you already have a group of slave laborers here in the complex? I've never seen them?"

Kammler: "Of course we do. You don't think we would waste the lives of our own people to build this complex or to build our new base on the moon. If the situation is dangerous which I'm sure it will be on the moon it is better to sacrifice the lives of inferior people then our own.

Von Weber: "The General has a good point. Even here at the complex a few dozen of the laborers have died from accidents during the complex's construction. Falling ice, slipping into the freezing waters and a myriad of dangerous other activates. It's expected that things can go wrong and it's better we lose a few inferior people then to risk the lives of those that w be needed to run things in the new order."

Parky: "That sounds like a splendid plan. No need to risk the lives of us with a strong Germanic or Nordic stock background. People like us are destined to be leaders and not menial laborers."

Asil: "Will you be taking both men and women slaves to the moon?"

Kammler: "Slaves. That is such a nasty word. We prefer to call them laborers. To answer your question. Yes. Mostly men will be going to do the hard labor. The women can do the cooking, cleaning and menial labor jobs."

Asil: "In other words you hope to duplicate the Germany envisioned by Hitler using slave labor which allows you to work them to death. Only on the moon if you do that you will soon have no workers."

Von Weber: "Asil, we are not as cruel as that. Our system, will not be like the concentration camps. We know that we have to keep laborers healthy and treat them well enough that they will eventually be domesticated like sheep. Of course those that get badly injured or too old to work will have to be exterminated as they would be a burden on society. As for the women we will do our best to keep them happy and content at their assigned jobs. They will also be used for breeding stock to replace the laborers who are no longer useful."

Kavan: "Sounds sort of like you are operating a farm and people are just livestock to be worked and bred."

Kammler: "Precisely."

Asil: "Just where are you keeping these laborers. I've not see any since we arrived."

Kammler: "There is a large dormitory near the submarine base that houses the men and a smaller dormitory next to it that houses the women. The reason you have not seen any of them is that they are put under lock and key during the day. At night the guards escort them to their work station and then they take then back to the dormitories during the day. We prefer not to let them work around our own people. These inferior beings are like wild animals, they will steal anything they see and if they get the chance they will use any means they can find to escape. That includes attacking our own people to get a weapon or take a hostage."

Von Weber chuckled. "If they did escape where would they escape to? Outside in this frozen wasteland? They would be dead within an hour. It just goes to show you how mentally inferior they are."

Parky: "Just how many are there?"

Von Weber: "We try to keep seventy-five here at all times. Mostly men and about a dozen women."

Parky: "Do you plan on taking them all to the moon?"

Kammler: "No, Maybe fifty to start. The others will be needed here to maintain the complex. All the major work is done here and once we leave for the moon this complex will be kept operational so we can continue to build more 'saucers' as you call them. It will take only a minimal amount of people needed to keep things operational for time being."

Von Weber: "Colonel Parkurkarkus. Now that you know what is expected of you and your collogues I suggest we return to our apartments and get some rest You and your associates have a lot of work to do to develop a perpetual motion drive system to power our moon saucers."

The General's went their way and our group went our way.

Einer: "I think we should take them down right now. We've got both Generals here and the moon saucers are in our sight. We could destroy them all in one quick blow. Freeze 'em and break 'em into ice cubes. Who's with me?"

Parky: "I for one am not. I have to disagree. I think we should give ourselves enough time to gather up some of the more important papers and plans associated with the saucers and the strides that these people have made in aviation. It might be some very important information we could share with the United States and Britain who are striving to build a peaceful world."

Asil: "Parky, you're a dreamer. If we share any of the knowledge here and no matter how peaceful a nation's intentions are there will always be someone who will turn that knowledge into an instrument for their own evil ambitions. Take a look back at Hitler. He started out by creating jobs and building an infrastructure under the guise of bringing people out of a depression and leading them towards prosperity. Well, you all know how that turned out. However, we do need to bide our time until I can talk to Kavan so we can figure out a way to rescue the laborers that are here. Hopefully we can fit them all on board the U630 or if not find some way to transport them to safety."

Parky: "I suppose you're right. Innocent humans should come first and foremost. We must also try to separate those German workers here that are under duress. Some of them don't believe in the dreams of the General's and their cohorts. But, don't you think it would be all right for me to bring just a few souvenirs home with me?"

Ole: "Parky you'll never change. You'll always be a bit of a scoundrel."

Parky laughed. "Awful hard to break old habits my friends. Just think if I could bring out one of the smaller flying saucers or at least get the plans to build one how much fun I could have. I could scare the wits out of people all over the world. I'd add some multi-colored flashing lights to the outside perimeter and hook up some loud speakers to make strange noises. I might even dress myself up in a green costume with a set of four flailing purple arms and eyeballs that move attached to the breasts. I'd have on a green helmet with a mirrored   face shield and occasionally I'd land in some remote area and just let a few people see me. I bet the news agencies would have a field day spewing out the existence of a strange flying saucer, they'd probably have headlines blaring about the SFS. Being piloted by a big green man with multiple arms and eyes for breasts. Oh, what fun I could have."

We all laughed so hard picturing Parky dressed up like that that I lifted my leg and peed. I regained my composure enough to suggest. "Parky, SFS would probably not be figured out by most people, after all they would think it was a flying disc like they were calling it here at the complex. Even calling it a saucer might confuse them. How about you get the word out that it's an Unidentified Flying Object."

Parky: "Unidentified Flying Object. UFO. I like that, makes it sound other worldly. Mind if I use that Sven?"

I quickly answered "Not at all you big alien from outer space,"

Asil: "That's enough you two. Parky, you are not to take anything from here. Also, promise me no UFO's to terrorize the world after we leave here."

Parky looked a bit dejected. His eyes cast down to the ground and his shoulders slumped as he muttered "I promise."   However you could never really be sure what Parky might do or how he would find a way to renege on his promise. I tried to glance at his hand which had conveniently moved to his back and out of sight of Asil. Were his fingers crossed? Maybe.

Parky and Ole decided to head back to their apartments to ponder our options for the near future. Asil decided to go and see Kavan who had returned to the U630. I was still wound up and not tired so I asked Ole if he would mind if I accompanied Asil and Einer to the U630. He didn't care, so off we went to visit Kavan.

Arriving at the submarine pens we approached the U630 at its berth. The first mate was sitting in a chair on deck with his feet propped up on a wooden keg. He had a large tankard of ale in his hand and looked to be passed out. He didn't seem to notice as we walked up the gangplank. A number of people on the docks were watching. Most likely they were hoping to see some sort of confrontation take place as no one was allowed on the U630 other than her captain and crew. The first mate stood up as soon as our paws, or in Asil's case feet stepped onto the deck of the U630.

We looked at the first mate who had not stirred so much as a muscle as we stood before him. He lifted his head and then he smiled.

Asil: "Some guard you are. I could have conked you over the head or froze you in that position and you wouldn't have been any the wiser."

He gave a hearty laugh. "You know darn well my senses knew you were here. I just did this as a benefit for the bystanders to see what their reactions would be. No need to disappoint them, now is there." With that said he jumped up grabbed Asil in a big hug and kissed her on the cheek. She pushed him away as she said "people are watching."

I looked at the people on the docks and sure enough they were watching and most were smiling at the antics of the big man. Getting a closer look I saw that the First Mate was none other than Aegir. Asil looked at me with worry in her eyes.

I looked at her and I felt sad for Ole for I knew where her affections now lie. "I didn't see a thing" was all I could say to her.

Aegir: "Nice to see you again my lovely. What brings you here?"

Asil: "I need to talk to you and Kavan. It's rather urgent."

Aegir: "Well, what are we waiting for? Follow me to the Captain's cabin. Einer you stay on deck and keep watch."

I could have stayed with Einer but I was curious as to what Asil was planning so I went with her. The door to Kavan's cabin was open as Aegir said "Go right in."

To Asil to just walk in was not the polite thing to do so she knocked on the open cabin door. Aegir was not so cordial as he bellowed out "Kavan, you've got guests. Hope you're dressed and presentable, it's a lady and her canine companion."

Kavan was lying on the couch reading a book with the title Buffole on the cover. He quickly stood up and greeted Asil and bent down to give me a quick pat on the head. His cabin was much like the rest of the U630, oversized and rather elegantly furnished. The floor was made of teak, brass lamps and fixtures were in abundance. A book case took up a quarter of one wall and a mahogany desk was cluttered with notes about what Kavan had so far seen and found out about the complex.

Kavan: "Asil, nice to see you again. What can I do for you?"

Asil: "It's D-day gentlemen. Time to stop this juggernaut from going any farther. We do have a slight snag to deal with. There are approximately seventy-five forced laborers here that need to be rescued before we destroy the complex. There may also be a number of innocents that are working here under duress that don't agree with the General's plans for world domination. We will have to do our best to weed them out and rescue them with the others. The diehards will most likely put up a fight and we will gladly accommodate them."

Aegir: Nothing I like better than a good fight."

Asil gave Aegir one of those don't butt in when I'm talking looks. "Kavan we need you to get as many of the innocents on board the U630 that you can and take them to safety. As for the overflow I was hoping some of your crew might be able to take control of some of the other submarines so that all those who deserve to leave here can."

We hadn't noticed that someone else had entered the cabin as we were talking until a familiar voice broke in.

"No need to fret. Me and my trolls will commandeer the other submarines."

Asil: "Krympe! What are you doing here? Odin will have both our hides for this. He ordered you to stay back at my cavern."

Mad or not Asil scooped Krympe into her arms and hugged her for all she was worth.

Krympe: "No need to worry Asil. I got permission from Odin to accompany Kavan and Aegir. They needed a crew for the U630 and my trolls are the best crew in the whole wide world. You just say the word and we'll take over this whole darn submarine base."

Kavan: "Krympe's right. We are at your command."

Aegir smiled, "For sure my darling, anything you wish we are at your command, as for me I'd climb the highest mountain, swim the deepest sea…"

Asil: "Enough already. Aegir you must have been listening to the music of the future for I've heard the lyrics of that song when I went into the future with Sven and Ole. Let's plan to make our move at midnight tonight. I'll inform Parky and Ole to get prepared. The captive laborers are somewhere near here under lockdown. You three can see to their rescue and help any of the complex personnel that we send your way. Krympe you can read the minds enough of most humans to tell if they are good or evil, if the evil ones try to escape deal with them as you see fit. Parky, Ole, Einer, Sven, Tony and I will be busy destroying the flying saucers and the rest of the complex so that they it can never be resurrected to house anything other than the ice of the frozen north. As soon as we are finished we will all meet at the U630. If we are not here by 0200 hours leave without us. Krympe once you and your trolls have filled the other submarines with those needing saving I want you to leave immediately. Drop the innocents at a neutral port and make sure to erase any memories they have of what happened here and the trolls that saved them. When you have finished scuttle the submarines and return to our cavern in Norway."

Aegir: "Krympe, when you get back to the cavern make sure to have Odin set up the place for the biggest party ever."

Asil: "What party? This is supposed to be our final mission and then we all go our separate ways."

Aegir: "Of course Parky, Sven and Ole need to return to their humdrum human lives but not you and me. We're going to be married as soon as this is over,"

Asil: "I don't seem to remember you asking for my hand in marriage."

Aegir: "Whoops, I missed that part didn't I. Just been so hectic around here I guess it slipped my mind. Although, seeing you have no immediate family I did get the approval of Odin and Krympe." He got down on one knee and took Asil's hand in his. "Asil, would your hand and the rest of you consent to be my bride?"

Asil: "You big jerk, is that any proper way to propose?"

Aegir: "Sorry, just trying to add a bit of levity to the dangerous situation we are facing."

He now got a very sober sincere expression on his face, "Asil, we have known each other for a long time and in my heart I always knew it was you that I dreamed would be my lifetime companion. Would you please allow me the honor of accepting my proposal of marriage?"

Asil: "Much better. Then there was a minute of silence as we all waited to hear her answer. "Yes, I will marry you."

Kavan and Krympe were exuberant and I did my best to wag my tail and act happy. Of course my heart ached for how Ole would take the news. I knew that he and Asil could never be. Things as they were, her a demi-god and he a human was just too big of obstacle to overcome. Even Ole would realize deep down that as a human he has a limited lifespan and Asil would live forever. Certainly he would not want to burden her life with him growing old and dying. It was time for us to get to work and I hoped I could break the news to Ole as gently as possible before Asil or Aegir told him. Better for it to come from his best friend and partner so he could be prepared before he heard it from them."

CHAPTER 20

I went back to our apartment and informed Ole of the plan to start the destruction of the flying saucers and the rest of the complex. He was excited that we were finally going to make our move. We decided to rest up as best we could but we were definitely to keyed up to actually get any sleep.

The plan that Asil had mapped out to me was that Parky and the rest us were to meet at Parky's office. Asil and Parky had been slowly pilfering and making their own timers and explosives. Plans of the complex were in Parky's office and with Asil and Einer's knowledge of ice they had marked out strategic area's that would be the weakest. Those areas will cause the whole structure to collapse into itself once the explosives were set and activated. Each explosive had a timer so we would have time to make our escape.

By midnight, Asil, Einer, Parky, Ole, Tony and I were huddled in Parky's office. Tony had proven his loyalty to us and we needed a sixth member to round out the three two-person teams that Asil had figured for the job.

Parky was still apprehensive about destroying so much valuable new technology that he felt would be useful to the world. However, he had to agree with Asil that no matter how good a human's intentions might be there was always someone who would figure out how to use that technology for evil. Mankind still had to struggle between good and evil. Hitler, Stalin, Mussolini and Tojo were good examples.

Asil: "Parky and Tony you take this section, you both know it well and if any of the guards should see you just pull rank on them and they'll hopefully back down. They know you both so there should be no issues. If a problem arises, Tony you're armed so if you need to shoot them.

Ole, you and Einer will take the assembly and fabrication areas, you worked there for a while so you are familiar with the layout. If you have any problems with the guards Einer will take care of them for you.

Sven and I will take care of the hallways, apartment areas, and dormitories. Once we have finished there we will move to the top secret section and destroy all the supplies and the flying saucers of project Green Cheese. That of course is our priority objective.

The timers are set for 1 hour. Once you have placed the explosives make your way to the U630 for extraction before the whole place blows up. Kavan has patched into the loud speaker system and he will make an announcement that any individuals who are here under duress are free to leave and they will have twenty minutes to assemble at the submarine pens.

Aegir and Krympe are in charge of freeing the slave laborers and commandeering the other submarines that are at the docks which can then be used to transport the majority of the refugees."

Tony: "That means the guards will be alerted to trouble. Isn't that going to put us in even more danger then we already are while we are setting the explosives?"

Asil: "It will, but we still have the element of surprise on our side. No one expects that this complex can be breached so that is to our advantage. If we are lucky the guards may abandon their posts and report to the submarine pens. If that's the case we can only hope they can be contained by Kavan, Aegir, Krympe and the trolls. Any other questions?"

Ole: "Just one. What if we can't get to the U630 on time?"

Parky: "That's an easy one. Just like every other assignment. If you don't make it you're on your own."

Ole: "I was afraid that might be the answer."

Parky: "Times a wasting. Let's grab our satchels of explosives and get to work."

I was still angry with Asil and hadn't felt the time was right to break the news to Ole about her and Aegir but being assigned to work with her was still a bit of a privilege.

Parky and Tony began to work their way around the perimeter of their section. One advantage they had over the rest of us was that they were already inside their assigned area so they didn't have to cajole their way past the guards at the entrance. As Parky placed the explosives Tony kept watch. The area was patrolled by four guards. Two were stationed at the entrance and the other two were patrolling the perimeter going in opposite directions.

Tony: "Parky, this place is carved out of ice, won't the explosives just blow holes in it without collapsing anything?"

Parky: "Oh, my uneducated little friend. Asil is the quee.." then Parky stopped before he said too much. Tony was unaware that Asil was a demi-god and the queen of ice so he continued with an answer to satisfy Tony's question. "Asil's has been studying the complex since we arrived here. There are weak areas with fissure cracks that with the force of the explosion will split wide open and the weight of the ice above them will collapse the cavern's ceiling like ice breaking off from a glacier. Asil is an amateur geologist. If anyone knows how to bring this place down she does. If you noticed the explosives are only a few dozen yards apart and our instructions also include placing a few of the explosive on the saucers near their fuel tanks. That way if the ice doesn't completely crush the saucers the explosions caused by their aviation fuel will blow them to kingdom come. Won't be anything in here worth finding when we get through. You don't regret teaming up with us do you?"

Tony: "Not at all. I came to the complex with the impression that these people really cared about the German people and that they wanted to help humanity. It didn't take me long to realize that men like Colonel Kempler and General Kammler were still filled with Nazi ideology. At first I thought General Von Weber was all right but his tune would change like the wind depending on who he was talking to. He's like a politician his agenda flows with the tide. He seems to be doing only what is best for himself with no concern for others."

The first guard they ran into stopped our intrepid pair and asked what they were doing out after curfew. Parky explained that he needed to check out some structural anomalies in the cavern wall that had been worrying him.

Parky: "You wouldn't want this place coming down on your head would you?"

Guard: "No. Except why are you doing this so late at night and not during the day?"

Parky: "If I did this while the place was full of people it would cause undue worry or rumors that the place might not be safe. I'm sure you see my point. So keep a lid on it ok?"

Guard: "Yes, sir. I for one would not relish being buried in ice. That would be a cold nasty way to die."

Once the guard was out of sight they continued placing the explosives.

Tony: "I feel sort of sorry for that guy. However, I know him and he's pro-Nazi so not much more I can say about him perishing with the rest of this place."

They were just placing the last of the explosives when the loud speaker crackled and an announcement in Captain Kavan's voice said: "Now hear this, now hear this. Any persons who are here under duress or are anti-Nazi please report to the submarine pens for immediate removal from the complex. You have twenty minutes to report. At that time all vessels containing refugees from the complex will be gone."

No sooner was the announcement made then alarms throughout the compound were sounding.

Tony: "Hurry up, this place and the rest of the compound will be swarming with guards in a few minutes."

One of the guards was in sight and he turned to head back to the entrance to take his post with the other three guards.

Parky: "Tony, just act nonchalant as we approach the guards as if we are as surprised as they are about what's going on. Let me do the talking."

The guards stopped them as soon as they approached. With rifles at the ready the Sergeant of the guards took commands.

Sergeant: "Colonel, what are you doing here after curfew?"

Parky looked at the Sergeant. "As I told your sentry who was patrolling we were making some after hours structural tests of the cavern walls. I felt it best to do so after hours so as not to alarm the other workers. You know how people can be, seeing someone taking ice samples or examining cracks in the ice would surely start rumors concerning the structural reliability of the caverns."

Sergeant: "Why do you have a guard escorting you?"

Parky: "He is here for my safety and he has been assisting me by taking notes as we went along. After all he is one of your people."

Sergeant: "What's in the rucksack Tony?"

Tony: "Just an ice pick and some chisels that the Colonel needed to do his examination of the ice walls."

Sergeant: "Take it off and hand it to me, real slow and easy."

Tony did as he was told and the Sergeant found only what he was told would be in the rucksack.

Parky: "I hope you are satisfied. We really need to be on our way. I've got to find the General's and see what all this commotion is about. Also, who has control of the audio system that's making those absurd comments about people wanting to escape from here?"

Sergeant: "I'm not sure what's going on Colonel. All I know is when those alarms sound everything goes to lockdown. You two will have to stay here until we get the all clear."

Parky: "Sergeant, I understand you have orders but I am a Colonel. I outrank you and I am ordering you let us by so I can meet up with General's Kammler and Von Weber to get this mess straightened out. I would hate to have to put you on report for disobeying the orders of a superior officer."

The Sergeant got a worried look on his face. He looked at the other three guards who offered no suggestions.

Sergeant: "Yes, sir. I see your point. You may pass. I hope that you might see fit to put in a good word for me and my men to the Generals."

Parky: "I'll do that Sergeant. I'll tell them you did a 'bang-up' job here."

As they walked away Tony commented. "Bang-up job, that was certainly rubbing salt into the wound wasn't it?"

Parky: "Nasty of me, but appropriate. Darn, I forgot something important in my office. You hurry to the submarines, I'll catch up with you in a few minutes."

Meanwhile, Ole and Einer were at the entrance of the manufacturing and research area. Two guards were posted at the door.

Ole pulled out his pass to enter and was stopped by one of the guards.

Guard: "Sorry sir, no admittance after working hours."

Ole: "Come on boys, you know me and Einer. My first assignment was here to work on improvements in the material department. My new assignment is as an assistant to Colonel Parkurkarkus. He wanted me to have a look around here to see if there is anything in development that might interest his department. It's rather important as he is working on a very special project by orders of both the General's."

Guard: "Sorry sir. Our orders stand. You'll have to wait until morning."

Einer stood back and a breath of icy fog left his mouth as the two guards were frozen solid.

Ole: "Einer, was that really necessary? I'm sure I could have talked our way in if you had given me more time."

Einer: "We don't have time to waste. They would have died anyway once the explosives went off and brought this place down on their heads."

Ole: "I think you enjoyed doing that."

As they walked into the development and research area Einer kicked one of the guards with his rear leg which caused the guard to fall against his partner. The two of them hit the floor and shattered into a thousand ice cubes.

Einer: "Freezing them was fun, but I really didn't enjoy it until I tipped them over."

Ole: "Sometimes you do have a nasty streak in you. Now let's get to work. Do you think there might be more guards inside?"

Einer held his nose high and sniffed for the scent of more humans. "Nope, just those two ice cubes at the door. We're free and clear to set the explosives."

With no one to interfere they finished setting their explosives and were just leaving the area when Kavan's announcement came over the loud speakers. The alarms went off and they hurried past running guards and civilians that seemed to be heading in every direction.

Ole: "I wonder how the guards are handling those who wish to leave."

Einer: "They were trained by Colonel Kempler a dyed in the wool SS officer. How do you think they will handle deserters?"

Then they heard gunfire. There were shouts and screams filling the air. If the guards were shooting the refugees it would prove to be a very one sided battle as none of the workers in the complex were allowed to have weapons.

As they came upon the entrance to the submarine pens they could see a large group of workers huddled in mass as a dozen guards held them at bay with machine guns at the ready. About a dozen workers bodies were sprawled on the floor in pools of blood. The captives could see that resistance meant death. It was an insurrection and chances of escape now looked futile to those poor prisoners.

Ole: "Einer, I don't have a weapon, mine was confiscated some time ago. Can you handle this?"

Einer: "I was hoping you'd say that. Einer hunched down and then he launched himself like a missile into the air weaving in and out of the guards as he froze each one in passing. When Einer came to the last guard he spun around and knocked him over unfrozen. The guard's machine gun slid across the floor and as the guard quickly crawled to retrieve. Einer jumped in front of him and growled. The guard still on his hands and knees stopped and looked at Einer eye to eye.

Guard: "Nice puppy. I bet you'll let me pick up my gun so I can shoot you dead, won't you? You dumb animal."

Einer wagged his tail as the guard started to move forward. Then quick as a lightning bolt Einer froze the guard in his tracks. Einer picked up the strap of the machine gun with his teeth and trotted over to Ole.

Einer: "Here you go. Now you've got a gun. Let's get these refugees to the submarine so they can get out of here."

The refugees were still standing there, mostly in shock at what they had seen Einer do.

Ole hollered at the top of his voice. "What are you staring at? Just a bunch of dead Nazi's. You're free to go. Everyone to the submarines. Time is running out. If you want your freedom, move it. Move it now!"

The refugees went off at a run. We could see the trolls with hoods covering their faces directing the newly freed workers to the various submarines that they had commandeered. Other trolls were at the gangplanks reading the minds of the refugees to make sure they were legitimate refugees and not Nazi's hoping to blend in and escape.

On the far side of the submarine pens Kavan and Krympe were grilling the subs Captains and crews to see if any of them were eligible to man the submarines and take the refugees to safe ports. None of the submarine Captains were eligible, they tended to be die-hard Nazi fanatics. However, some of the officers and crew had been shanghaied into service and they offered their assistance in manning and guiding the submarines to safe ports in exchange for their own freedom.

Meanwhile, Asil and I had approached the top secret section which contained the saucers and supplies for the moon operation.

Asil now had clearance for this area so she flashed her badge at the entrance which was inside General Weber's there were three guards plus their Sergeant guarding the secretive bookcase. .

Sergeant: "What's your purpose for wanting to visit this section so late at night?"

Asil: "Colonel Parkurkarkus and I are working on some changes for the large saucers and I need to take some measurements."

Sergeant: "Seems a bit irregular but I have heard the General's talking about trying to get the project completed as soon as possible so I guess it will be all right to let you in."

Asil: "Are there any other guards on patrol inside that I may need to talk to concerning my mission?"

Sergeant: "Just the four of us. It's a pretty secure area. Usual two of us are on foot patrol but we're taking a break at the moment. If you're worried about your safety one of us would more than happy to escort you."

Asil used her feminine charms and did a bit of flirting as she answered. "Nice of you to offer but I think we will be just fine. Maybe you would be so kind as to stay here until I get back. I'd hate to get spooked by running into one of you unexpectedly while I'm inside."

Sergeant: "No problem, we'll be here when you get back. We don't see may beautiful women around here. We could set up a little picnic for you when you return if you'd like."

Asil: "You flatter me. Let me think about your offer, might just be that I'll accept your invitation."

We went inside and made our way to the first section on Asil's list and set the explosives. I told Asil I was rather surprised how nice she was to the guards.

Asil: "Better to be nice and have them on our side. Sometimes it helps to be a woman when you're dealing with men."

"I see what you mean, especially in a place like this with so few women."

Asil: "Exactly."

We set the explosives in key spots on the caverns walls and then we set additional explosives near the fuel tank on the saucers that were destined to go to the moon. More explosives had been placed amongst the stored equipment that was to be loaded on the saucers before their departure. Asil used her powers of freezing to attach the explosives instead of taping them on with our special tape that Parky had deigned to stick to the ice. This made our job go much faster and all went smoothly, especially since we did not have to worry about the guards.

Asil: "Well Sven, we're done here. We made much better time than I thought we would. I hope the others are doing as well. We should hurry to the submarine pens in case Krympe or the others need help."

That sounded good until we got back to the guards station. As with most soldiers these fellows seemed to have had access to things that surprised us. The General's desk had been covered with a white table cloth and had been set up with a small feast.

Asil was in a position that if she refused their offer of the picnic it would arose suspicion and possibly turn he guards against us so she graciously accepted their offer and she had a seat at the desk as I jumped onto her lap to join in.

Sergeant: "We gathered up a few items we thought you might enjoy. We have wine from France, Schnapps from Germany, caviar from Russia and bread and cheese, all for your enjoyment."

Asil held up the stemmed goblet from the table as the Sergeant poured her some wine. Kavan's voice interrupted the moment as it came over the loudspeaker. The Sergeant pouring Asil's drink froze and the wine ran over the top of her goblet. He quickly stopped pouring and apologized for the mess as the sirens began to wail.

Sergeant: "Sorry, we have to lock down the facility right now. You had best return to your apartment. Sounds like something very strange is going on around here. If you are worried about your safety I could personally escort you."

Asil: "Thank you for the offer but I'm afraid it would get you in to trouble with your superiors. I'm sure Sven and I will be just fine. He's a wonderful guard dog. Thank you for trying to make my day a bit more pleasant."

We hurried along towards the submarine pens. Soldiers ignored us as they ran past and took up stations along the corridors and entrances to the different sections of the compound.

We arrived at the submarine base and had to weave our way through throngs of refuges that were being interview by Krympe to make sure they were not Nazi's or sympathizers as Kavan and Aegir kept them moving and turned over those who were unacceptable to the trolls to be escorted to the now empty laborers barracks. Ole, Einer, Parky and Tony had yet to show up.

We heard gunfire and saw some of the refugees fall in pools of blood just as Ole and Einer appeared. We watched as Einer took care of the guards and Ole was soon armed with a machine gun and they now seemed to have the situation under control.

Tony soon joined them, as a regular guard he had a sidearm and drew it from its holster to help Ole stand guard at the entrance to the submarine base. The flow of people had stopped and the submarines filled with refugees were now leaving at regular intervals.

Soon only the U630 remained. Kavan had loaded all the refuges aboard the other submarines. Once are small band was ready we could leave.

Asil and I joined Ole and Einer at the entrance of the base as Tony headed for the U630. We were about to leave when General's Kammler and Von Weber approached backed by twenty well-armed soldiers dressed in black SS uniforms.

Kammler: "Somebody shut those damn alarms off." One of the soldiers hurried off to do as he was told. Both the General's glared at us until the alarms went silent.

Von Weber: "What the hell is going on here?"

Then the explosions started. The walls of ice in the submarine pen shook and icy stalactites started to fall from the ceiling. Cracks in the icy walls began to open with sounds like gunfire.

We stood our ground to make sure all the refugees had escaped and their submarines were clear of the base. Kavan was impatiently standing on the deck of the U630 and the trolls had done their jobs of erasing the refuges memories of what had happened here and they were getting the U630 ready to depart.

Kammler: "Traitors! Von Weber I told you not to trust them from the first day they arrived. Kill them all now!"

Asil: "Einer, You know what to do."

Einer took flight which caught the soldiers off guard, as they hesitated Einer swopped down and turned the whole group into a pile of frozen statues.   All that remained now were the two General's in front of us. The other Nazi's were being buried in ice as the complex crumbled from the explosions.

Von Weber: "I can't believe you betrayed me. I trusted you. All of you. I was fool."

Kammler: "You could have been part of the new order. We could have ruled the world together."

Von Weber: "What's to become of us?"

Asil: "Sorry gentleman. You made your decisions long ago. You're no better than your Fuhrer was. World conquest is not in the cards for you or your minions it's time for us to go. You will be spending eternity in your underground paradise."

The General's stood watching as we quickly boarded the U630. Then suddenly General Kammler pulled a luger from his holster and aimed it at Asil. Aegir was on deck and with a flash of his hand appeared a trident from thin air that skewered Kammler to one of the ice walls.

Aegir smiled: "Odin said I couldn't help the humans, he didn't say anything about helping another demi-god."

Kavan: "Hurry up, everyone to the U630, this place is coming down around us."

General Von Weber stood at attention as he watched us leave. Ever the soldier he would stand at his post until the very end.

The hatch of the U630 was still closing as it moved ahead and dived beneath the frigid waters. We could hear chunks of ice hitting the hull as we pulled away from the Nazi complex of world domination.

CHAPTER 21

Tony: What's that sound hitting the hull, are they shelling us with hidden guns?"

Kavan: "Just ice chunks falling from the cavern. Be thankful that's all it is. I lived through that sound before when they were depth charges from enemy ships."

Finally we were clear of the cavern and all became quiet. Asil wrapped her arms around Aegir's neck and kissed him.

Ole watched them and I could feel his hurt as I had not had time to warn him.

Asil and Aegir finally finished and she walked over to Ole. "I'm sorry, but you know the gods would never let us have a life together. Aegir and have known each other for a long time. He's a good man and so are you. I'll never forget you."

Einer looked at me and gave a chocked whisper "Goodbye my friend."

Asil gave Ole a kiss on the cheek and then Einer, her and Aegir disappeared in a swirl of fog.

I could see Ole doing his best to hold back the tears that welled up in the corner of his eyes. "I'm here for your partner" was all I could say.

He choked out a very quiet, "I know you are. I also know she was right but it still hurts."

Kavan could see we were both in pain. I would miss Einer terribly. He was a great friend.

Kavan: "If you two would like to be alone I understand. If not we can go to the parlor and celebrate a successful final mission."

We decided to suck up our loss and join Kavan. He poured us all some SvenBrew beer from his private stock and we sat in silence for some time. Suddenly we all realized something. We looked at Tony.

Ole: "Parky was with you wasn't he?"

Tony: "He was. He told me he forgot something important and went back to his office to get it. He said he would meet us at the submarine pens."

Kavan: "I never saw him. A man of his size would certainly have stood out even in the sea of people we loaded onto the submarines. It looks as if our big bulky friend didn't make it."

As if things were not sad enough with the departure of Asil, Einer and Aegir now it seems we had also lost Parky.

Tony: "I have a question. What was that business with Einer freezing those soldiers and Asil, Einer and that big fellow just disappearing into thin air? Was that just my imagination or is there some type of hocus-pocus going on here?"

Ole: "A little of both my friend. Just think of it as an illusion of war. One where in the thick of battle our mind can play tricks on us."

Tony: "Pretty tricky indeed. I best keep it to myself because no one would believe me. They'd probably lock me up in the looney bin if I tried to tell them what I saw, or think I saw."

Kavan: "That they would."

Ole raised his glass in a toast. "To Parky may the heavens beware when he joins their ranks. Also, to Einer, Asil and Aegir. May the three of them live happily ever after."

That last toast was hard for my partner but he was doing his best to understand that demi-gods and humans are not meant to be together forever. Our lifespans are just too short to share with the immortals.

As for our last mission we could revel in a job well done. The refugees had their memories of the trolls and of this place erased. They would be dropped off at safe ports in the darkness of night so no one would know how they actually got there. The last vestiges of an evil regime were now buried under tons of ice.   The submarines that carried the refuges each had two trolls in disguise aboard them and once the refugees and crews were safely ashore the trolls would take the submarines back out into the deep recesses of the ocean and scuttle them. For now the world was safe.

Kavan had moved to the ornate Wurlitzer pipe organ and started to play Bach's Toccata and Fugue in D minor. Under our present circumstances the haunting tune seemed eerily appropriate. As Kavan continued to play our tiredness overtook us and Ole fell asleep in his chair as did I as I curled up on his lap.

Kavan shook Ole awake and I looked up from his lap to see what was going on.

Kavan:"Rise and shine boys. I've got orders to drop you two off here."

Ole: "Here? Where's here?"

Kavan: "Come up on deck and I'll show you."

We followed Kavan topside. It was cold, but at least the sun was shining. All around us was the ocean. No land in sight. A boat that was dwarfed by the size of the U630 was tied next to our hull. A bosons chair was swinging back and forth with the swells of the waves. Kavan and one of the trolls grabbed the chair and held it steady.

Kavan: "It's time we part my friends. If you ever get to England look me up. We'll talk over the good old days when we helped to save the world from the evil of men."

Kavan and Ole hugged. Ole looked apprehensively at the bosons chair as he sat in it. Kavan picked me up and gave me a peck on the head with his lips. "I'll miss you too my furry comrade. You watch after Ole and keep him safe." Then he handed me to Ole and we were winched up and onto the ship that was waiting for us. The U630 was already slipping beneath the water by the time we set foot on the deck of the ship.

To our surprise we were greeted by the Captain and crew of none other than the Carolsea.

Captain: "Welcome aboard matey's. We have orders to deliver you to the coast of North America."

There wasn't time to visit as the seas were swelling high and the Captain and crew were much too busy keeping the Carolsea under control to be visiting with us. We were only a few hours from our destination so our little nap aboard the U630 much have lasted a lot longer than we had thought.

We were put ashore in the dead of night somewhere along the Canadian coast. There was little time for goodbyes as this was a clandestine operation and the Carolsea quickly departed under the cover of darkness. With a hearty farewell and a good luck from the Captain and crew.

Was it luck or providence we weren't sure but we made our way inland and within a quarter of a mile we saw a light. We made our way towards it and found that it was a tiny unmanned way stop train station. We put out a flag to signal the train's engineer that passengers were waiting. Within an hour we had boarded a mixed freight and we were on our way home. Two days of switching trains finally brought us back to where we belonged. We settled into our old haunts knowing the days of being adventurers had come to an end.

A week went by and Ole was sitting on the dock listening to the radio as he watched the Mississippi river flow by. I dropped a newspaper in his lap. He opened it up and a strange look came over his face.

Ole: "Listen to this Sven. Sounds like the world has gone crazy according to these headlines. The government denies all rumors of a strange unidentified flying object that has been reported to have been seen in a number of locations around the world. The Military denies all these claims as just being a case of mass hysteria or of people looking to get attention. However in a few rare instances the object has reportedly landed in a few secluded areas and witnesses have said that it is manned by strange other worldly creatures. The object itself has been described as disc or saucer shaped with colored lights flashing around its perimeter. The object is black in color with a clear dome on that top that is lit up with a green hue. It makes a whirring sound and occasionally a garbled voice sounding like an injured animal can be heard coming from the object.

In the rare instances that the object has landed eye witnesses reported that a gangplank lowers to the ground and a strange creature emerges. The creature is said to be much larger than an average human, it is green in color with multiple purple arms and two large jiggling eyes where its breasts should have been. Where there should be a head there is some type of yellow helmet with pink antennas on the top that flop around as the creature moves. Absolutely hideous claimed the witnesses.

Could it be a creature from outer space? Certainly sounds like a hoax to this reporter."

Ole smiled and I gave a happy tail wag as Ole laid the paper down. It sounds like our friend the old con artist Parky had escaped after all.

I jumped up on Ole's lap as he reached over and turned on the radio. The announcer came over the airwaves. "Well folks, this is different. I have a request here in my hand with a record that was just handed to me by one of our staff. Seems it came by special courier and was dropped off with a request that it be played immediately. The note says that this song and the singer are from the future. Once the record finishes playing it will self-destruct. And everyone who has heard it will forget about it, except, mind you for the one special person and his canine companion who the song is dedicated to. What do you listeners out there in radio land think? Should I play it? Sure, my curiosity is aroused let's check it out. The song is called 'I will always love you' by a singer called Dolly Parton. Dedicated to Ole and Sven."

'If I should stay

I would only be in your way

And so I'll go, but I know

I'll think of you each step of the way

And I will always love you, I will always love you

Bitter sweet memories...'

Needless to say by the time the song finished we were both teary eyed. As the song ended we heard the announcer. "Damn! Records on fire! What the hell! Whoops, sorry folks, pardon my language. The note about the record self-destructing was true, not only that, but the damn notes on fire too. Never in all my born days have I seen anything like this before. By the way, who was that singer and what was the song? For the life of me, I can't remember."

Ole and I sat teary eyed and choked up, but that was the way it had to be.

THE END